To:
abbie,

Again, Alabama

Susan Sands

♥ Enjoy!

Susan Sands

TULE
PUBLISHING

Again, Alabama
Copyright © 2015 Susan Sands
Print Edition

The Tule Publishing Group, LLC

ALL RIGHTS RESERVED

No part of this book may be used or reproduced in any manner
whatsoever without written permission except in the case of brief
quotations embodied in critical articles and reviews.

This is a work of fiction. Names, characters, places, and incidents are
products of the author's imagination or are used fictitiously. Any
resemblance to actual events, locales, organizations, or persons, living or
dead, is entirely coincidental.

Dear Reader,

This book, in its many forms, is the realization of a dream. Seeing my work in print is nothing short of a miracle made possible by lots of generous people. I would be remiss in not naming as many as possible.

Writers need mentors who are willing to take time out from their busy schedules to give a hand up to others. Karen White picked me up from my house and drove me to my first Georgia Romance Writer's meeting (and she'd never met me). She still answers my calls! Thanks and love to Eloisa James aka Mary Bly. She knows her role in all of this. I will be forever grateful to call these ladies my friends.

To Christy Hayes, Tracy Solheim, Laura Butler and Laura Alford, my dear friends and critique partners: Through it all, you gals have been there for me and I love you for it. Such a wealth of support and fabulous brain trust we are combined! Also, to my sister-in-law and fellow writer with whom I took that trek to the west coast for our first writer's conference. Thanks for allowing me to drag you all over the country in pursuit of this dream. Yours is still coming.

Rest in peace to my grandmother, Alice Noel, who recently passed away. She read everything I wrote and was my biggest fan. I was able to tell her my good news just a few months before she left us, and she was so proud.

To my parents, Ray and Linda Noel, who never even gave me a funny look when I told them I wanted to write a book. They've supported me from word one.

To my husband, Doug Sands, who bought the laptop

and sent me across the country for my first writer's conference without complaint, and to all the RWA conferences since.

To my children, Kevin, Cameron and Reagan: Sorry about all the time I've spent at the computer. Y'all have been champs.

To my agents at Inkwell Management past, Allison Hunter, and present, David Forrer: I so appreciate your continued support and encouragement. I can't thank you enough for taking a chance on me!

To my fantastic editor, Sinclair Sawhney: You made my story shine with your focus and insight. Thanks for your willingness to roll up your sleeves and tackle this one!

Chapter One

CAMMIE STEPPED FROM the tiny bath into her childhood bedroom. She'd brushed her teeth, and briefly considered a shower after catching a terrifying glimpse of herself in the mirror, but opted for caffeine instead. Between her two a.m. arrival and very little sleep once she'd finally fallen into bed, the prospect of facing the siblings this morning made it a sound decision. And nobody was here to get a look at her like this anyway, thank God.

Cammie groaned and stretched. Right now, she required a gallon of coffee. Where *were* her clothes? Darn it, she was certain she'd dragged that suitcase upstairs—

A sudden, loud banging outside her bedroom window nearly shot her through the roof. Whacking her shin on the corner of the antique, four-poster bed, she lunged toward the closed curtain and apparent source of the infernal noise. *What the hell?*

Someone or something was trying to hammer its way inside—on the second floor.

Flinging back the heavy drapes, Cammie was momentarily blinded by bright sunshine. She blinked, focused, and struggled to process what met her tired brain through her equally exhausted eyes.

She made out a shirtless and very manly muscled chest. As the chest moved downward, Cammie squinted hard, and recognized the strong chin centered with a deep dimple.

She thought she might vomit. Or faint. Or something equally humiliating. Over the years, the very thought of home, of Ministry, Alabama, had brought him to mind in the worst possible way. It was why she'd hardly been joking when referring to this town as "Misery" instead. He'd been her misery.

Jumbled still-shots of memory flashed of an intimate and disastrous history with Grey Harrison, who currently stood outside on a ladder, gaping at her through her childhood bedroom window, while she sported her tiniest lacy, black panties and matching push-up bra. Beefy-eyed, with mascara smudged down to her cheekbones, she likely resembled an outmatched boxer gone a round too long with a superior opponent.

If ever she'd envisioned another face-to-face scenario with him, this one bubbled straight from the blackest sludge of her cruelest nightmare. It was like one of those naked dreams where she'd forgotten to put clothes on before heading to the grocery store. Only, this was real.

It took a minute for her stunted brain to crank back up and shift into self-preservation mode. Mortification switched anger to action. *How dare he?*

Cammie spied the ratty old University of Alabama t-shirt she'd carelessly discarded last night, still hanging from the bed post, and snatched it over her head in a swift motion. She didn't stop to check if it was right-side out. Lord, she hoped it was. Her jeans were in a heap at the foot of the bed, but before she bent down, she glared at Grey, who continued to gawk as if he'd been struck dumb.

Pointing toward the ground, she hit him with her most effective stink-eye, hoping to convey a clear message. *Get the hell off that ladder and stop staring at me, asshole!*

This seemed to do the trick. He flashed a quick—and possibly appreciative—grin and descended the ladder.

Hadn't she endured enough, like in a gigantic steaming pile, these past weeks? Grey Harrison, *here*, after all this time? Really? She looked up to the sky questioningly.

She'd indeed come home to Misery.

>>>«««

IT NOW OCCURRED to her on her way downstairs that she could have immediately just pulled the stupid curtains shut. God, what an idiot he must think her. *And why was he here?*

She took a deep breath and yanked open the door.

"Grey." His name on her lips after so many years sounded very strange.

"Hello, Cammie. It's been a long time."

Ya think? She ignored his shaggy hair and boyish grin. Instead, she said with as little peeve in her tone as possible, "I didn't expect to see you here—banging on the house." *Outside my second story window, in this town, while I'm in my skimpiest underwear.*

"Sorry about that. Your mom, she uh, hired me to do

the work on the house."

Her childhood home and family business, The Evangeline House, was a century-plus, old plantation home that hosted nearly all the towns weddings, anniversaries, and sweet sixteens. No event was too large or small.

"What work?" She raised her eyebrows. She searched her spinning brain. Was he a handy man? Surely not. No, no, it was coming back. He'd majored in architecture.

"The old place has some pretty serious structural issues. It's going to be a big job."

"Are you living back in Ministry?" Did she sound shrill? She tried to keep her voice neutral, a pleasant expression pasted on her lips as her mind kicked into full-on freak-out mode. She'd loved him since middle school. Before makeup and sex. Since childhood. And he'd loved her too back then.

"For a little over a month now—with Dad. I'm helping him renovate the old house."

No one thought to mention that Evangeline House had big problems or that Grey Harrison was back here, living just through the back gate with his dad. "It appears my family has seen fit to keep me in the dark." She experienced an invisible punch in the gut that her siblings had kept this all from her. Or was it because he was standing here in the flesh?

She tried not to clench her jaw. According to her dentist, she was a world class bruxer—a clencher—especially during stress. This caused headaches and neck strain. Had she remembered to pack her night guard and those muscle relaxers?

She'd arrived in her current clench-worthy situation as a direct result of her four siblings' web of guilt, effectively woven to trap her in Alabama for an indiscernible amount of time.

Cammie was to handle the daily running of things while their mother recovered from today's back surgery. Of course, she wanted to be here to support her mother, but they'd dumped the entire thing on her now that she was unemployed. How long she stayed depended entirely on how Mom's surgery and recovery went.

"I'm sure your family didn't want to worry you with everything you've had going on—" He dropped his eyes, as if he'd said too much.

And he appeared to know what was happening in her life, though admittedly, some of it was pretty public knowledge. "Yes, I imagine you've seen the whole thing on TV or heard about it from someone."

"I didn't mean—"

She held up a hand to ward off the stuttering apology. Accustomed now to the awkward and frequent foot-in-mouth syndrome folks were recently struck by, Cammie rolled her eyes and sighed. But on the inside her knees were wobbling and she was losing it, big time. He was *here.*

"It's okay. I get it all the time these days," she said. They were chatting, like old friends.

"Bet it's not a lot of fun when people recognize you from television, I mean, not anymore." He referred to her former recognition as the fan-type, not the latest finger-pointing and snickering variety.

"A grand plan to hide out in Alabama, right? My family may have held off on letting me in on the house troubles, but it didn't stop them from dragging me back here to take over. I guess they figured springing everything all at once after I got here would be more fun." She shot him a look that said, "*you know how they can be.*"

As in, they didn't tell me about you being *here,* the assholes.

"Sorry to be the bearer of bad news about the house. But if it's any consolation, Jessica Greene's eyebrows will grow back," he said, referring to her other, rather unpleasant situation.

Cammie could do this. She could chat with him as if the world hadn't just spun off its freakin' axis.

"If she's lucky. She's getting so much press from this; it's likely she'll shave 'em off if they start growing in too soon." Jessica Greene was the South's most famous television foodie, and Cammie's very recent former boss.

"I'm not sorry to say, she looked like a drowned dough ball with all that flour and water you dumped on her hair." His shoulders began to shake. "Then, when they hit her with the stream from the fire extinguisher—" He didn't sound especially sorry either.

Her lips twitched. Despite the awful debacle that followed, she could admit it had high entertainment value on playback. "Yes, I was there." Cammie couldn't laugh about it yet though, it'd cost her too much. Her job, her pride, her reputation. The infamous Crepe Suzette hair fire hadn't really been her fault, but the world believed it was, and there wasn't a thing she could do about it. *Breathe, Cammie.*

"So why is she trashing you on all the talk shows?" And suddenly, as if a marvelous idea occurred to him, he asked, "Why don't you make the rounds and tell your side of it?"

Brilliant. As if she hadn't thought of that. "My contract doesn't allow me to discuss what happened. Her contract does." That was her official position. Cammie smiled tightly at Grey. Grey Harrison, who was *here.*

"Oh. Bummer." His mirth died down.

Changing the subject abruptly, she swept her hand, indicating the interior of the house. "How bad is it? We have several events booked next week." She had to focus on the immediate problems, besides his being here in her mother's house.

He shrugged his well-toned shoulders, cleared his throat, and began, "I've put up yellow caution tape across the entrances to the doorways to indicate structural problems. Most of the larger rooms for entertaining are safe, but ask me before you head anywhere with the tape." Now he was all business.

"Sounds pretty serious." She remembered now that he'd studied at Auburn to be an architect and engineer—something to do with restoring historic structures. He'd been in his second year, and she in her first at rival University of Alabama when their insanely happy little couple bubble had ended so abruptly.

"It'll take some time." He looked pretty somber.

"Well, that really stinks." He was really *here. Oh, my God.* Cammie tried to keep her expression from revealing her inner freaked-outedness.

"Sorry to be the messenger, and sorry I, um, surprised you upstairs like that." He didn't look especially sorry, she noticed. If she wasn't mistaken, his eyes appeared hot with the memory. *Oh, hell no.* He wasn't allowed dirty thoughts about her ever again, not after everything that had gone on between them.

"Yeah, no problem. Nothing like getting caught with your pants down." She tried to blow it off like she was unaffected, and wipe that smirky turned-on expression off his face.

It didn't work. He was still smirking and still held her eyes with his smoky, heavy-lidded gaze. It was all she could do to keep her eyes above his belt and not crotch-check him. She was certain that the sweeping heat in her face had just turned it bright red.

Her head was beginning to pound from the delay of caffeine reaching her bloodstream. "Mom's surgery is in a couple of hours and I'm heading over to County General in a few minutes. Do you have what you need to—do whatever you do here?"

He nodded. "All set here. Give Miz Maureen my best." Still smirking.

"Sure, thanks." She turned on her heel. Getting out of this house as soon as humanly possible was the most important thing she'd ever done, or so it seemed. Too bad she couldn't leave just like she was: beefy-eyed, barefoot, and in yesterday's clothes. *Damn. Damn. Damn.*

Like in a slow motion horror flick, she'd almost made it

to the stairs and in the clear of the danger when he said from behind, "Oh, and Cammie—"

She turned, "Yes?" *Aaaaghh!*

"It was really nice to see you again." He fixed her with another killer grin that once upon a time had made a younger version of herself weak in the knees.

"Uh, yes, you too." Somehow she turned and made the final getaway on two sturdy legs, resisting the urge to run like hell upstairs.

That thermostat needed bumping down a couple degrees, she thought. She locked the bedroom door, fanning her face, then threw herself on the bed. She started shaking almost immediately, sucking in deep breaths. She'd only ever had one real panic attack, and she'd thought she was dying then. This was a close second, but instead of sensing her imminent death, she was pretty sure she was gonna kill somebody. Her entire freakin' family was in for it. Just as soon as Mom made it through surgery, they all had it coming.

Somehow, she had to dress and get herself past him again so she could see her mother at the hospital before she went in for surgery.

>>><<<

AFTER CAMMIE LEFT, or, more accurately, slammed out and spewed gravel trying to get away from him, Grey still couldn't believe it. *She was back.* She'd slipped out while he was down the hall working in the library. His heartbeat sped up a bit as it again struck him that he'd finally had the opportunity to lay eyes on her after all this time. And she hadn't tried to gut him with a sharp implement. Better than he'd imagined it might go.

Grey'd nearly lost his grip and tumbled off the twenty-foot ladder the second he'd seen her, wearing next to nothing, through the window. Tearing his gaze away from her luscious body, their eyes had locked—hers, a bit dazed for an instant, but no less gorgeous as she soon recovered from her obvious confusion.

Maybe he had stared a bit too long, considering that she had been wearing the sexiest excuse for underwear on her sizzling, hot body, he should be congratulated. But surprised didn't quite describe his gut-clenching reaction to seeing her through that window. Blown away was more like it. He'd finally torn his eyes away and climbed down before she called 911 to report a prowler.

Yes, he'd heard she was coming back, but wasn't prepared for his reaction to actually coming face-to-face—and other equally dazzling parts—with her. He wished he'd taken the time to get a haircut before she'd blown into town.

Her hair was still honey-blonde, just below shoulder-length. It had been longer back then...and the rest of her, good Lord.

He shook his head to clear it. Grey had the feeling her family members would catch all kinds of grief for their failure to inform her that he was here at the house—or judging from her reaction—back in Ministry.

He'd imagined facing her again over the years, had actually spent time playing it out in his head, known it would sting, though this was more like a soul-shattering explosion. But never had he envisioned their meeting again as the second story window farce of fifteen minutes ago.

He didn't care in the least that she'd pulled on her shirt wrong-side out. He'd hardly been able to process at that moment.

She was lovelier now than ten years ago. Back then, she'd been everything he'd ever wanted, until he'd slept with her best friend. Yes, ten years ago things had gone horribly wrong.

Her mother and siblings had gotten to a place of civility toward him nowadays, especially since he'd offered to do the work on the family home at cost. He owed them all that much for what he'd dished out in grief and gossip to their family, but he especially owed it to Cammie. He was planning to make amends. Now that Deb was gone, it was time.

After he'd married Cammie's best friend, Deb, ten years ago and moved a few cities away, visits back here to see his parents often placed him in the path of one or more of Cammie's relatives. For quite awhile they'd been chilly toward him, but over time, they'd let bygones go.

Grey and Cammie had grown up together, and while their parents had been friendly, though not super close, had always been good neighbors. Nowadays, his dad kept a protective eye out for Miz Maureen because she was alone in the house, and their properties adjoined in back. Since Grey's mother had passed away six years ago, he was glad they looked out for one another. And he would further ingratiate himself with Cammie's mother and the rest of the family by doing all he could to save their home—and business, since they were one and the same.

Grey's recent, and possibly permanent, return to Ministry hadn't been on his life's plan. Back just over a month now, he continued to struggle with the adjustment to a less hurried lifestyle where people were overly interested in his personal life. Of course, how could he blame them? He did have quite a history here with and without the town's most famous, and currently infamous, citizen.

The expected pang of guilt and frustration swept through him, as he allowed memories of his combined past with Cammie and his late wife, Deb, to intrude on his task. He nearly smashed his thumb with the hammer.

"Damn!" Shaking his head to clear away the angsty emotions Deb unfailingly evoked, even beyond the grave, he began to get an idea of how complicated Cammie's reentry into his world might be. At least for him.

Besides the whole 'caught you in your underwear' gaffe, his impact on her appeared mostly to surprise her and piss her off equally. She'd seemed pretty shocked, and maybe a little shaken up, but the great big engagement ring she wore spoke volumes that her personal life was rocking along just fine. He wanted her to be happy, didn't he? She deserved it after the awful way their relationship had ended, thanks to his youth, stupidity, and misplaced sense of responsibility gone horribly wrong.

Turning, Grey caught sight of a Laroux family photo

fixed on the richly paneled library wall. Cammie must have been about sixteen then, still sprinkled with those freckles she'd hated so badly. He remembered as if it were yesterday. They'd been each others' first and only love—until Deb'd figured out a way to manipulate them. Not that he was blameless. How could he have been? He'd fathered Deb's child. His daughter.

Chapter Two

CAMMIE WAS SO distracted by this morning's deeply disturbing events and overwhelmed by intense annoyance with her siblings that she'd left without her much anticipated coffee. She hardly noticed Ministry's familiar wrought iron benches, colorful window planters, and crisp awnings as she drove through the historic treelined town square. Ministry was the name on the map. *Misery* best described the fiercest of emotions churning within her as she'd hightailed it out of here ten years ago.

It was hard to pine for a place that held such bitter memories, no matter how historically quaint and lovely the town. Or for that matter, the gorgeous, old plantation house where she'd grown up. The one with the huge deep-rooted, oak trees and gardens that connected to Grey's parents' property. Where he now lived—again.

Cammie's three sisters and twin brother, not to mention Mom, had deliberately kept her in the dark to drag her back here. They must realize how awkward it would be for her to face Grey again—especially with no warning. But somehow he didn't seem as surprised to see her as she'd been. Hmm.

She had loved him with all the innocence, passion, and hope reserved for *the one.* He'd been rock solid and mature at such a young age, steady in his dedication to their future. Nothing or no one could have persuaded her of his betrayal, except proof of his own actions.

Yes, it had been ten years; but the whole town had witnessed her humiliation, if not firsthand, then by word-of-mouth. Maybe ten of those people had left Ministry since. Now the whole television watching population of at least the North American continent had feasted on her latest professional and personal humiliation.

Her family had been in cahoots here, even knowing the craziness her life had been the last few weeks. Courtesy demanded at least a heads-up. Family demanded even better. She was once again fodder for the local gossip mill, and with Grey back in town, folks here might book parties at Evangeline House just to enjoy a front row seat. Another bonus she could provide her kin.

It wasn't as if she'd not wanted to come here and support her family right now. Likely, she would have flown down for Mom's surgery and stayed a few days without anyone asking. Hell, she'd missed them all. But right now, she felt wrestled to the dirt and hog-tied.

Without much enthusiasm for the many coming weeks, she dragged her feet toward the hospital's main entrance. She supposed she was a little over-dressed for small town Alabama on a Tuesday, but her slim, black pants and striped tunic were at the top of the suitcase, plus accessories. She couldn't very well not wear any jewelry, could she? So, she would be called uppity by the locals—again. Ever since she'd moved to the city, gotten a good job, and learned to love pretty clothes and accessories, she caught hell about it when she came home. Well, just because she was a laughingstock didn't mean she couldn't put on some armor. Better to be talked about because she looked too good than shabby and downtrodden. No more, "Poor Cammie."

As Cammie approached the volunteer desk, she asked the young woman for directions to the surgical waiting area. So far today Cammie had yet to speak with any of her siblings. She figured they would all be gathered at the hospital by the time Mom went in to surgery.

"Hey, wait a dang minute. Don't I know you from someplace?" The blonde's candy pink nails suddenly wrapped around her wrist like a vice just as she turned to leave the desk.

Oh, crap. She'd been made. The girl's head lolled around, as if tuning in her brain like an antenna to the right station. "Yep! I got it. You're the one who caught Jessie Greene's hair on fire. Girlfriend, that was about the funniest thing I ever saw." To prove it, she hooted with such laughter that Cammie became concerned for her bladder.

Cammie smiled tightly at the airhead and disentangled her arm. She'd forgotten how quick folks in town were to reach out and touch a stranger, or in her case, a semi-stranger. She turned to search for the elevator. It was bound to happen—especially here at a public place. Locals would recognize her and spread the word.

Punching the elevator button extra hard, she waited in

the slow moving cage filled with George Jones going on about how he'd stopped loving her today and a wreath upon her grave. Poor song selection at a hospital. Not very uplifting for families of the sick and dying.

Finally the elevator dinged at the third floor and came to a rocking halt. Stepping out, Cammie took a deep, calming breath. Time to face her screwy family. She hoped for this reunion it would only be her sisters and brother. There would be plenty of opportunity later to see the in-laws and offspring.

Rounding the corner, she heard the ruckus. It was as if they'd scented her. She first caught sight of her middle sister, Emma, the pageant queen, and noticed her head swivel and eyes lock onto her as she approached.

"Well, hey there, honey. It's about time you showed up." Maeve, her oldest sister wrapped her in a great big hug the moment she entered the carpeted waiting area. Beyond Maeve, Cammie spotted Ben, her twin brother, on his cell phone holding a cup of coffee. Jo Jo, her closest sister, and Emma lined up to greet her warmly.

"How was your trip?" Jo Jo, closest to Cammie in age and the one who best understood her, held Cammie out at arms' length for close scrutiny.

"I got in really late," Cammie defended her dark circles to deflect any comments on the subject.

"Mmmm. Hmmm. I can tell. Aren't you getting enough sleep?" Jo Jo tittered.

"Doesn't look like she's slept a wink in weeks. Maybe just enough for her eyes to puff up." Emma's observation came on the heels of a very tight hug. The former hometown beauty queen and current junior pageant coach firmly believed in the "God's honest truth." Cammie recognized her sister's unflattering comments as concern for her lack of sleep.

"Thanks, Emma, but I gave up on my puffy eyes long ago. Where's Mom? Are we allowed to see her before surgery?"

"They're prepping her now and said they'd bring us back to say hi to her before she goes to the operating room. Starting her IVs and whatnot," Jo Jo answered for the group.

Cammie nodded, but noticed her three sisters continued their close inspection. "Stop eyeballing me. I'm fine. I just need coffee," she snapped.

"Somebody's protesting just a bit too much, don't you think?" Emma muttered, eyebrows raised.

"What's wrong?" Ben approached, late to the conversation after ending his call, placed his arm around her shoulders and frowned as he scanned her features for trouble.

"Nothing is wrong," she answered, "except that you all are a bunch of buttheads." Had she not been so deeply angry and frustrated by their keeping things from her, she might have been amused at their shocked expressions.

Ben responded first. "My dear sister, I don't doubt that we are, but to what are you referring?"

"Right. Like you didn't know ahead of time that Grey Harrison was back in town," Cammie accused the group.

Their surprise at her statement turned quickly to comprehension. Jo Jo reddened. She would, because Jo Jo understood more how Grey's betrayal had shattered her.

But no real admission from the others emerged. The expected bluster came forth. "Honey, that was years ago. You're engaged. We didn't realize Grey's coming back would cause you to get all het-up," Maeve, her eldest sister, said, then shrugged as if she was a moron.

"He was hammering outside my bedroom window when I came out of the bathroom this morning." She shuddered, remembering. "I jerked open the blinds."

"Oh. That must have been quite a surprise," Jo Jo had the grace to appear shamed.

"I was in my underwear." Cammie clarified to her family.

"God Almighty. Tell me you weren't in some old granny drawers. I have a recurring nightmare about being in a car wreck and the hot paramedics finding me in granny drawers!" Emma, obviously aghast at Cammie's morning horror, hadn't worn cotton underwear since—well, likely never.

"No, I wasn't in granny panties." Cammie shook her head at how easily they'd derailed her. "You're missing the point. Had I known—had any of you bothered to tell me— he was working on Evangeline House, I wouldn't have opened the blinds—in my underwear! I might not have even come to Alabama."

"Mom hired him a couple weeks ago to do work on the house. We obviously didn't know he'd be there bright and early this morning outside your window," Ben said. "And we certainly weren't of the mind that you'd freak out."

She ignored her brother. "Were any of you planning to fill me in about Evangeline House's problems?"

She nailed them with a glare. Guilty. Dead busted, all of them.

Maeve stepped up. "You've been covered up with your own problems lately. Nobody wanted to dump more on top of you just now," Maeve said, her expression oozed sympathy.

"You didn't feel badly enough to take over for Mom while she's down instead of guilting me into taking over. I'm putting my life on hold to come down here and run things. I didn't realize I'd be in a construction zone while I was doing it," Cammie said, unforgiving.

"And we can't tell you how much we appreciate it, honey. It'll fill your time while you figure out what to do next. And you can finally spend some time with all of us," Emma said.

They'd gotten together and made a plan to bring her back home to Alabama, apparently for her own good.

She could almost hear the twanging of banjos. God help her.

"You manipulated me." She said, angry and hurt.

"Don't look at it like that. We have your best interests at heart," Emma said.

"Maybe staying home with my fiancé and taking some deserved time off is in my best interest. Did you think of that?" She thought of Jason waiting for her back home in

Virginia Beach. She missed him. And right now it would have been nice to have him here helping defend her.

"You're never any better than when you're surrounded by your family. Plus, pretty boy can come down to Ministry and visit while you're here. It'll give us all a chance to meet him," Maeve said.

"His name is Jason." But the idea of her family having a go at him made her palms actually become instantly clammy, so she rethought the good sense of his being with her.

"Well, you're here now, and we need your super special skills to run things. You and Grey will just have to forgive and forget. That's ten year old stuff and it shouldn't matter anymore anyway."

Cammie supposed Emma was right in theory. But all that 'ten year old stuff' hadn't happened to any of *them*.

Just then, a pretty young nurse entered and suggested two or three family members at a time go back where mom was ready for surgery.

Cammie turned to her sisters. "This isn't over."

They collectively shrugged, looked sheepish, or avoided her black glare.

Ben put an arm around Cammie's shoulders and turned her toward the nurse. The woman did a double take when she recognized Cammie and, unlike the bimbo up front, wisely refrained from comment. But she blushed deeply when she got a good look at Ben. An expected reaction, as he had quite a reputation with the ladies within a tri-county area. Ben grinned and winked at the flustered girl.

"Behave," Cammie hissed, slid Ben the stink-eye and

elbowed him in the ribs as they fell into step behind the lovely girl down a series of hallways until they entered their mother's room.

Maureen Laroux lay in a narrow adjustable bed, propped up on pillows. She appeared relaxed and resigned to having her back repaired. Her lovely face split into a sleepy smile as Cammie approached with Ben. "Darling, I'm so glad you're here, safe and sound."

Unaccustomed to her mother in a vulnerable position, Cammie experienced an inexplicable urge to curl up beside her. Cammie had been hurt and abused by the world, and seeing her mother spurred a childish need to blubber like a baby. Of course she didn't. She'd never do such a thing.

"Hi, Mom." She leaned down to gently embrace her mother instead. "I'm so glad we're allowed to see you before you go in."

"Don't worry. I'll be fine. But if something does happen, you all know where the keys to the safety deposit box are, don't you?"

"Mom, nothing bad is going to happen. And, yes, we know where everything is. Now you go get yourself fixed up. We'll let the others come in and say hello," Ben said, patting Mom's hand.

She blew them both a kiss as they waved and departed the tiny room.

"You okay?" Ben stopped alongside and placed a hand on her shoulder. Head bowed, she indulged in her emotions for a moment before wiping the moisture away and pulling herself together.

"I'm alright. We'd better go tag the sisters so they can head back and make a fuss over Mom." She and Ben were the youngest two siblings by three years, Cammie technically the baby by six minutes. The three older girls were spaced closer to each other in age, Maeve separated by two years from Emma, and Jo Jo only eighteen months behind her.

"They can be quite a gaggle of mother hens." He slung an arm over her shoulders as they headed toward the others.

"So, what's on tap for this week?" Ben asked when the sisters were gone from the waiting room. He was referring to events scheduled at Evangeline House.

"We've got a wedding, a seventy-fifth anniversary, and a few other minor events. Oh, and the Little Miss Pecan Pie Pageant is coming up next month. God willing, I'll be long gone before that rolls around." Cammie barely controlled a shudder.

"Emma will have your hide if you miss her big shindig." Ben snickered. Their sister lived and breathed the junior pageant scene, and Little Miss Pecan Pie Princess was the year's culmination of her hard work. The event was cause for great pride and bragging rights to the winners but had sparked feuds the likes of which made the Hatfields and McCoys seem like a tiny misunderstanding.

"I've had more than my share of drama lately, so I'll take a pass on the pageant mamas, if you don't mind."

"Might miss an Aqua Net flame-up."

"At least it won't be a full-on explosion." She grinned at him.

"Jessica Greene's hair didn't actually explode—more like

went up in a ball of fire. I've never seen you move that fast. She was lucky. That flour rained down on her before her scalp was singed." Ben was her twin—her other half. He understood her mind, scarily.

"Let me guess, you've got it recorded for posterity."

"You're famous—infamous, I mean. Heck yes, it's recorded. I play it back whenever I need a good laugh. I've run through it in slow-motion too. Junior does this awesome voice-over. I swear it'll make you pee your pants."

She shot him a dirty look. Junior was Maeve's husband, and her nemesis brother-in law. Cammie and Junior had been engaged in a never ending, practical joke war since Cammie was a teen and he'd married Maeve. With e-mail, the internet, and Skyping, they could carry on from several states away. He was a taxidermist, a barbaric trade. Junior never passed up an opportunity to poke fun at Cammie in some of the most inappropriate ways.

"It was *funny*. Like, off the charts hilarious, Cammie. If Jessica Greene had been seriously injured instead of howling like a banshee at you for messing up her hair, it wouldn't have been nearly so comical. Her problem right now is that she looks the fool, not you."

"That's what Jason says." She sighed. Her phone was turned off because she was in the hospital. He'd likely tried to reach her.

"Jason does sound good for you, perfect or not."

"He's a great guy."

"So, when *do* we get to meet him?"

"At the wedding, if I have my say." She was only partly

joking.

"Oh, come on. We're not that bad. Or maybe you're worried we won't like him." Her handsome brother's dark eyebrow's furrowed. "When's the wedding, by the way?"

"We haven't set a date." This was one of the conversations she'd hoped to avoid. Ben was way too perceptive.

"Are you waiting because you aren't sure, or because he hasn't met your family?" Ben asked.

"No, it's definitely you people and your bad behavior I'm concerned about." They would eat Jason, and his slick-city self, alive down here in po-dunk Alabama. With everything else happening, sitting down and discussing dates just hadn't happened yet. Maybe Jason had tried and she hadn't been ready at the time. She couldn't remember why.

"Grey Harrison is available if you think Jason won't measure up," he said.

She shot him another nasty look. "That's low, even for you." She knew better than to take his poor humor seriously. "The man just lost his wife." While Cammie hadn't lived in Alabama for years, her siblings hadn't kept her completely in the dark regarding her former best friend's death.

It was one of the emotional scabs she'd hoped might one day fade into a barely discernable scar. No chance for the two women to gain or give forgiveness. It all lay squarely on Cammie's heart. Deb had rarely crossed her mind anymore, until she'd died a year ago.

≫≫✂≪≪

THE DOCTORS WERE satisfied that Mom's surgery had gone

exactly as it should and she wasn't in danger, so everyone besides Jo Jo left the hospital for the day. Jo would take the first shift at Mom's bedside after the anesthesia wore off. Cammie headed back toward Evangeline House with the intention of first showering.

Her stomach did a sickening little flip at the knowledge that Grey might still be there when she arrived back at the house. How could she face him daily? The old questions she'd shoved down in the stinky sealed pit of their shared past began to nag at the edges of her thoughts. She guessed it was normal, since it was the first time they'd seen one another after all this time.

Cammie was happy now with her love life, but that big, awful painful break with Grey had changed the course of her life, and now they were thrown together again after so many years, and the pain seemed far fresher than she would have imagined.

Grey and Cammie'd been so young and crazy in love. Sure, they'd argued the night he'd turned to Deb, but it hadn't been a huge blowout. When her best friend had turned up pregnant out of the clear blue with his child, Cammie had simply run from the horror and humiliation of the situation, refusing to talk to Grey. She hadn't even wanted to know why. His betrayal had just been too painful.

As she pulled into the drive at Mom's, she noticed two things—Grey was out in the front yard, and he was with a young girl. Cammie felt like she'd been hit as realization struck. The child looked like him. How could she have forgotten about his and Deb's daughter? More like, she'd avoided thinking about her so far.

Lucy, her niece, was also there. Great. Lucy and Grey's daughter must be about the same age. Perhaps they were friends.

Lucy turned with a giant grin when she recognized her aunt inside the car. By the time Cammie climbed out, Lucy was waiting to greet her.

"Hi, Aunt Cammie." The child flung her arms around Cammie's waist.

She returned the enthusiastic greeting, though it continued to baffle Cammie how huggy her entire family had always been. They considered Aunt Cammie the least outwardly affectionate of the bunch. Everyone loved her, but she just wasn't the touchy-feely type. That was how they often described her, anyway. It wasn't a compliment.

"Hi, Lucy. I think you've grown a foot since I saw you at Christmas." She took in her lovely, young niece's auburn hair and startling blue eyes. Her oldest sister, Maeve, was the only other one in the family who'd come into those blue eyes from somewhere back on the family tree.

"My mom had to buy me a bunch of new clothes when school started 'cause all my jeans were too short." Lucy did seem rather tall for ten years old.

"Well, that's not such a bad thing." Cammie continued to try to ignore Grey.

She really did love her nieces and nephews. They were the closest thing she had to her own children. Sadly, she didn't get back to Ministry as often as children should see family members. It was entirely her fault—though it had been easy to blame her high-flying career—until now.

"Aunt Cammie, this is my friend, Samantha. She moved here when school started." Samantha took a few steps toward Cammie for the introduction. She raised her eyes shyly. Cammie was stunned at their deep green, so like Grey's. Her hair was straight and silky and black as midnight—Deb's hair.

"It's very nice to meet you, Samantha." She extended her hand toward the child, who reciprocated.

She was an undeniably gorgeous little girl. A perfect combination of her parents, without a doubt. Cammie turned as Grey approached them. "Sammie, are you ready to head home?"

Sammie to rhyme with Cammie slapped her in the face— hard. Cammie and Grey's starry-eyed teenaged plan had been to name their first born child of either sex Sam or Samantha. He and Deb had taken that special plan and made a mockery of it. Hadn't she shared the name with Deb once? Just one more insult to Cammie via Grey and Deb.

Disgusted by the grimy memories, Cammie turned her back on Grey and excused herself to go inside. Hearing his daughter's name made it impossible for her to even muster the courtesy of a greeting. As she entered the house through the front door, Cammie stomped straight inside with the rest of her bags and spent the next couple hours unpacking and playing mindless games on her laptop and watching TV in her room. She'd given up on social media since it'd become her worst nightmare.

Ben was picking her up later, and they planned to visit with Mom and go out for a quiet dinner to catch up. Though, here in Ministry and surrounding areas, having a quiet dinner with her brother was an unlikely event due to his almost obscene popularity with the locals, both women and men, but mostly women.

Once Mom was out of the hospital, Cammie would be doing double-duty running Evangeline House and helping out with her care, so her time visiting with Ben would be sparse at best. In addition to his bizarre local popularity, which amused them all greatly, he remained continuously slammed with his family law practice. Busy to the point of nuts. From neighborly disputes over cattle to defending criminal cases, his was a wide and varied caseload.

Avoiding Grey for several weeks might be tricky if he was underfoot inside the house; but it was a really big house. This lingering animosity wasn't bringing out the best in her. She wondered at her surge of fresh anger over the past. Ten years seemed like yesterday.

Chapter Three

❧

"**N**O, I'M FINE," She again reassured Jason. Cammie'd been so happy to hear his voice this morning.

"Just checking. So, what's on your agenda today?"

"I'm getting started on things here in Mom's office and then heading to the kitchen to check out the supplies."

"I figured you'd have gone straight to the food first thing."

Mom had told her not to worry about the food for the upcoming events, which seemed strange. Evangeline House had an excellent reputation for its strong catering menu.

"Gee, thanks." She laughed, but understood his meaning. The kitchen was her thing, her love. She was in her creative element there. "I really haven't had a chance yet. I even left yesterday without coffee, if you can believe it."

"Was there a fire?" Of course she didn't say what had her so upset she'd left her mother's house without her shot of caffeine.

She often wondered how she had gotten so lucky with Jason. He seemed not to care that she was odd and from the real-life setting of Deliverance. He found her adorable—

after really getting to know her, and he continued to proudly escort her out in public despite her infamous fall from grace.

"I want to fly down south in the next couple of weeks."

"It's not winter yet. You might not have all your feathers."

"Funny."

"I thought so." She had to find a way to talk him out of this madness of meeting her family.

"No really. I want to catch a flight down to Alabama and meet your family."

"Not if I can help it." She joked, sort of.

"Oh, come on, they can't be that bad."

"My family will eat you alive and pick their teeth with your bones." There wasn't a trace of laughter in her tone.

"Lovely image," he said.

"You've been warned."

She heard someone call his name in the background. "Sorry, hon, I'll call you later. Keep your head up. Love you."

"Love you, too."

She was still smiling when the phone rang on her mother's desk and startled her out of her happy bubble. "The Evangeline House, how may we assist you?"

Her morning went along, as might her mother's, making appointments, providing answers to questions she was able, and promising to call back those she couldn't immediately satisfy. Half the day slipped by somehow, and as Cammie ended a call regarding particular provisions for petting zoo animals as part of a themed outdoor wedding reception, a ruckus caught her attention.

A little girl with bouncing blonde curls, no older than three, came shrieking around the corner with a barefoot boy hot on her trail. The boy, maybe seven, held the largest bullfrog Cammie had ever seen, the long legs dangled below its body, and bored and bulging eyes stared blandly amidst human excitement.

Spotting Auntie Cammie behind Granny Maureen's desk, Blondie seized her opportunity. The tiny tot obviously understood the universal unspoken law about girls sticking together when threatened by boys and slimy creatures.

The tot launched herself across the desk into Cammie's arms, wailing and begging for protection. Cammie instinctively wrapped the shaking, little body in a tight embrace. She could feel her harsh breathing and sensed real fear of the harmless frog. Flashbacks of torture by slimy creatures from her own childhood prompted instant empathy for this frightened child.

The little boy stopped dead at the door's threshold, causing the big-eyed toad's legs to sway. He seemed— flummoxed. "Well, dang it, Susie. This little fella can't hurt nobody. You didn't have to go runnin' to the grown ups." He admonished his sibling, then turned to Cammie.

"Pardon us, Aunt Cammie." He flushed under his freckles, head hung.

Cammie made a quick decision on how this would go. She pried the little girl's face from the front of her blouse and looked down into gorgeous, saucer-sized blue eyes.

First, a proper greeting. She smiled what she hoped was an unintimidating smile, "Good morning, you two." She'd not seen them in awhile, but knew her mom wouldn't allow them to run around, frogs a-flying, with potential clients in and out.

"Mornin', Aunt Cammie." They replied in unison.

"Does Granny Maureen let you run around here while she conducts her business?" At their grimaces, she figured not.

"Well, she won't hear about this from me if you promise not to come tearing through here again, especially carrying creatures that belong outside."

Both children heaved a sigh of what she took as relief. Hoping to smooth out the situation, Cammie added, "I do believe that bullfrog is a girl."

"She is?" This from Susie, whose eyes grew even rounder. She adorably lisped every 's.'

Cammie continued, "She might even have babies of her own." Shame appeared on the face of her nephew.

"I didn't mean to keep her away from her babies. Just looked like a plain old frog to me." He defended his position.

Cammie nodded at Dirk and turned to his sister. "Susie, your brother is right. This bullfrog won't hurt you. She's not very pretty, but she doesn't bite or sting, or anything. Dirk, bring her over here so Susie can have a closer look. It's alright, I'm here." Susie wasn't totally convinced, but she appeared less afraid.

"Perhaps we should give her a name," suggested Cam-

33

mie.

"Could I name her?" Susie asked.

"What do you think, Dirk?" Cammie deferred to her nephew.

"Sure—I guess. But I never named a frog before." Dirk tried his best to hide his skepticism for what Cammie figured he believed a ridiculous idea.

"Penelope. Her name is Penelope. Her's not so ugly." Everyone eyed the amphibian in question. Penelope continued to quietly dangle from Dirk's grasp, eyes bulging.

Cammie had to agree. "No, she's not. Would you like to go with Dirk to take her home in case she has tadpoles or baby frogs looking for her?"

"Yesth. C'mon, Dirk, but you still have to hold her. Her might jump 'way from me." Susie hopped out of Cammie's lap and sidled up next to her brother.

"Thanks, Aunt Cammie. We promise not to go tearin' through here no more," Dirk said.

"Yes, we promise," agreed blue-eyed Susie.

"Good. And, do you promise you'll stop in to visit after you've cleaned up a bit and checked to see there aren't any cars parked outside?" They both nodded.

After the pair trotted away, toad in tow, a wistful smile continued to play about Cammie's lips. The scent of little girl tears, sweat, and the sweet essence of baby shampoo clung to her blouse, triggering an unexpected longing for—something she didn't want to think about right now. She and Jason hadn't gotten that far.

SO FAR THIS morning, Cammie hadn't noticed any signs of Grey's presence. No obnoxious hammering outside her window to start the day, thank goodness. Maybe he was home with Samantha instead of spending the day under her feet or up on a ladder.

After making a couple of lists and notes in the calendar's margin for the next few days, she decided to check stock for catering. Amazingly, Cammie hadn't yet entered the main kitchen since her arrival so early yesterday. She'd made coffee in the caterer/butler's nook outside the family dining area and grabbed a yogurt from the mini fridge there early this morning. So, now it was time to get a handle on how things were running around here if she was going to be in charge for the next few weeks.

As she entered through the swinging door and flipped the light switch, Cammie could hardly process the scene that greeted her. It was a proverbial ghost kitchen. Normally, the bustling heart of this thriving home and business, it was dark, quiet, and devoid of all supplies—save a few half-empty staples on the sadly deserted open pantry shelving.

Her mother hadn't put a great deal of money into overhauling the entire kitchen area in a while, but until recently, it had been in nice shape. She'd fixed problems as they'd arisen, replaced appliances as needed, and maintained a neat and workable space for a business that served memorable food and catered the largest events in town.

This—this was disturbing. One of the ovens was obviously not working, judging by the items stored inside. There were folded dishtowels stacked, clean, but sitting atop the counter. The open pantry space, normally full to overflowing with staples for making fresh pastries, cakes, and hors d'oeuvres gaped with empty spaces. A few bags of flour, rice, and some large cans of tomato sauce hunkered in an otherwise bare shelf. But all the fresh items were either sadly dried up or absent.

She made her way to the subzero refrigerator and discovered milk, eggs, and a few of the normal items one might have inside, or for a single person's sustenance.

Confusion gave way to frustrated anger. Why had no one told her about this? How were they still catering events? It was obvious just then—they weren't.

"H-hello?" She was jerked out of her shocked, angry state by a timid and uncertain sounding young voice.

Naturally assuming she would come 'round to face one of the many related kinsfolk the place was so often virtually teeming with, Cammie found herself at a loss.

She hadn't expected Grey Harrison's daughter in the kitchen just now. "Samantha. Can I help you?"

"I was looking for Lucy. I didn't mean to interrupt—" She was a tiny thing, with silky, straight, and black-as-midnight hair. Her emerald green eyes appeared huge against translucent skin and prominent cheekbones that promised great beauty. She was stunning, but thin and angular, in that 'tween stage where nothing fits together quite right. And she probably thought Cammie looked like she was ready to take off someone's head—which she had been.

"I haven't seen her in here, but I can help try and find

her if you'd like." Having some notion of what the child had been through recently, she'd never take the chance of embarrassing her or making her feel unwelcome. After all, she was a child.

"Thanks." Sam's young voice was barely above a squeak.

"There you are, Sam!" Lucy came scuttling in sideways on one foot from a full run, rounding the corner inside the doorway. "Hey, Aunt Cammie."

Then she turned to her friend, "C'mon, Sam. Let's go play Frisbee."

Cammie understood two things. If Samantha was in her home, so must her father be nearby. And judging by the state of this kitchen, her doggone family had misled her about more than what they'd admitted so far.

>>>><<<<

CAMMIE RIGHTED HERSELF after the kitchen discovery and the unexpected encounter with Samantha. Instead of heading out of the kitchen, she decided the best course would be to continue her assessment of exactly what she had come home to.

Calling her sisters in the middle of their work day or while their kids were around likely wouldn't be a good time to get to the bottom of things. And she had a meeting with a potential client on the books any minute. She'd have to postpone ripping someone apart until later. Instead, she muttered about stupid sisters, stupid broken ovens, and other stupid things and people while continuing on with her newly imposed role.

Part of that role included meeting with more stupid people, apparently. It seemed the entire town had been made aware of her reentry to their culture. Cammie pasted on a smile as she answered the door and wished immediately she hadn't done either.

"You *are* here! I told you she was back, Judith. Oh, honey, let me look at you. She's still pretty as a picture, isn't she, Judith?" Judith nodded, but Jamie, eyeing the top she wore, had more to say, "Wow, who'd have thought you'd have gone designer on us?"

"Uh—" Cammie started to reply to the awkward bombardment, but Jamie wasn't finished with her assessment of Cammie.

"You do look a little tired, though, what with all that Jessica Greene business, I wouldn't get a wink either. But we don't believe a word of it, do we, Judith?" Both women were shaking their very blonde and well-coiffed heads like misinformed bobblcheads.

"Hello, Jamie and Judith. How long has it been? Ten years?" Not long enough.

"Cammie, where are our manners? We haven't even given you a hug yet." Cammie fought the urge to run away screaming.

"Oh—that's okay—" But it wasn't okay with Jamie and Judith. Cammie was enveloped by clouds of what she thought might be Calvin Klein's newest scent. Jamie and Judith were from some of the oldest money in Ministry. They were a year apart in school and had married brothers from Greenville. It was nearly incestuous in Cammie's book.

After she'd managed to get her breath back, and step away from the heavily scented sisters, Cammie suggested they have tea on the back veranda. Mom often met with clients out here, surrounded by the garden. It was better than being cooped up with these two within four walls and little ventilation.

After gathering the tea tray and cookies she'd prepared from the remains of the kitchen supplies before they'd arrived, Cammie got down to business. But there really wasn't any business. This was a gossip-gathering expedition thinly-disguised as a business meeting. Both women were former schoolmates of Cammie's and Grey's. They were here to get the scoop.

"So, Cammie, we would looove to hear your side of what happened with Jessica Greene." Jamie was nearly sparking with curiosity.

"Sorry, ladies. I'm not at liberty to discuss any of it with you. There's a clause in my contract with the network." Then, "Would you like to discuss options and possible dates for your parent's anniversary party?"

Blank stares. Then, Judith, the quieter sister admitted, "We aren't quite sure when we want to have the party, or if we want to do it indoors or outdoors. We really are just starting to think about it." Jamie elbowed her in the ribs.

"We're keeping our options open. Your place seems nice," Jamie said, all drippy and drawly.

"It's been around awhile and we do know how to throw a nice party here." Cammie handed Jamie a folder with glossy brochures. "Feel free to give my mother a call if you decide you're interested in scheduling here at Evangeline House. We're more than capable of accommodating a celebration of any size or budget."

Just then, as if on cue, Grey sauntered around the back of the house, wearing tight, faded jeans, boots, and a t-shirt that stretched across his toned torso in a way that elicited a breathy, "Oh…my," from the bee stung lips of either Jamie or Judith, Cammie couldn't be certain, as she wasn't looking at them.

"Afternoon, ladies." He shot them a killer grin.

"Hey there, Grey," they returned in unison, sweeter than iced tea with real sugar.

As soon as he'd lifted a hand and waved at the Sugarbakers, his gaze locked on Cammie, and he approached. Her stomach did not just do that. She was hungry; that was all. "Do you know if there's any Mexican tile left over from when your mom renovated the sunroom?" Grey asked.

"If there is, it would be in the storage shed out back." She managed, her tone crisp and businesslike.

"Okay, thanks." He turned and dipped his head toward the two gossip-mongers. "Have a nice day, ladies." As he retreated, Cammie dared a glance to judge J & J's reactions. They were staring at vees on the back pockets of Grey's jeans. The ones that covered his rear so nicely.

Cammie cleared her throat.

"Cammie Laroux, what in the world were you thinkin,' letting that man get away?" Judith muttered, fanning herself with a napkin.

"Sister!" Jamie chastised Judith for her speaking her mind, then turned and gave Cammie a conspiratorial grin and said, "You didn't hear it from me, but he's entirely too hot to stay single in this town, if you know what I mean."

Cammie couldn't begin to guess, but decided that no matter how she replied, it would only open her up for more speculation and conjecture. And the smaller her gossip footprint while she was back here, the better.

Cammie ushered the sisters toward the front door with as much haste as courtesy allowed. "Do let us know when you decide about the party."

"Will he be working here *every day?*" Judith blurted.

"Not sure. I hardly see him. I'm busy in the office and will be helping with my mother's care. So nice to see you again, ladies." Cammie thought her face might crack if she had to continue smiling another second.

She slammed the door and hoped she didn't hit anybody in the butt on their way out.

Barely a moment later, the door burst open again, and she was bombarded by excited girls begging for ice cream. "Please, Aunt Cammie, we won't be late and my mom isn't home yet—please, can we go? We've finished our homework." Lucy's voice carried the loudest.

"Let me get this straight, you want to go to the ice cream parlor in town on a school night? I'm not sure about this." She hoped this was how her sister, Maeve, would handle things.

Sammie piped up. "My dad is waiting for us right outside and he said it was fine, if it's all right with you."

Her dad.

"Lucy, call your mom on her cell phone and check with her." She would do almost anything to avoid going out there. Hopefully, Maeve would answer, and that would be the end of it. She would make the decision, and Cammie's involvement here would be over.

The doorbell sounded. He'd just seen her moments ago, so he knew she was inside. At least he'd bothered to ring the bell.

No! I don't want to talk to you!

It rang again. "I'll get it!" Lucy tore off toward front door. "Aunt Cammie, it's Sammie's dad. Could you please talk to him? He's waiting outside."

I don't want to!

What was wrong with her? She'd already seen and spoken with him today. The memories were returning. And she'd rather avoid dealing with him whenever possible.

"I'll be right there, Lucy." She was a sucker for her nieces and nephews. That was the only reason she could give to explain why she didn't go tearing upstairs like the hounds of hell were at her feet.

She turned back to the huge, carved mahogany front door where the late-day sun streamed every direction through the mullioned panes of inset glass.

Sending up silent thanks that she'd taken a moment to freshen up after the bullfrog incident earlier, thereby entering into this less than a total mess—at least it was something. She opened the heavy door to face Grey Harrison again. He turned as she did, and greeted her with the sideways grin she'd tried for nearly ten years to erase from her memory.

The old clock chimed on the wall, like in a horror movie.

Damn him.

>>>><<<<

"HI," HE SAID, feeling a bit foolish standing here as if they'd not spoken to one another and broken the ice yesterday or he hadn't seen her and had a short conversation barely ten minutes ago in plain view of the Doublemint Twins.

"Hi." She answered, her expression completely neutral.

"The girls were hoping to go out for ice cream. I offered to take them if you think it's all right."

She nodded coolly and asked, "What time do you anticipate having Lucy home? It *is* a school night—" Her gorgeous eyes revealed nothing, like they hadn't already done this. What had happened?

So this was how she was playing it, huh? He would see about that. Smiling, he turned to Lucy, "Lucy, do you think we could persuade your lovely aunt to join us for ice cream?"

Lucy's smile positively lit her face. She turned to Cammie and all but threw herself into her aunt's arms. "Oh, Aunt Cammie, pleeeaaassee—please, please, come with us. I never get to spend any time with you, and it's a special occasion!"

The glare of frustrated, black angst Grey received might have struck down a lesser man. In truth, he nearly staggered backward under the intensity. It was quick, and almost instantly concealed and replaced by a polite smile, but it filled him with childish and inordinate satisfaction to realize she wasn't as unmoved by his presence as she pretended.

This might be the perfect opportunity to spend a little time with Cammie and clear the air regarding Samantha. Kid pressure was an impressive influence on people to do things they might decide not to otherwise. Judging by her expression, she hadn't appreciated his underhanded tactics.

⪼⪻

OH-NO-HE-DID-NOT! HOW DARED he? Using Lucy as emotional blackmail to drag her to the local ice cream parlor where half the town would see them together after all these years was low. Stiffening her spine, Cammie stood taller. Soon enough, she would be back in Virginia Beach with dreamy Jason—not here. Not with Grey.

Cammie shot Grey another quick, nasty look before she could stop herself. She barely managed to keep bitter, scathing words from streaming forth. He'd named his daughter Sammie. Instead, she tightly accepted his mal-intentioned invitation. "That would be lovely, thank you." The syrup from her tone might cause cavities.

Lucy whooped her delight, grabbed Samantha by the shoulders, and spun her around. Samantha, clearly not exhibiting the same gusto as Lucy, smiled wanly and turned toward the truck with Lucy bringing up the rear, completely oblivious to her friend's lack of enthusiasm.

Grey must have noticed his daughter's cooling off, because he turned his attention from tormenting Cammie to trailing Samantha with a worried stare. In fact, he turned his back on Cammie and followed Samantha to the truck, leaving Cammie standing and watching.

"Come on, Aunt Cammie!" Lucy called her to follow. Oh, boy. What next? She hoped he stepped in dog poop. Too bad Mom didn't have a dog.

The girls piled inside the truck's rear cab, enabling them to all fit comfortably. Scoops was the only ice cream parlor in the county. It was the very same establishment they'd repeatedly visited as young children up through their teens. Back then, they'd ridden bikes from Cammie's house most months of the year, before they were old enough to drive or weren't able to catch rides with her older siblings.

As it was only mid-October, the weather was still mild in this part of the country. Early December through late February typically became too chilly for outdoor ice cream eating. The children here usually outgrew winter coats long before wearing them out. Today was a lovely fall day.

Scoops appeared largely unchanged. The red and white striped awning matched the umbrellas out front, casting shade onto the tables to shield those preferring not to have their cones melt before eating them during warmer weather. Several locals milled about, a few noticed Cammie and whispered to one another. A slight murmur went around. Cammie tried to ignore their overt curiosity. She saw faces that were vaguely familiar, though she refused to make eye contact.

While the four of them stood in line, the girls took their

sweet time deciding on a flavor, taste-testing, discussing and mulling over the choices. Fortunately, there was no one behind them to annoy with this tasting frenzy. Cammie could remember doing the exact same thing as a kid, though with many fewer flavors to choose from. She glanced behind her at Grey and saw the reminiscent smile playing around the corners of his lips. Apparently he remembered, too.

Ice cream was a common denominator, kind of like bowling, knowing no age, color, weight, or class discrimination. Cammie found it very hard to remain pissy while plowing through a double scoop of rocky road.

She sat with Grey, at the same table, but as far from him as possible, enjoying her cone, and ignoring him. The locals she hardly remembered continued to cast openly speculative glances. No problem. She really did love ice cream.

"Are you okay with Samantha hanging out with Lucy some at Evangeline House while you're here?"

Oh boy, there it was. She wasn't ready to have this conversation. Not here, not now.

She started. "Of course. Why wouldn't I be?" Her pitch was high and brittle, though she tried to simmer down.

"This is awkward for us all, you know? She looks so much like Deb." He said, carefully approaching the large white elephant that was his lovely black-haired, green eyed child.

"Yes, she does. But she's a child and I don't hold it against her." Her muscles felt so tight and rigid, she might just break in two. Cammie realized she was being childish, but her heart was pounding in her chest, and she wanted to cry.

"I'll make sure she doesn't get in the way. She and Lucy often are together after school and do homework, but they can go to my dad's house most days until Maeve gets home from work since your mom will be recovering." Grey had obviously picked up on her weird/angry vibe and her stiff posture and sought to smooth things out.

"I said it's not a problem. Whatever they normally do is what they should continue to do." Cammie's words came out through gritted teeth. Cammie felt like the nastiest, most horrible human in the world at that moment.

"We'll figure it out," Grey sighed.

Cammie realized he'd have to be a giant doofus if he didn't get it. He had to understand how his beloved child was a living, breathing reminder of what he'd done to her and the feelings that brought back. Cammie also realized it wasn't Samantha's fault, and with their back yards connected, it made sense that Samantha would be around while he worked at the house. Lucy lived two doors down, about a quarter mile, on the same side of the road as Evangeline House. The next couple of weeks would be—interesting for them all, Cammie especially if the way she felt right now was any indication.

"It's not like I'm staying long."

"Fine." Now his tone and posture was equally stiff and rigid.

⫸⫸⫷⫷

THEY RODE IN silence from the ice cream shop. The girls,

full and tired from a long day at school, stared out the window, likely distracted by tomorrow's Geography quiz and considering wardrobe choices for the next morning. If he knew his daughter, she had much more on her mind. He'd give anything for her thoughts to be so simple.

Facing Cammie again brought back the wrenching discomfort, and yes, the guilt he experienced every time he allowed himself to think of her. She had run off immediately after hearing Deb was pregnant, and that he was the baby's father. He couldn't have denied the awful truth, so how could be blame her for leaving town?

Grey hadn't known where Cammie'd gone after she found out about Deb's pregnancy. He was up to his eyeballs in drama with Deb, which hadn't allowed for anything else. Only days after Deb's pregnancy was confirmed, the miscarriage began. She'd become emotionally unstable, and even though he would have expected a strong reaction to her losing the baby, this was much different. She hadn't believed the baby was gone—had threatened suicide, even then.

Grey shook himself out of the past. It all felt so fresh again. And now, with Cammie's obvious discomfort with Samantha, it made everything so much worse. He'd believed he could at least earn her forgiveness while she was here.

When he pulled up in front of Cammie's house, she thanked him politely, as she likely would any stranger, then she and Lucy were whisked away by a gaggle of sisters as they stepped out of the truck. Each one quickly acknowledged both he and Samantha. None of them were likely happy with the way his and Cammie's relationship had ended years ago, but they weren't overtly mean to him anymore, and they were quite lovely to his daughter.

"Dad, can we go home now?" Samantha sounded tired and a little sad. He immediately turned his attention to his daughter, hopeful that she might end her day on a positive note. He recognized signs of the scale tipping at any moment from okay, to very not okay. It happened often enough he knew to tread carefully.

"Sure, honey. Did you have fun with Lucy today?"

"Yeah, I guess."

"Everything okay?"

"Fine."

"You know, if you want to talk to me about something, you can."

"I know." Then, "Do you like Lucy's aunt?"

"Which one?"

"Dad, you know I mean her Aunt Cammie. Why won't you answer me?"

"Yeah, I like her fine, honey." But it was so much more complicated than that.

"I thought so." Sam's silence filled the truck.

He wondered where that had come from.

Chapter Four

HER THREE SISTERS were waiting when she arrived home from the ice cream parlor with Grey. Cammie wondered how they'd managed to free themselves up at this time in the evening. Where were their children? It was near dinnertime. Surely someone needed feeding.

They all lived within a mile or so of Evangeline House, so their getting here quickly wasn't an issue. Dropping everything and running put Cammie on alert, though.

Junior had arrived to instantly shuffle Lucy into a waiting pickup. Evidently, there was urgent homework waiting for her along with dinner and preparations for bed.

Cammie guessed they'd gotten the alert from the message she'd left on Maeve's phone that she'd taken Lucy out for ice cream with Grey, so it wasn't overly surprising the sister brigade had banded together for whatever it was they'd decided needed inquiring about. Ducking into the powder room while the rest headed upstairs gave her a moment before she faced them.

Cammie figured she may as well go on up or be dragged out of the bathroom. She could hear them talking and laughing—anticipating. Taking a deep breath, she headed upstairs toward her mother's bedroom.

Maeve took the lead as soon as Cammie entered. "Lu Lu from the ice cream shop called and said the two of you were arguing at the table, and you looked ready to fall to pieces." This from Maeve.

"Yeah, honey, we've been sittin' here dying to know what the heck's going on between y'all." Emma shamed her for making them wait—classic.

"Cammie, are you alright?" Jo Jo tried to be patient and kind but Cammie detected an edge to her voice.

Cammie stared mutely around her at the curious and concerned faces of her sisters. Her eyes filled, she hiccoughed, and then she burst into tears. She sobbed and wailed while they patted, soothed, and murmured softly comforting words and sounds.

"Its okay, pumpkin, let it all out—then you can tell us what happened," Maeve soothed.

"Shhh—baby," Emma cooed.

That hadn't happened in—never in her life, as far as she could remember. Resistant to showing her emotions in front of others, her family included, she was horrified. What the hell was wrong with her? No doubt they were as baffled by this behavior as she was. Cammie dared a glance through her wet lashes.

Still hiccupping a bit, she accepted several tissues thrust her way and did her best to blow her nose and dry the remaining tears.

She heard a giggle. It was Emma.

"What?" She snuffled.

"Honey, you might want to go into the bathroom and…um, freshen up a bit." She bit back a grin as she said this.

"Yes, dear, I think that's Emma's way of implying you look like dog shit," said Jo.

"I would never *say* such a thing," Emma huffed.

"Of course you wouldn't, darling," Maeve said.

"We'll hear all about it when you get back," Jo Jo said.

When Cammie saw her reflection, she understood. Dog shit, indeed.

She returned to the bed scrubbed clean and prepared to spill. One of the girls had efficiently whipped up bloody Marys for everyone.

"Now, what went on with Grey this afternoon that's got you fallin' apart?" Jo Jo asked.

"Well, duh!" said Emma.

Cammie sighed. Her resistance was futile. "Nothing really happened. It's just that everywhere I go, people recognize me. I've gotten used to it. It's alright, really. And the stuff with Grey, that'll be alright, too. I—just don't typically cry like that, especially in public."

"Well now, first off, honey, we're not public, so a good ugly cry is okay, and at some point all the deep down stuff finds its way out—" Maeve cut herself off from her rant and cleared her throat prettily. "I mean, maybe we haven't really thought about how Grey's being here might bring back some of the old hurt."

Cammie closed her eyes, took a deep swallow of the

bloody Mary, opened them then let it all out. "I've been so far away from this for such a long time, you know?" She shook her head, trying to understand the outburst of emotion. "I knew how badly he'd hurt me, I just didn't know it would still hurt and I didn't know seeing him with his and Deb's daughter would have this effect on me after all these years."

"It's because he's a rat bastard, honey, that's why you're mad," drawled Emma, whose history with men was legend—legendarily tragic.

She knew Emma didn't really think that about Grey. "This whole thing makes me uncomfortable is all—having him here at the house. It's like I suddenly seized up when he was talking to me about having Samantha around."

"Have the two of you ever just talked about what happened with Deb?" Jo Jo asked.

"No, I didn't want to hear anything he had to say to me at the time. There wasn't any excuse for what he'd done. It wouldn't change anything now." She lowered her head, for a moment, allowing herself to remember how his betrayal had injured her to her soul.

"True. You can't get your girlfriend's best friend pregnant, then say, 'Please try and understand,'" Maeve said.

"It's just so strange. He's the same, but different. I guess I tried really hard to *not* think about it." She hated exposing herself this way to her sisters, as supportive as they'd proven themselves. Vulnerability wasn't comfortable for Cammie.

"Maybe you should ask yourself what kind of friend you had in Deb back then? She was always so jealous of you, you know." Jo said.

Jo had suggested something Cammie hadn't wanted to dwell on. "Deb is dead, and I don't want to discuss her now. I can't see any way to excuse either one of them." Cammie wrinkled her nose and shook her head. Maybe she would just go with the rat bastard theory and move on.

Wait. They'd distracted her from what she's really wanted to address with them. There were other things bothering her before all this had gone down with Grey today. The kitchen. Nobody had explained what the hell was going on around here with the kitchen and heaven knew what else. She had them all here, and it was time for answers. Grey Harrison wasn't going anywhere tonight.

Time to kick the hornet's nest.

She cleared her throat, wanting to make sure her voice was clear and they knew she meant business. "I want to know from the three of you what the hell is going on around here and why nobody told me about the mess in the kitchen or the house falling apart before I came down." There.

They eyed one another as if to figure out who would lead here. "Like we told you before, you've been pretty busy with other things." Maeve took on the oldest sister mothering role.

"This is my home, too, you know," Cammie defended.

"We don't hear from you much these days," Emma said, not meeting her eyes.

"What are you all trying to say—that I should never have stepped foot out of Mayberry, Alabama? That I'm no longer part of this family? You don't think I had a good enough reason to leave?" Cammie spoke what she believed they'd not said.

Jo spoke up for the group, always the bridge between the older and younger siblings, and the family peacemaker. "Cammie, we know you got your heart broken and were humiliated to show your face around here, but that was an awful long time ago. Maybe people don't forget in a town this size, but they move on. It's been nearly ten years, honey. And this is still *our* home, whether or not you think we're the sharpest tools in the shed for living here and loving our choice."

"And, baby girl, we do miss you," Maeve added as a buffer to Jo's last statement.

Cammie's lip quivered. She'd just been called out for being a prissy absentee sister. They really didn't understand. "None of you had done to you what Grey did to me in front of the whole town. You weren't laughed at and humiliated." She almost took it back when she thought about Emma's history.

"Honey, I know more than anyone that bad things happen to good people all the time—especially when we're young and don't know any better than to wear all our emotions right out there like a red flag in front of a charging bull."

"I'm sorry y'all don't think I've been a good daughter, or sister, or aunt for that matter. But it's always been hard to come back here and hold my head up when everybody I see is whispering behind my back. Especially now, after what happened with Jessica."

"Mom thinks you're a wonderful daughter. And there's no better sister and aunt," Jo Jo reassured her. "We just wish you could enjoy being here more and not worry so much how people in this town react. When you breeze in from the big city after not coming around, it just gives them something fresh to sink their teeth into. If you'd come more often, you wouldn't be such a big deal."

Emma rolled her eyes and said, "Girlfriend, *I* still live here and God knows some shit went down way back that shocked even the most liberal-minded around these parts—though I know that's not saying much. So, I get it, but I don't, you know?" Emma had a point. She'd had awful things happen, and she'd rode out the storm right here in town.

Jo Jo and Maeve nodded, though Cammie knew it had been huge for Emma to even reference her past. *Nobody* discussed Emma's downfall. It simply wasn't done—especially by her.

"And Jessica Greene is an A-number one bitch wagon and everybody knows it. You're famous around this town," Maeve said, likely trying to push through Emma's discomfort.

Cammie could agree completely with Maeve's assessment of Jessica, but added, "Infamous and a laughingstock is more like it." Cammie couldn't change what had happened in her recent professional life. But she'd rather be anywhere but here to experience the consequences.

"But all of you, my entire family, conspired to keep me

out of the loop. You didn't tell me about the house or about Grey being here before I got back." She shook her head. "That sounds like you decided *not* to tell me in case I changed my mind about coming home."

Again, they either cast downward glances or avoided her eyes.

Emma finally spoke, "You're right. We wanted you to come home for you to mope and feel better, and we thought you wouldn't if you knew Grey was back in town, and especially if he was working here at the house. Lord knows, you'd have had every right to refuse."

Maeve put a hand on her shoulder. "Truth is, we needed your help to get things back on track, we just didn't tell you *how* much help we needed," Maeve said.

"We never meant to hurt you, Cammie. But we couldn't take the chance that you wouldn't come home. This is where you need to be, with us, for lots of reasons," Jo Jo added.

She skewered them again with a pissy glare. "Mostly for your own selfish purposes because you need slave chef labor. I think you all suck," Cammie said.

That was the best she could do for now.

They nodded and agreed that they did indeed suck, patted her and hugged her, then left her to her mood.

It would be easy to sit here and sulk about all the wrongs dealt her. But if she was honest, and she usually tried to be, her sisters had been right about some of it. Cammie had stayed away for selfish reasons. She'd hurt her family. But they'd hurt her by not taking the time to understand her need to escape from here and take time to heal. True, she'd fled the scene after Grey'd blown her out of the water, and except for the quick holiday visits home, she'd not looked back.

Cammie had thought her emotional outbursts over for the year after what had happened fifteen minutes ago as tears threatened again. She wondered if she might have a brain tumor or something that had drastically changed her personality.

Drying her eyes, she retreated to the privacy of her bedroom, where she worked to find a tidy box in her mind to lock up this wellspring of unexpected messy emotions. They had to go away somewhere and leave her to her mission at hand—taking care of Evangeline House and getting the hell out of here.

She saw she'd missed a call from Jason. Cammie would definitely burst into tears if she talked to him right now. She texted him a quick goodnight and promised they'd speak first thing in the morning.

>>><<<

HE CALLED BACK first thing in the morning. "Hey, hon, how are things?" he asked.

"I wish I had a teleporter like in Star Trek, and I'd have you beam me back up there."

"Uh-oh, that doesn't sound so good."

"Things are a mess down here. My family tricked me into coming back so they could take care of me while I'm "recovering" from my disaster. But I swear I'm going to have to put in a month's worth of work in a couple weeks on this place. Can you believe they manipulated me like this?" She omitted mentioning anything about Grey. There wasn't any reason to bring that up.

"Sounds like they care about you and wanted to make certain for themselves that you were alright. You have time to spend with them now. It's a gift, and I think it's a good idea, Cam. You've been really stressed lately."

"What does that mean?" Cammie demanded.

"Whoa. Nothing, except that I think you could use a little downtime to slow your pace and hang with your family." His voice was soothing, in the way one would speak to a mental patient on the edge.

From his perspective it probably sounded reasonable. "I guess you're right, but really, things here are a disaster; the house is falling apart and Mom let the kitchen staff go."

"So sorry, Cammie. Maybe they really do need you. If anyone can dig in and set things to right, it's you, and I'm sure your siblings know it."

Cammie sighed. Jason had yet another point. She was maniacally organized and handled projects with a single-mindedness that allowed for no interference until the job was done. And yes, her siblings and mother were well aware of this talent/flaw in her makeup. "You get points for your insights, smarty-pants," she said, smiling into the phone.

"You see? It's the rainbow after the storm," Jason laughed.

"You have no idea."

They hung up and Cammie felt better, calmer after their

conversation. Jason had cheered her up, as usual. That was why she loved him and planned to marry him. He made her world make sense. He was gorgeous, funny, kind, and had a kick-ass future.

She'd omitted any mention of Grey, not because she had anything to hide from Jason, but because she wouldn't know where to begin a comprehensive explanation. Grey was the past. Jason was her future.

Jason knew a version of her back story with Grey, but not his name or the whole sordid tale. She hadn't wanted to appear too damaged when they'd met, and after things progressed between them, it hadn't seemed to matter.

Someday, she told herself, she'd be able to come home, make eye contact with folks in town without knowing looks, and meaningful sympathetic glances. Up 'til now, this small town's long memory continued, just like in an old rerun of Andy Griffith she used to watch at her grandmother's knee as a very young child.

Everybody's famous in a small town, or maybe they die famous. Wasn't that a song or quote? Well, it was true.

Between her past and this recent press, she may as well be a walking neon sign. For now, Cammie was headed to the kitchen. It was the one place where she commanded complete control, no matter the situation.

She planned to tackle the things she could begin to resolve. The kitchen's lack of food and supplies had nothing to do with structural issues. Mom's cutting staff and persistent back pain had prevented her from preparing quantities necessary for large events. Cammie had no such physical disability—cooking was her passion. Some people painted or waxed poetic to express creativity and emotion. Cammie baked, sautéed, sliced, diced and souffléd. She especially loved crafting Southern foods with her own special twist.

Jo Jo worked part-time answering the phone, and she'd agreed to pick up a few more hours while mom was recovering. This would allow Cammie time to focus on putting the kitchen to rights. Jo's skills leaned more toward bookkeeping and secretarial. Her youngest child, Susie, was in preschool three days a week until one o'clock. Dirk was in the third grade. So, while the kids were in school, and on the weekends, Jo helped out. The others had jobs outside the Evangeline House, so they lent a hand whenever possible.

Mom had outside catering lined up for the booked events, but Cammie wanted to have a closer look at exactly what those arrangements entailed.

She would make certain the food served at the upcoming functions would equal or surpass Evangeline House's previous standards. The events this time of year were scheduled in the two main ballrooms, outdoors or under tents, as the weather was predictably mild. There was always a backup plan in place for when Mother Nature didn't cooperate, though.

Fortunately, this week's bookings were minimal, due to Mom's surgery and everything happening with the house. The entertaining wing was deemed solid for formal parties and could also accommodate smaller meetings, showers, and teas.

Cammie took a few minutes to meander through the twenty-three-room home/mansion of her childhood on the way to the kitchen. The old wood and beeswax smells drifted into her nostrils and memories of growing up in a noisy household full of laughter and arguments among family members permeated her emotions.

Meandering the rooms and hallways, she realized how hard over the past ten years she'd worked to block out her life here. Not wanting to remember, because she would have pined for her home. It had been easier to look ahead. Admittedly, she'd had a wonderful childhood in this beautiful, old house, full of adventures and people who loved her.

She avoided the area toward the rear left corner of the house upstairs and to the back center where there were obvious cracks in the molding and settling dips in the floors that showed evidence of instability and were already blocked with large sheets of plastic and caution tape Grey and his crew had put up.

The old sunroom, a connecting hallway, a couple third floor bedrooms and the library were deemed currently at risk.

The many bedrooms—every one was special in some way, either a sibling's bedroom at some time, or the backdrop of a childhood experience. Old houses, especially, held their character, Cammie thought. People lived and died in them over the decades. Houses truly absorbed life and the character of the occupants through time.

The memories from her childhood and teen years

seemed as if they'd occurred ages ago, and she wasn't the same girl, was she? She hadn't thought she was until she saw Grey yesterday. Long suppressed memories had boiled back up to the surface in a rush of painful emotion. She'd wanted to shriek at him and demand why he'd made such awful choices, never really allowing her any closure—leaving her heartbroken and grieving his loss.

But now that she'd created something real with Jason, she owed it to their future to set this recent surge of old soreness behind her. She couldn't risk opening up wounds and stirring the anger and questions about the past with Grey. She could ask, but wasn't sure if she wanted to go down that road, no matter the answers.

Cammie had never considered herself vengeful, and though there were times she'd wished Deb a painful existence, she never wished her dead. By the time she'd returned home to the family interrogation, she'd been filled with unspoken emotion.

As Cammie rounded the corner, lost in yesterday's events, she was nearly deafened by a shrill scream. Her lips formed a surprised, but joyful 'o' as she found herself face-to-face with a large, ageless black woman—one she'd known and loved since childhood—one who obviously hadn't expected to see Cammie here either.

"Rosie! Oh, Rose, it's so good to see you." They embraced. Well, it was more like being picked up by a grizzly bear and twirled around.

"Oh, my baby! How you been?" Rose still wore the old type uniform of a pale grey underdress with a full starched, white apron, bib-style, covering her ample bosom all the way to mid shin and tied at her thick waist. "Honey, just look at your sweet face."

"Rosie, I've missed you. How are you and your family?"

"Oh, honey, we're just fine, like always." Rose dabbed at her eyes with her apron. Then, her expression became fierce. "I seen you on the television with that woman all screamin' and her hair on fire. Darlin' you didn't do that? I know you didn't."

"No, I didn't, Rosie. But she had to blame somebody, and that was how she chose to handle it." Cammie shrugged.

"People who lie go to hell, you know?" Rose's face was dead serious. Cammie nearly burst out laughing at her expression.

"I don't want anybody going to hell on my account, Rosie," Cammie reached over and hugged Rose again, just to wipe away her grave mood.

"I guess you saw that boy, Grey, working here on your momma's house?"

"Yeah. I saw him. They didn't tell me, Rosie, they just let me run right into him after all this time."

"I told your momma they'd better tell you before you got here that he'd be under foot. Ain't no way they should've let that happen, honey. I'd have called you and told you myself if I'd known they didn't fill you in. If you ask me, she should have sent him packing when he showed up here."

"What do you mean he showed up here?" Cammie

wasn't sure she wanted another reason to be pissed at her mother or the rest of the bunch, but she had to ask.

"I was cleaning when he came by the first time, I don't want to be accused of eavesdropping." Rose shrugged. "You'll need to ask your momma about that. Like I said, she didn't ask what I thought, so it's not my business what she decided to do about her money and doing work around here. But you had a right to know the boy was back and would be here in the house before you came home."

It was so like Rose to tell her something without telling her anything to make sure she was in the loop and knew what questions to ask. So, Grey had come to Mom. Very interesting. Why would he have done that?

Cammie changed the subject. "I'm surprised to see you still working. I thought Mom said you'd planned to retire last year."

Rose's shoulders relaxed, "I'm mostly retired from heavy work, but I come by to make sure my girls are handling things like they're supposed to. Your momma still needs me around here, you know? Who else is gonna make sure everything's done just so?" They were standing on the second floor landing at the foot of the stairs.

"You've got a point there. I feel better knowing you're here to help take care of things. Especially now that Mom's had this surgery. Rose, can I ask you about the kitchen?"

"Your momma's been real funny about her kitchen, lately. She ain't let me near it except to make sure it's surface clean. I think since she's not been cooking, she feels bad about it. But I'm danged determined to get in there today and do some scrubbing. I've got a couple of my girls with me to do the heavy cleaning. I'm getting too old to get down on my hands and knees anymore."

"You certainly don't need to be down on the floor. But I'm planning to stock up on supplies, so it would help to have the kitchen ready when I haul things in later today. Mom won't have much of a choice how I deal with the kitchen while I'm here."

"Don't you worry, none. She'll be just fine before ya know it, honey. Do whatever you got to, and I'll help all I can. I got to get back to work, but just holler if you need me." Rosie gave her another quick squeeze and ambled down the stairs.

Cammie felt like a little girl again just knowing her Rosie was in the house and just a squeal away. Rose'd always been there when they'd been children to kiss boo-boos, break up sibling fights, and make things sparkle. Cammie's day had just improved.

Judging by the banging and scraping noises she'd overheard from the library down the hall, Grey was hard at work. That was a room she planned to steer clear of, if possible. She'd noticed he'd come in just after eight o'clock this morning, likely once Samantha was off to school. It gave Cammie one more piece of information to file away in her plan to avoid any new awkward situations.

She pushed all thoughts of Grey to the back of her brain where they belonged. Right now, there were more important matters to focus her energy and attention on. Food and the Evangeline House kitchen.

Today, she planned to shop at the local Costco and stock up on the main staples. Then, she would put a dent in the local organic market outside of town.

Cammie'd looked them up on the internet to see if they were open this week. Always preferring to use as many fresh ingredients as possible when cooking and baking, she loved the idea of the farmer's market and the organic methods employed in cultivating their produce. She'd prepared the menus and made a few calls to clients aligning her specialties with their tastes. They would have the opportunity to stop by and taste test items before the events.

The changes were slight, but well worth it. This weekend was the Forrester event, an intimate wedding anniversary, and the Dupree wedding reception. She would have the family representatives from each event swing by Friday to double check everything was in perfect order. Her mother had booked and prepared for these events for months ahead.

Outsourcing the catering was a killer in this business, even though she now understood that her mother's back pain and staff cuts necessitated this drastic measure. Bob, the electrician with more butt-crack showing than two plumbers combined, was working on the oven. And after today, the rest of the kitchen should be good to go.

Martin's, the local independent grocery/deli had been contracted to cater the food for the weekend's events. Cammie had read on the invoice of their forty-eight hour cancellation policy. They were pretty much the only game in town besides The Evangeline House and a couple local hotels and restaurants several miles away. She would cancel the food even though it wasn't very neighborly.

She decided to head there first and get it over with. She hesitated to walk in and take away business from them. On the other hand, Evangeline House couldn't afford to lose the revenue either. Especially with the repairs Grey was making. Who knew how much that would cost them?

She had gone over the menu and could easily replicate and improve on it. Obviously, she would do a far nicer spread than the local grocer—not to belittle their talents. Martin's did a decent job for this area, or her mother wouldn't have considered using them. But canceling the order would be tricky, mostly because Cammie and the Martin's daughter, Jenna had a strained relationship.

Hopefully Jenna wouldn't be around. They'd been good friends way back. All that business with Grey and Deb from years past pretty much did a number on Cammie's friendships around here. Mostly because she hadn't maintained steady contact with anyone in town. Several of her old friends had tried, but had given up after a while. Who could blame them?

Twenty minutes later, as Cammie entered the store, the bell hanging from the handle tinkled. When she approached the deli counter, a female voice called from the back room, "Be with you in just a sec—"

Cammie recognized the voice, when a woman appeared through the door. "Well, look here, it's Cammie Laroux as I live and breathe." Hand on her hip, with what looked like fresh, disposable clear gloves on her hands, a butcher's apron over top of jeans, and a white t-shirt; Jenna Martin was posed in defiance.

Crap. "Hey, Jenna. It's good to see you again."

"Right. So good, you thought you'd come in town and not call, as usual? Of course now that you're famous, should I expect something different?"

"I was going to call as soon as things settled down at the house. You know my mom just had back surgery?"

"Uh, yeah. That's why we're taking care of the food this weekend for her. You know we've been doing that a lot lately." Jenna was still a pretty girl, though she'd gained a good fifteen pounds since high school. Her curly dark hair strained at its confinement, her cupid's bow mouth twisted in a less than pleasant smile.

"Jenna, I'm sorry."

"Save it, fancy pants. What can I get for you?" Jenna's dark eyes narrowed. Obviously she wasn't going to make this easy for Cammie.

And it was about to get worse. Cammie cleared her throat, "That's why I'm here. I'm going to handle the catering this weekend. So, we won't need your services."

"Are you kidding?" Cammie was very thankful Jenna didn't have a meat cleaver in her grasp at the moment.

"No, I can easily handle the catering while I'm here. I read in Mom's notes that you have a forty-eight-hour cancellation policy, so I wanted to let you know ahead of time that we've changed plans.

"Forty-eight hours is for a *sandwich* tray, maybe." Jenna sneered.

"It did sound generous." Lame, and they both knew it.

"I've already purchased fifty Cornish hens, a twenty-five pound sack of risotto, tons of phyllo dough for the desserts, and more butter, vegetables, and other supplies than I can cover the loss for. So, your, 'Oh, so sorry, I'm going to cater my own wedding and birthday party for over a hundred people,' kind of screws me over!" Jenna's face was an angry red.

"Hey, Jenna, take it easy. I'll buy the supplies and the hens from you. It's the least I can do. I'm sorry for canceling so late and I do apologize for taking back the catering business. My mom wasn't able to handle it all while she's been down. But we can't afford to send it out, either. It kills the profit margin. You're a business owner, you understand."

Jenna narrowed her eyes but her complexion lost some of its mottled appearance. She grudgingly gave in, "Fine, I'll go get the stuff. I hope you brought a truck."

"Nope, just mom's U-boat of a station wagon." That almost brought a smile to Jenna's face, she was sure of it. They'd had some good times in that station wagon.

As they were loading frozen fowl on a dolly back in the freezer, the bell jingled on the front door of the shop. "Just a couple more back here. Check and see who's out there, would you?" Jenna directed her.

"Yeah, sure." Cammie's teeth were chattering, and she was happy for an excuse to escape.

"Hey, what are you doing here?" Grey Harrison, his brows raised in surprise, stood on the other side of the counter. His navy blue t-shirt fit snug, reminding her of their recent ladder encounter. A handsome smile played around his lips.

She wished herself back inside the freezer.

Smiling tightly, she said, "I'm picking up supplies from Jenna for this weekend's events." Was the man following her? Or just picking up lunch? The grocery made the best deli sandwiches in town. Cammie must figure out how to put a damned tracker on him so she could avoid him. Her breath caught in her throat and she felt her cheeks redden. Great.

"Cammie, who's out there?" Jenna called from the back.

"It's me, Jenna." Grey called back to her.

"Oh, hey, Grey. I've got your order ready. Give me a second." Jenna came out then; her apron and gloves had vanished, hair expertly tousled, the transformation nothing short of miraculous. Most transformative was her expression. Gone was the sour, pinchy Jenna. The now-beaming Jenna must haven eaten her predecessor, as she was nowhere to be seen.

"Can I give you ladies a hand?" Grey asked.

"That would be great. We're about to load up Cammie's car," Jenna was quick to answer, now all syrup and honey instead of piss and vinegar like she'd been before. That was how Cammie remembered her. She'd never been a real softie until the cute boys rolled by. But she had been fun to go out with on a Saturday night.

"It would be my pleasure to help with that." He sounded so Southern, if he said Ma'am, she might swoon.

He suggested they load some of the items in his truck for additional space since he'd be heading back to Evangeline House shortly, but Cammie declined the offer.

By the time they'd stuffed her car to the brim, Jenna was behaving in an oddly girlie manner and obviously wished Cammie off the nearest cliff. *Sorry, girlfriend, no cliffs in this part of Alabama.*

Cammie couldn't tell much by Grey's relaxed, offhand behavior. He should have been a poker player—he would be filthy rich. Or a stripper—that would likely be profitable as well, based on the way every muscle rippled under his shirt as it stretched taut across his shoulders, chest, and biceps as he lifted and carried the heavy items to the car.

Cammie was damned uncomfortable and couldn't wait to be on her way. Before she managed to make her way out to the car, slam the door, and get the thing in reverse, Grey was knocking on her window.

What?

"Do you need help unloading the car once you get home?"

Really?

"No, I'll be fine. Enjoy your lunch." Again, she tried to turn away and put the car in gear. Another knock at the window.

Geez.

She rolled it down, trying not to appear as impatient and bothered as she felt. "Yes?"

"Are you sure?" He asked.

Was he freaking kidding? "Cross my heart. Rosie is there

with two helpers and the gardener will gladly lend a hand. So, thanks."

"Okay, I'll see you later." He grinned and waved.

This time she waited a moment before attempting to back up to make certain she wouldn't run over a foot. When he showed no signs of stopping her progress, she began her short trip home in the massive station wagon. She was shaking by the time she made it to the road heading toward her house.

Why am I behaving like such an idiot? It was lucky for her the spell was broken the second he was out of range.

As she drove back toward Evangeline House, Cammie's thoughts weren't focused on the road as they might have been, and when the station wagon suddenly crashed into the gigantic buck that appeared out of nowhere, Cammie's forehead and chest slammed forward into the steering wheel without the impediment of an airbag.

While wheezing air back into her lungs, relief flooded through her the she hadn't slid down the steep embankment beside the road. Something drizzled down her nose. She wiped at it and took a look. Blood. Darkness surrounded her vision and swallowed it.

Chapter Five

❧

"CAMMIE LOOKS GOOD, don't you think? It must be hard on her—being such a laughingstock and all." At the sound of Cammie's name, Grey's head had whipped around. They'd all been friends, back in the day, but there was an edge to Jenna's tone and a gleam in her eye that didn't give him such a friendly vibe at that moment.

"Huh? Yeah, she looks good." He decided not to bite on Jenna's laughingstock comment.

Jenna's eyes narrowed. "The two of you seem to be getting along pretty well, considering."

"I'm grateful she's speaking to me," Grey admitted.

"Can't say I blame you after everything that happened back then. Too bad Cammie has her work cut out for her over at the plantation with the place falling down and all, bless her heart." The dreaded 'bless her heart.' It was the South's most effective way to cut down on the sting of an insult or bad news. "God love 'em" came in a close second.

"I'm working over at Evangeline House and so far see no evidence of it falling down, Jenna. Where did you hear that?" He had to be careful around here with the gossip mill working over time now that he and Cammie were both back in town.

"Well, I'd understood they're close to shutting them down altogether because it isn't safe for folks to be anywhere near there. I wouldn't want to have my wedding there—might turn into a funeral, if you know what I mean."

That kind of unfounded and mean-spirited talk could potentially cause real problems. How could he best turn this around without raising Jenna's hackles?

"Jenna, seems to me you wouldn't want anyone thinking you were spreading a rumor that might hurt their business, would you?"

A shamed flush spread across her cheeks. "Certainly not. Cammie's my friend. I mean, we haven't been so close lately, but I'd never do anything to hurt her or her family on purpose. You don't think that of me, do you, Grey?" She blinked like she had something in both eyes and was trying to clear them. Oh wait, she was batting her eyelashes at him.

He pulled out his wallet, intending to pay for his lunch order. "Of course not, Jenna. But I hope you understand that Evangeline House is going to be just fine?" There, that ought to fix her gossip wagon.

Grey paid for his lunch and marveled at the cattiness he'd observed over the years of some women. Who knew Jenna Martin could be so hateful? The cerebral warfare females waged, fueled by jealousy and anger, terrified Grey. Guys settled disputes with a punch in the nose and a shared beer afterward. Very little lasting damage that way.

The old plantation would require a lot of work still, but

after an extensive evaluation of the property, he didn't expect to find any more serious problems with the place.

After he left the grocery, Grey headed back toward Evangeline House, but couldn't get through due to a traffic delay. By the looks of things, there'd been an accident. The red lights of an ambulance ahead, along with several police cruisers blocked the right lane.

Slowly, he approached an officer waving traffic around the scene. As Grey inched closer, he recognized the station wagon he'd helped load only an hour before. It was sitting askew in the lane with the driver's door open, the windshield shattered and a deep indention in the hood. Cammie wasn't anywhere that he could see.

He swallowed convulsively, the blood roaring in his ears so loudly he was deafened by it. "Oh, God." The ambulance pulled away while he'd been several cars back.

Rolling his truck window down, Grey managed to find his voice, "Do you know if the driver is alright?" He asked one of the young officers on the scene.

"Looks like she got the business end of a twelve-pointer. Quite a bit of blood, but I don't think she's critical." Grey must have reacted because the officer asked, "Hey buddy, you okay?"

"Uh, yeah."

He headed straight for County General, calling his father on the way.

He asked his dad for a couple favors during the call. His father reassured him. "Son, she's going to be fine. I'll take care of the car and its contents. Don't worry."

His dad owned the local towing company, and Grey wanted to get the car picked up as soon as possible and all the food back in refrigeration. Even with her accident, he didn't want her to lose all the frozen Cornish hens if possible. At least he could try and do that.

By the time he arrived at the hospital, she was back in the triage area and he wasn't able to go back and see her. Ben appeared through opened elevator doors. "What the hell happened? Someone called the nurses station upstairs and said Cammie hit a deer in Mom's car."

"I drove up on it. I was a few minutes behind the ambulance, but she'd already been taken back by the time I made it here."

Ben approached the desk, "Excuse me, can you give me an update on Cammie Laroux's condition?"

The woman spoke quietly to Ben in a husky tone while thrusting her chest toward him, as if he would become turned on while asking about his sister's accident. Female reactions to Ben boggled his mind. Ben then turned to Grey. "She's okay. Only a bloody nose and a bruised collarbone. Thank God."

Grey exhaled hard, not knowing what he'd have done if Cammie had been seriously injured.

"I'll call the rest of the family before they hear it from someone else and the story gets worse." Ben excused himself to use his cell phone.

Grey sat down hard in one of the faded chairs. His hands were trembling.

"I'm going to head back and check on her myself. Want

to come with me?" Ben asked.

"Sure." That was an understatement.

"The nurse says she's got a cut on her forehead, a fat lip and will be sore for a few days, but was lucky to be in Mom's tank, even without the airbag."

"I guess the deer wasn't so lucky."

"Junior says it wasn't pretty, though he plans to mount the rack for his showroom."

"Sounds like Junior." Cammie's taxidermist brother-in-law wouldn't pass up that kind of opportunity. He dealt with dead animals all the time, and the county often called him to clean up when such matters needed dealing with.

As they reached the treatment room, Grey sucked in his breath at the lump on Cammie's head. "Oh, wow. Hey, how are you feeling?"

"Like I hit a brick wall at fifty miles an hour, but fine otherwise."

"Dad did a quick clear out of the station wagon and managed to save the hens before they thawed. He's dropping them at Evangeline House with Rose and her daughter. She says to tell you not to worry, they have things under control."

Cammie's relief was evident by her exhale and soft, "Thanks for thinking of the food. It would have been such a waste to lose those hens. What about Mom's car?"

"Retired, I'm sorry to say."

Ben sighed. "Lots of good times in that old wagon."

"For all of us," Cammie agreed, then asked, "Can I go now? I want to see Mom before I head home."

"Simmer down. They're finishing your release forms now. Junior says that buck had quite a rack on him." Ben said.

"Tell Junior I'm fine, thank you." Cammie said.

"He did ask." Ben grinned.

"After he checked out the rack, I'm sure." Grey had to agree with Cammie's assessment of Junior's priorities.

Thankfully, Cammie moved carefully, though better than he expected as she rose from the bed, even though her clothes were pretty bloody.

"How's your chest?" Ben asked.

"What a thing for a brother to ask." She winked at Ben, but winced at the movement.

"The nurse said you'd hit the steering wheel pretty hard and would be sore for a few days, weirdo."

"I was kidding. It feels like somebody stomped on me, but I'll be alright," Cammie reassured him.

"I don't want Mom to see the blood all over you shirt. It would upset her. You can come back tomorrow. Go home now and get some rest." Ben shuffled her hair, but gently.

"I'm fine," Cammie sighed, exasperated.

"Go home. I'll stay here with Mom, and Grey can take you," Ben said.

Grey hurried to reassure them. "Of course. I'll be happy to." He was more than happy to help; his relief was so great that Cammie wasn't hurt more severely than she was.

Cammie opened her mouth to protest, but Ben cut her off. "You'll do as we say unless you prefer to be admitted for a night's observation." She stared at her brother in angry silence.

The matter was settled.

"I'll bring my truck around," Grey said.

The nurse was already insisting Cammie have a seat in the wheelchair. Grey headed toward the exit and decided to let Ben handle that fight as well.

>>><<<

GREY TREATED HER as if she would break. "I'm okay, you know," she said.

"You've just been in a car accident and you have stitches in your eyebrow."

He stood too close, in her estimation, close enough for her to detect a wisp of his breath on her brow and the scent of spicy soap as he reached across to buckle her in. He tried to keep his weight off her, she knew, but he indented just a tiny pressure for an instant when the buckle clicked, causing her to inhale suddenly, which caused him to startle. "I'm fine. I'm not going to die. In a few days I'll be good as new."

"And today, you have to take it easy. I promised Ben that I would see to it."

"I know. I'm sorry to be such a pain in the butt." She was trying not to complain that he was the one taking her home.

"Are you hurting?" He did seem concerned.

"Not too bad. The nurse gave me some pills for that." Her breastbone and head had begun to throb at the hospital, but the meds were starting to kick in. She could feel a distinctly warm sensation stealing around her middle.

"Do pain pills still make you, uh—silly?" He asked, smiling.

"What do you mean?" She couldn't quite put her finger on—something, but had the uneasy feeling she was about to find out what it was.

"I seem to recall a wisdom tooth removal surgery and your first exposure to narcotics." He turned, starting the ignition, a huge grin spreading as he obviously recalled details.

That grin brought back the incident in foggy remnants including her begging him to kiss and touch her. "Of course I remember having my wisdom teeth out, but I'd forgotten about the pain pills." What a liar. She now remembered her first orgasm as clear as day. Before that, she'd either completely blocked out the event, or shoved it into the disremembered storage place in her brain with the countless other Grey-related items. Dear God, would she react that way to the drugs again? "I haven't had any pain meds since then."

"Did you already take the pills?"

"About a half hour ago." She swallowed her panic as she fought the sensuous relaxation creeping in, easing her pain and inhibitions.

"Uh-oh." He obviously still held close a clear memory of how the medication affected her.

"I remember enough to know that I want to be alone when they take effect." Cammie couldn't help but notice the way his faded blue jeans encased his muscled thighs.

"Let's get you home—and stop looking at me like that."

She still had every reason to hate his guts. But he really had aged well over the last ten years.

⟫⟫⟪⟪

CAMMIE WAS A near-puddle; soft, pliable and boneless in his arms, by the time they reached Evangeline House. Grey lifted her gently and carried her toward the house, but she protested. "I wanna go to the back yard."

"I'm carrying you upstairs to your bed."

"No! I wanna go and lie in the gazebo, like we used to. You remember, don't you?"

Boy, did he. Their make-out spot. He glanced around. The weather was mild with no rain forecasted. Maybe the fresh air would do her some good and sober her up a bit. He could work for a while then carry her up later. The gazebo was nestled in the center of the yard, shaded by oak trees and well-appointed with clean, comfortable cushions on wrought iron furniture.

He laid her on the chaise and had to disentangle her arms from his neck, as she'd locked them tight around him. Though the rest of her body was extremely relaxed, her arms seemed reluctant to disengage. He opened the nearby storage chest to pull out one of the blankets kept inside for chilly evenings.

Tucking it around her feet and placing a clean pillow under her head from the storage box, Grey tried to speak to her. "Cammie?"

"Hmmm?" She opened her eyes and seared him with a sleepy, sexy gaze as she stretched like a lazy cat, arms over her head, her still-bloody shirt accentuating her breasts. Fortunately for him, the blood removed any lingering lustful thoughts. Concern for her wellbeing was squarely at the forefront of his mind now.

"I'm going up to the house to get you a clean shirt. Any one you prefer?" He would check to see if Rose was there to handle it, and hopefully he could get to work on the house. Plus, the idea of aiding her in changing her blouse brought back in sharp relief his struggle between good and evil intentions toward a drugged and weakened woman.

"Doesn't matter," She slurred and waved him on his way.

"You alright for a few minutes out here?" She nodded. "I'll be right back."

He sprinted from the gazebo toward the back porch, which was roughly twenty-five yards or so. Did she have to look so hot in a blood-covered t-shirt? Most slurry, fawny women would have him running the other direction for far different reasons. He should really let someone else handle the garment change. Cammie was riling up his manhood in the worst way—a dishonorable way.

It must have something to do with the other time she took those pain pills. Way back when they were young and so hot for each other. Back when their bodies ached through denim for the slightest brush of bare flesh, when the heat of the other's proximity caused a painful longing to press just a little closer.

He entered the house in a near lather. "Rose?" She wasn't in the kitchen, but he did notice it looked as if a hurricane had come through.

But no Rose. He called all around. Upstairs, downstairs, and no Rose. Damn. He would have to handle Cammie's blouse change himself. He headed toward her room as if he'd grown up here as well. He had, in some ways, he supposed. They'd begun "going out" in middle school.

He'd gone inside her bedroom when Maureen had initially hired him to work on Evangeline House. His emotional response had surprised him. So many things inside were the same as they'd been years ago.

Her pom-poms were stuck at the corner of an old cork board filled with faded photographs overlapping each other at the corners. There were lots with her sisters, girlfriends, clubs; but not a single one of either Grey or Deb. Obvious gaps stood out where pictures had been removed.

He had a flash of nostalgia again as he crossed the threshold of her bedroom in search of a blouse.

Finding her suitcase empty, he started with the top dresser drawer. There weren't any clothes in it, but something caught his eye just before he shut it. It was an old, navy blue bandana he'd worn as a teen. He recognized the pattern because his mother had bought several yards of the fabric and made him and his dad both each at least a dozen neckcloths.

As if unable to stop, he touched the fabric. There was a small item, something hard and round wrapped within. He shouldn't snoop, of course he was trespassing, but he had to know what was inside. Carefully unrolling the somewhat weighty item, it fell with a thud, clank and then rolled underneath the bed.

"Damn it." He stooped down to his hands and knees.

"What in the world are you doing up here—under my sister's bed? And where is Cammie?"

Those were all very good questions. He managed to identify the object as his high school ring, tried to ignore the hard punch in his gut, and decided to leave it be. "Oh, hey, Maeve. I came up to get Cammie a shirt and I dropped something."

"Okay. But where is she?" Maeve was no-nonsense.

"She's out in the gazebo," he said, willing himself to focus on the moment and not think about the high school ring still under Cammie's bed like a tiny ball of emotional dynamite.

"Why isn't she here in bed after her accident?" Hands on her hips, she resembled Cammie, though not quite as much as the other sisters because of her oddly dark blue eyes.

"Because she insisted I take her out there. I'm not quite sure why. Hey, can you help me find her something to put on? Her shirt is pretty bloody."

"Oh, my Lord. Ben said she was okay." Maeve's eyes teared.

"She's fine, Maeve. She has a small cut on her eyebrow and it bled some. Uh—she's also a little woozy from pain meds. So, don't pay much attention to what she says." He made a circling motion with his index finger next to his ear and grinned.

"You're scaring the snot outta me, Grey. Go on down

and check on her. I'll get her some clothes and be down in a sec."

"Okay." He headed down the stairs, his class ring still at the edge of the bed and the edge of his thoughts. Stopping by the kitchen, he filled a glass with ice and water for Cammie.

She was sound asleep by the time he'd made it back to the gazebo, her mouth wide open. He'd only been in the house a few minutes, but it seemed an eventful space of time.

The back door slammed and Maeve tottered toward them on her espadrilles, calling out to her sister. "Cammie, are you there? Honey, you scared the bejeezus out of us!" Maeve bent over her sister. "Dang, that must have been some smack on the head to bleed so much. What's wrong with her? Is it okay for her to be asleep?"

"They cleared her to sleep, so I'm assuming she didn't have a concussion. She's medicated and very relaxed."

"Let's get her inside and put her to bed. I'll worry about changing her shirt later. Can you carry her?"

"I managed to get her out here from the truck. I figure I can tote her back inside." He bent to gather her now-limp form in his arms for the second time today. At least she wasn't squirming against him just now.

Grey couldn't say he was put upon just now. In fact, this would most likely be the only time he'd hold Cammie close again in this lifetime. He wanted to savor it. She still smelled the same. How could that be? Did she wear the same perfume? Or, after all these years could he recognize her by scent? How sad and desperate that sounded.

He laid her down on top of the bed, pulling up the quilt—the same one he remembered from when she was a teen, handmade by her grandmother. Maeve had disappeared into the bathroom to get a warm washcloth. He quickly bent down to pick up his ring from under the bed before her sister returned.

What to do with it?

Grey quickly slid it in the top drawer of the bedside table just as the water shut off in the next room.

"Okay, I can take it from here. Thanks so much for bringing her home and handling things until I made it back." He'd been dismissed.

Cammie stirred, opened her eyes, and reached out, her fingers encircling his wrist. "Hey, you." Her smile, though sleepy, was dazzling.

Grey's breath whooshed out, so unexpected was his response to her touch. He cleared his throat. "How are you feeling?"

"Good to see you awake, honey." It was obvious by the narrowing of her eyes that Maeve hadn't missed the sexy tone Cammie'd sent his way.

"Oh, hey, Maeve. I'm alright. A little sleepy." Cammie yawned, then refocused her attention away from Grey toward her sister.

He took the opportunity presented by her change in focus. "Glad you're feeling better. Guess I'll head downstairs and get something accomplished this afternoon before it's time to get Samantha home."

"Thanks for taking care of me." Cammie glanced toward him, but her earlier sexual haze seemed to have lifted.

"Let me know if you need anything." he was backing out of her bedroom as he spoke the words.

He needed a beer and a cold shower to calm his nerves—and everything else.

≫≫≪≪

MAUREEN LAROUX THOUGHT about the ten year old letter again—for about the thousandth time. She may never know if she'd done the right thing where Cammie was concerned. Her bright, beautiful daughter had moved on, become successful, and achieved things she might never have attempted had she known the whole sordid truth surrounding the mess with Grey Harrison and his deceased wife. Not that Cammie had lacked ambition or drive, she simply had been so deeply wrapped up in a future with Grey that she would've stuck with him had she thought they had even the tiniest chance of a happy ending.

Cammie would've held out hope, no matter how dismal. She probably wouldn't have left home—or might've tried harder to stop him from marrying Deb after the miscarriage. At the time, Maureen had been determined Grey wasn't to be trusted, that he would hurt her daughter even more in the bitter end. Once a liar, a cheat, always one. That was the way of men in her experience.

So, the letter continued to burden her conscience. Maureen hadn't destroyed it, though she'd been tempted many times during the past ten years. She had enough scruples or whatever the character trait was that kept her from destroying the truth, even if she'd made the long-ago decision to keep it deeply hidden. She had her principles. Cammie might never forgive her if she found out. But maybe, if it ever came to light, or if Maureen had a fit of conscience too strong to resist one of these days, Cammie would hopefully understand that Maureen only had her best interests at heart. Always.

Of course there was the very real possibility that some-day Grey would tell Cammie about the letter. Maureen realized that by hiring Grey to work on the house, she'd made that scenario more likely than it ever would have been. Though she could hardly have turned down his help considering the generous offer he'd extended.

What would be would be, and they would all live with the consequences.

Before Maureen had met James Laroux, the father of her children, she'd been deeply hurt and disillusioned. Admit-tedly, her righteous intentions in protecting Cammie from heartbreak might have roots hidden within Maureen's own painful past. This wasn't something she wished to dredge up and examine so many decades later.

She'd hated that Cammie was forced to come back and handle the family business while she was down from this blasted surgery. But her other children hadn't Cammie's skills and acumen, either in business or in the kitchen; that girl was a magician with food. Maureen had known she'd discover the empty kitchen and set things aright.

She'd not had the energy or the time to restore things,

but her daughter was a left-brain/right-brained whiz. Creative and organized, and could solve a problem using both skill sets like no one Maureen'd ever seen. Evangeline House's kitchen didn't stand a chance without Cammie in residence. Things would be set to rights in no time.

Her conscience bothered her, knowing Grey Harrison was living in Ministry again and they hadn't alerted Cammie, but The Evangeline House was the family lifeblood. And Maureen thought he might be the reason Cammie stayed away. Maybe clearing the air—even yelling at him or finally demanding an explanation for what had happened ten years ago would gain some closure to the entire matter.

Maureen of all people understood unresolved emotions and never having the opportunity to close the book on an unfinished chapter in life. Closure was vital to move forward without regrets and what might-have-beens.

Chapter Six

CAMMIE WAS EXCITED but exhausted after last night's exertion; she'd cleaned, organized and prepared for the weekend's cooking frenzy. Rose arrived first thing this morning with her helpers in tow to give the place a super-duper scrubbing down.

By the time she'd dressed, gone through a few things in the office, and made her way to the kitchen, she was nearly buzzing with the anticipation of throwing herself into her recipes. Finding a clean apron hanging on a hook next to the back door, she once again blessed Rosie's like-minded determination to set things right around here.

Her chest was still somewhat sore, but not nearly so much as she'd expected, and though she had a nasty bruise surrounding her left eyebrow, all in all, Cammie supposed the deer had fared far worse.

Allowing for her less than a hundred percent status, she'd made detailed lists by task, cook times, and temperatures, items that would require refrigeration, etc. Organization was key to efficient execution of all that required doing. This afternoon, she'd scheduled food tastings for the weekend's events. That way, there would be no surprises when she tweaked the originally planned menus.

Completely engrossed in her pastry dough, Cammie was dragged from her sore, but happy place by a ruckus of what might be barking and—*squawking*—outside? This couldn't be good. Startled, and more than a bit curious as to what the disturbance might be, Cammie poked her head out the back kitchen door.

Her attention was drawn immediately to the formerly-empty wire chicken coop. The large containment now confined chickens. Not happy chickens, unfortunately, as they were currently set upon by a large dog dead set on catching a chicken snack. The dog barked and howled madly while the flustered fowl flapped and screeched—as hens are wont to do when threatened by a hound nurturing unholy intentions.

Cammie saw Grey enter the fray. Whistling urgently for the dog to cease and desist, but likely only causing more chicken heart failure, he worked to gain control of the madness. It was almost too much. She hurried outside toward the maelstrom, not sure how best to approach this chaos.

Fortunately, her presence distracted the dog just long enough for Grey to grab him by the collar and haul him out of the wire containment.

The chickens continued their squawks of angst and outrage a few more moments before settling down.

She found her voice first. "Grey Harrison, what on earth

were you thinking? Chickens? Really? You could have given me a heads-up."

His surprise at her arrival on the scene was evident in his deer-in-the-headlights expression. He quickly recovered himself, attempting a manlier pose.

"A gift from my father." Sleeves rolled up, tanned forearms exposed; he extended his arms wide as if bestowing on her the greatest of treasures. The boxer sat beside him, chicken feathers hanging from his mouth and stuck to his nose.

She'd been trying, since making her way out the back door to keep a straight face, but she couldn't contain her laughter a moment longer. Her shoulders shook, and it took several minutes before she could speak without tears rolling down her face.

"What? Who doesn't like chickens?" He was filthy and boasted more than a few fowl feathers attached to his own person.

She managed to get her mirth under control finally, and answer truthfully, "But why would I want them? I'm only here for a few more weeks."

"Evangeline House has always kept chickens—it's tradition." He had her there. She was surprised he'd remembered and wondered where the chickens had gone. As far back as she could recall, there had been chickens and fresh eggs on the property.

"I assume the chickens went the way of my mother's kitchen, but I will say thank you. I have a ton of cooking to do and I prefer to use farm fresh eggs. Once I get things back up and running, and Mom is back to her lively self, I can't imagine her not wanting the chickens."

"You're welcome. My dad asked me to bring them over and put them in the coop and check on you and your mother. How are you both, by the way?"

"Please tell him we appreciate his thoughtfulness," she said. "Mom's obviously still in the hospital, but recovering nicely, thanks."

"You're quite the sight, aren't you?" He seemed amused by her appearance.

"I tried to cover the bruise with makeup, but figured it didn't really matter." Comprehension dawned on Cammie that he wasn't referring to her bruised face, but at what a hot mess she'd become during her cooking frenzy. Her apron was literally coated with remnants of the ingredients she'd used in several recipes thus far.

Lifting a flour-infested hand, she patted her hair in a Marilyn-esque fashion—she'd twisted it into a messy bun and quickly clipped it up out of the way. Based on what she could feel, half of the messy bun was down and she felt some pretty significant chunks of—what was that?

Cammie pulled something out of the back of her hair, and realized it was a medium sized blob of dough. She smiled sweetly at Grey and held out the offering, "Hungry?"

His lips twitched as he unsuccessfully tried to control his smirk. Those same lips that made her ache with sensations she hadn't fully understood as a young woman.

"Um, nope. Just ate." Chuckling a bit, he turned toward his truck, whistled for his dog, and ducked as the dough flew past his head, then he flashed her a grin.

Realizing there wasn't hope for a graceful exit, Cammie simply said, "You have a little—I mean, be careful you don't get any chicken shit in your truck." She stared meaningfully at his rear end, pointing. It was hard to hold a grudge against a guy who had chicken shit on his butt and had just done a nice thing for her mother.

"Hang on; I'll get a paper towel from inside." Her face was burning, as was the rest of her, and Cammie was relieved for the quick escape. What was wrong with her? She shouldn't be noticing his butt. Or any guy's, for that matter. She hated guilt.

>>>><<<<

GREY PULLED UP beside Samantha just as the bus rolled away. She'd just begun her slow walk, dragging her heavy backpack down the gravel drive. The home was set off the road about a quarter mile. Grey tried to meet her at the bus at the front of their property whenever he could. Some days, since he'd been working for the Laroux family, she got off the bus at Evangeline House with Lucy. "Hey there. Did you have a good day?"

She didn't look up, just made her way to the passenger's side door, head down. "You're late."

Was she crying? Her eyes appeared a bit pink and slightly puffy, but he couldn't really tell as she hadn't yet looked at him straight on. Her behavior was erratic at times, and he knew to tread carefully. She climbed in and shut the door. "The bus just pulled away. I wasn't early, but I wouldn't call it late." There was definitely something going on here. "I delivered some chickens to Lucy's aunt so she would have fresh eggs for her cooking."

"Why do you like her so much? You never talk to other ladies like you do her."

"Do you see how Grandpa's house and Miz Maureen's house are separated by a gate in the backyard?" He asked.

She nodded.

"Well, I grew up with all of Lucy's aunts and her Uncle Ben. Ben and Cammie were the closest two to my age, so we went to school together and were all friends when we were kids and went back and forth to each other's houses. That's why I'm comfortable talking with her; it's because we grew up together."

Samantha took that in, then nodded solemnly again. "Okay, Daddy. It's good to have friends. I'm glad Lucy's my friend."

Grey felt a pang of guilt in telling a partial truth to his very intelligent daughter. He also worried that the whole truth would somehow find its way out at some point. But while Samantha was so fragile, he'd take things as they happened for now.

"So what's happened to upset you today?" Grey asked softly.

"Sophie's having a birthday party, and she was talking about her mom and dad putting up decorations and how they were going to grill out and how her mom was taking her to get her nails done." Samantha gave him a sorrowful stare. "It made me sad." Her lip quivered.

"Aw, baby, I know." He pulled her in close. Then, he extended a hand where she could see it. "My cuticles are awfully rough. How about a mani-pedi?"

He heard her giggle through her tears. "Daddy, I don't think so."

"Aw, come on. I wouldn't embarrass you."

She pulled back and said very seriously, "Thanks for trying, but Mommy and me never got our nails done together anyway."

He sighed. She was right. Deb just didn't do many normal mommy kinds of things with her daughter. "Well, let me know if you change your mind. I have some killer callouses," he said, trying to lighten the mood between them again.

"Got it." She moved back to her side of the truck, and seemed pretty much back on an even keel, for the moment.

⫸❈⫷

CAMMIE'S TASTING MEETINGS for this week's events with the Forrester's and Dupree's went quite well. She'd tweaked the menus slightly, but closely followed the original orders, adding a few embellishments. The clients' approval greatly relieved her mind, because frankly, she wasn't certain what she would've done otherwise. Tomorrow was Thursday, and she still had a few last minute items to attend in the kitchen tomorrow, but she'd completed the bulk of the cooking today.

Jo Jo would be her right hand on Saturday, along with any other family members she could manage to hog-tie and drag in as party helpers. Cammie wasn't certain if they'd scatter like roaches once she hit the scene, leaving most of the work on her shoulders. Normally, a couple sisters and various in-laws pitched in when there were two events going on, or so Mom had led her to believe.

When she'd been young, Cammie had thrived on the buzz of anticipation right before an event. The satisfaction of playing an important role in making someone's most special day memorable infused her with great delight.

The butterflies she now experienced reminded her of those past weddings, graduations, anniversaries, and all the many and varied other kinds of parties she'd been a part of in the history of this business that was her family legacy.

Cammie would do her best while she was here to see her family's business thrive. She would deal with the fact that Grey might be the best person to help preserve this heritage. Hopefully, once Mom was back on her feet, she could scuttle right back to Virginia and Jason and the tatters of her career.

>>>><<<<

CAMMIE WAS JUST putting the finishing touches on the Dupree lemon petit fours when she heard the swoosh of the kitchen door and a loud catcall from behind. She carefully lifted the icing tip away from the last, luscious square before turning around.

Her big, gorgeous brother Ben frowned. "Hey, are you sure you're up for all this?"

"And if I wasn't, do you have a replacement in mind?"

He surveyed her bruised face as if to reassure himself she was indeed on the mend.

"Alright, pretty boy, stop lollygagging and help me get these desserts into the ballroom.'

"Pretty boy? Ew, Cam, that's gross. I'll help you if you promise never to call me that again."

"Fine, but I could use an extra set of hands, here."

He bowed, "At your service, ma'am."

They carried the trays to the beautifully decorated ball-room, everything at the ready for the Dupree wedding reception. The guests would be arriving shortly.

"Wow. This all looks awesome. Who's getting married?"

"Wanda Dupree is marrying Logan Townsend. Do you know them?" She glanced over her shoulder and registered the sick look of fear on Ben's face.

"Yeah, I know Wanda."

"By the looks of you, you know her pretty well." Cammie wanted to laugh, but wasn't sure if she should, judging by his panicked expression.

"We, uh, dated awhile back."

"Was Wanda prior to the two-date rule?" Ben recently enacted a two-date maximum per woman. This applied to all women. He'd been having issues with them getting too attached. But in the spirit of fairness, he couldn't play favorites.

"She was the reason for it. Well, the main one."

"Well, if you don't want to renew your—relationship, you'd better clear out, brother. The wedding party should be arriving any second if everything went off as it should at the church."

"You don't need to tell me twice. Oh, you in for football later?"

"What?" No one had mentioned football to her.

"Are you kidding? Alabama's playing Auburn tonight. You telling me you didn't know? We're all watching the game—like we always do, Cam."

Surely he was joking. They were all going to hang out and watch football while she handled two events at the same time? Her open-mouthed irritated glare must have given Ben a clue.

"Oh, come on, the game's not 'til eight. Plenty of time to wrap this up and join the family at kick off."

"You all suck, you know that?" She tried to hide the fact that her eyes had grown suspiciously moist. She had a few extra hands from the rental company staff picking up the empty glasses and such, but she would be running her tukus off trying to keep up with both parties. Jo should be down in minute to help, but even the two of them would struggle with all this.

He grinned a great big sneaky grin. "Aw, honey, we're not so bad. Who gets married in Alabama on game day, anyway?" Then he walked out, leaving her fuming and sputtering at the uselessness of her siblings.

She hadn't gotten a firm commitment from any of them, had she? Cammie had assumed, like when they were kids that everyone would pitch in on the weekends. She supposed it was her own fault. No wonder her mother's back had gone out.

Just when she'd begun slamming things around in the kitchen and was about to start screeching at the top of her lungs, one-by-one, her siblings, their spouses, and available children showed up, dressed in appropriate serving attire.

"Thank goodness you showed up to help out. I was about to get in my car and drive home." She put them to work, but it seemed they already knew what to do and where to help out.

The evening was a blur of activity, but Cammie fell back into it with an easy familiarity that came with lifelong experience.

Besides bride Wanda getting stinking drunk, and making a scene by stumbling into the anniversary party during the toast after she'd cried on Ben's shoulder on her way back from the bathroom, everything had been a smashing success.

Cammie was exhausted, and fortunately minimal damage control had been necessary to smooth any ruffled feathers caused by the inebriated bride.

After the crowd had departed and her siblings had pitched in to help clear away any remaining dishes, she headed upstairs and changed from party attire into jeans and an Alabama sweatshirt. Hair in a ponytail, she headed to the kitchen to construct a few tailgating favorites. No football game was complete without the perfect appetizers. She checked her watch. There would be just enough time if she hurried.

Downstairs, much of the noise was male, but included thunderous footfalls of children barreling across old hardwood floors, her sisters' laughter, and the occasional parental correction of a niece or nephew thrown in. They were sounds of home, of fall, and family experiences so common, she'd nearly forgotten them. Cammie paused, tearing up like a ninny outside the large living area housing the enormous flat screen her brother bestowed a couple years ago upon the room for Christmas. It was simply called, the football TV.

"Pull yourself together, or they'll eat you alive," Cammie jumped a mile at being caught blubbering by her sister, Jo. She leaned into her sisters comforting embrace for a quick second, embarrassed, but glad it hadn't been Emma who'd discovered her in a weakened condition. She sniffed and straightened her shoulders.

"Nothing like the pecking order we've got going on around here," Cammie acknowledged.

"Just a little good-natured sibling rivalry—or survival of the fittest, however you choose to look at it. It's football day, honey. No crying allowed on football day," Jo winked, and pulled her forward into the crowed room. The sea of red and white was quite shocking—roll tide.

As she entered the room, they shouted her name in unison, "Cammie!"

"I see you're all sadly in need of pigs in a blanket and a few other items," Cammie eyed the coffee table boasting a bag of cheese curls, chips and salsa, and a bowl of pretzels.

Junior blew her a kiss, "Woo-hoo! Cammie's makin' snacks, everybody!" A loud chorus of cheers and whistles followed her as she made for the kitchen.

"Animals," she muttered with a smile. There were worse

things than making finger food for extremely appreciative people, she supposed.

She hummed softly and rolled out pastry dough, planning to cut out squares for wrappers. Cammie had purchased the cocktail sausages at Jenna's grocery on a whim. This bunch could eat their weight in the things.

As she slid a huge pan into the oven, the kitchen door swung open. Lucy buzzed in with Samantha in tow. Cammie said hello to Samantha, but the little girl quickly averted her eyes.

"Hi, Aunt Cammie! Sam just got here. We're looking for more cheese puffs. Do you know where they are?"

"Uh—yes, honey, they're in the pantry next to the pretzels, I believe." Cammie retrieved her wits and wondered what was up with the little girl.

"Hello, Samantha, welcome to football day." Cammie smiled broadly, trying to get a feel for what was happening here.

There was obviously something eating at Sam, something unique to Cammie for her to behave so oddly. She seemed to be a sweet-natured child.

"Thank you." She kept her head down, muttered her reply, and refused to make eye contact when confronted with kindness.

Lucy, oblivious to the tension, said, "C'mon Sam, lets go sit on the porch and work on our lanyards." Sam silently followed, not lifting her eyes again.

Then, it occurred to Cammie, was Grey here too? As the thought was formulating, she heard the good-natured ribbing. He'd attended rival school, Auburn. Of course any opponent who played Alabama was who an Auburn fan rooted for on game day. She supposed he would be sporting navy and bright orange, a hideous combination, with a fighting Tiger across his chest today instead of his own alma mater. That was always the case on game day, whether you had plans for the viewing or not.

She wouldn't go out of her way to find out though. Her best bet was to stay in right where she was. She cranked up her favorite country music CD and began caterwauling right along with Miranda.

She'd just turned the faucet on at the sink to rinse out the prep bowl when she was startled out of her chorus by a deep voice. "Hey, Cammie, did you see where Sam went? She left her bag in the truck."

He stood there in the kitchen wearing faded jeans, an old Auburn t-shirt, and holding a bright pink Hello Kitty tote. He was a daddy. Something shifted. He should have been *her* little girl's daddy. It hurt; it shouldn't have, but by God, it did.

Before she could answer, Emma came to the rescue the way only Emma would. She invited Grey to watch the game after insisting it was no trouble and of course he should.

Grey accepted the offer to stay because he'd just been bullied by a woman in tight jeans and high heels. Cammie shot her sister a glare after pointing him to the backyard where the two girls were giggling under the old oak at the picnic table working on their crafts. Emma winked innocently and headed back to join the rest of the family.

Avoiding Grey's eyes as he passed her and stepped out back required balling her fists at her sides and concentrating hard on the dark stained, old boards where she stood. She could swear she smelled him—in a manly, basic, rip-off-his-clothes way. Oh, God, that couldn't be good, for so many reasons.

The timer began beeping incessantly, which required her full attention. The heavenly scent of what surely must be among the unhealthiest snacks on the planet permeated the room as she juggled the large pan. At least she wasn't inhaling Grey anymore. What was up with her?

Cammie slid the large oven mitts on and concentrated on balancing the heavy tray as she carefully eased it from the hot oven.

"Need some help?"

She was so startled by the warm breath near her ear she nearly sent pigs and their blankets flying through the air. "Grey! Don't you know never to sneak up on a person taking something hot out of the oven?" Cammie slammed the pan down, accentuating her agitation at his stealthy arrival.

"Sorry, didn't mean to endanger you or the snacks. The music is a little loud. I just wanted to apologize for accepting your sister's invitation without asking you first. I hope it's alright that Sam is here with Lucy. I'd only meant to drop her off. But she forgot her backpack in the truck."

Cammie leaned toward the kitchen CD player and turned it down to a background volume.

"It's fine." Cammie still wore the huge potholder on the

arm with which she was gesturing.

She turned and began filling a tray with the piggy rolls and placed her back to him, trying to ignore how his presence in a room caused such a warming physical sensation in her lady parts. She'd been near men in kitchens countless times over the years and hadn't had the slightest reaction, certainly not the kind she was experiencing now.

He'd waited until she'd placed the tray on the counter and moved in closer again, his eyes seeking hers. "Cammie, when I saw your mom's car right after the accident and the blood—" He placed a hand gently on her shoulder and slid it downward in a comforting gesture.

At least, she assumed it was meant to be comforting. Honestly, she wanted nothing more than to lean into him at that moment, but that would be so wrong and stupid, wouldn't it?

She returned his gaze and smiled softly. "Thanks. I appreciate your bringing me home from the hospital and carrying me around when I was, uh, loopy on painkillers. Sorry if I said anything inappropriate."

Maybe she was just feeling fragile from her accident, and if she were honest, from the past month or so of being beaten half to death by life. She'd like to think this weakness toward Grey was an abnormal response.

"Are you kidding? You on the pain meds almost made it seem like old times." He cocked his head sideways and grinned.

Cammie flushed. After all, a girl could only take so much. She resisted the urge to fan her inflamed cheeks.

The roar of the family brought her back to the moment, and she realized how exhausted and sore her body felt just now. The accident and her confused emotions were taking a toll, not to mention the long day she'd had catering and entertaining. She wouldn't take the pain meds for obvious reasons, but a couple over-the-counter pain relievers wouldn't hurt. Hopefully, she would sleep, despite the upset and guilt currently rampaging through her.

⟫⟪

CAMMIE HAD JUST finished clearing up any remaining evidence of yesterday's parties. Most had been handled last night, but she'd been straightening furniture and returning things back to their normal state. Grey'd left her a message saying he was using today to head to a neighboring town to pick up supplies and take Samantha to an orthodontic appointment. She could admit a tiny bit of the excitement and anticipation had gone out of her day at finding this out.

"You know what you need once Mom gets home from the hospital, dear sister?" Jo Jo startled her.

Cammie stood up from removing an errant party favor that had fallen behind the potted plant in the foyer. "What? And don't sneak up on me like that."

"A girls' night out."

Cammie stared blankly at her sister. "Out to do what?"

"Are you ninety years old—have you forgotten what it's like to go out with friends and tear up the town?"

This whole idea seemed pointless. "I don't tear up towns—wouldn't know how to, actually," Cammie replied primly.

"Oh, sweetheart, you are in desperate need of a little innocent fun." Jo patted Cammie's hand as if she were two years old—or ninety. "After the month you've had, you need to cut loose."

Cammie still didn't see the value of going out and getting crazy for no good reason, but if her sister or sisters decided on a plan, then Cammie most likely wouldn't have a lot of say in the matter. "I'll think about it." There, that would put this nutty idea off a little longer.

"Good idea. Don't worry about a thing. I'll get together with the sisters and we'll plan everything. You'll have a blast, trust me." Jo's smile wasn't comforting in the least. In fact, Cammie knew that smile. If anything, it meant trouble. And Jo was the normal one.

"Oh, dear." And she meant that.

Jo Jo headed off to answer phones and left Cammie to her tidying up.

Cammie's cell vibrated inside her pocket. "Hello?"

"Hi there." It was Jason.

"Hey, you. What's up?"

"Just checking in on your mom's condition. And yours." Such a great guy.

"She's better, thanks. I'm heading over later this evening after I finish cleaning up around here."

"So, how *are* you?" he asked.

"I'm okay. Better now that I've gotten a couple events under my belt and everybody helped out. Stinks that Auburn beat Alabama last night though. I thought my family was going to rip the TV out of the wall."

"Big fans, huh?"

"You've no idea." She smiled.

Still, she didn't mention Grey. What would she say? By the way, my old boyfriend, the one that I would've married was here, and I got all hot and bothered but nothing actually happened.

⟫⟪

CAMMIE HEADED OUT to the hospital. She'd received a call that her mother was running a slight temperature and was being monitored for a possible infection. Nothing to worry about yet.

She passed a couple of old high school friends in the hospital parking lot, said a quick hello, and dodged uncomfortable questions. She assured them she was all right from the deer incident and shared a phony laugh over the Jessica Greene parody, then headed upstairs to see her mother.

A middle-aged man in a lab coat, who Cammie recognized as Mom's doctor was standing next to her mother's hospital bed making notes in her chart when she walked in.

Cammie's heart plummeted. "Is everything okay?" She asked.

Mom appeared to be resting comfortably.

"Hi, Ms. Laroux; yes, your mother's temperature is starting to come down and we've begun a second round of IV antibiotics, just in case. Her incision site isn't showing any signs of infection, so it's a precaution in response to the spike in her temp. I don't foresee any other complications, so rest easy."

"Is she alright?" Ben caught her as she left their mother's room.

"I just saw the doctor, and he thinks they've managed to prevent anything major. Just watching that her temperature doesn't go back up." He heaved a sigh.

They made their way to the waiting area just down the hall from Mom's room, leaving her to rest. Cammie wore headphones, her favorite classical music cranked up, as she sat in the hospital waiting room chair and entered notes into her PDA calendar for the next couple of months. She was working on ideas for opening her own restaurant, a lunch place and bakery. This was a positive way to momentarily fast forward to the next phase of her life. The one where her mother's health was good and she was back home in Virginia Beach, elbow-deep in what she loved, with Jason by her side. Blissful peace at the idea of the dismal present temporarily becoming a distant blip on her radar began to permeate her lovely daydream.

Ben had stopped by after work, and had brought his briefcase with him and worked on whatever lawyers carried in briefcases. Cammie hadn't bothered to ask, busy as she was trying to Zen her way through the evening. Hospitals made her extra antsy.

Without warning, or because she had the music so loud she hadn't noticed until it was too late, the matched pair of dark cowboy boots that sauntered just within her field of vision, startling her out of her happy place. As her eyes traveled up six feet and some change of rugged, muscled, sexy male in jeans, holding a bouquet of yellow roses, she realized her blissful peace had been blown all to—

"Hello, Cammie," His eyes held hers a brief but impactful moment before he turned toward her brother, who was making a hard study of his paperwork just then. "Ben."

"Oh, hi, Grey." She greeted him politely and took out one of her earpieces and turned down the volume to a reasonable level, still not quite ready to let the daydream go and face this reality. "I thought you were out getting supplies."

"I left early this morning. I stopped back by to check on your mom and bring her these," Grey said, holding out the lovely bouquet. Ben finally raised his eyes from the document he was scanning then nodded briskly at Grey. "Harrison."

Guys were so weird, Cammie thought as she took the flowers, then brought them to her face, inhaling. She adored fresh blooms. Not knowing what else to do with them, she gently laid them on the small end table.

"My dad said Miz Maureen might have an infection. How's she doing?"

"Oh. We hadn't really let anyone know—" Cammie began.

"Dad spoke with her earlier," Grey said.

"I appreciate your father's concern. She's holding her own right now. The incision site from where they installed the hardware in her spine still looks clean. Her fever is down now, so she should be on the mend. The doctor is supposed to be here soon," Cammie said.

Grey lowered his tall frame into the chair across from her and was focused intently on her face. Too intently for her piece of mind. His direct gaze gave her the heebie-jeebies.

While she appreciated his show of character in stopping by, Cammie could have done without the upset to her constitution. His presence during her visit home unsettled both emotionally and hormonally. She was engaged to be married. No, she and Jason hadn't yet set a date. But they would. Soon.

He reached out and touched her hand with his long, calloused fingers. Her hand trembled. It was nearly her undoing. She could feel herself weakening physically every time he came near her. Maybe it *was* time for Jason's visit to Alabama. It beat the desire to climb up into Grey's lap and seek comfort and physical gratification if she was honest with herself.

She abruptly stood, breaking contact before making a completely idiotic scene. She could feel Ben's curious stare boring into her back. No way would she turn and face him head-on.

Cammie cautioned a glance up at Grey, also standing now. His expression was guarded, and solemn.

"Do you want coffee?" She asked, unsure how to proceed.

"Sure. I'll walk with you."

"How's Samantha?" she asked.

"She's up and down. It's been a rough year. Make that ten years." His expression was rueful.

"It can't all have been bad." Careful, girl, or you might sound like you want to hear all about it, and she so didn't.

He stopped then, and held her eyes with his weary deep green ones. "No, not all bad, but rarely easy." His voice held a heavy wealth of deeply packed history that Cammie knew nothing about.

Ben appeared in the hallway just then, "Hate to interrupt, Cam, but the doctor's just come from Mom's room. He wants to meet with us."

Cammie immediately turned her attention to Ben. "On my way."

Grey fell into step beside Cammie, Ben having gone on ahead. "Can I call you?"

She sighed. "I'm getting married, Grey, and I'm leaving town soon. I don't see how it will solve anything."

He closed his eyes for a brief second, as if pained by her words. "Do you really love him?"

Who? She was so entranced by his soft words and wounded expression; it took Cammie a split second to remember. "Jason? Of course I do." They slowed and stopped a couple rooms down from where Cammie's mother and Ben were waiting with the doctor. She touched his arm lightly, her gaze soft and steady.

"I—have to go now. I'll call you when things settle down with my mother. Maybe we can talk before I leave town; I don't know, Grey. It might be better to let things alone between us. I really have to go now. Thanks for stopping by. Tell your dad hello."

His response was to stare at her with a sad longing in his

green eyes. He lifted his hand in a slight wave.

She walked backward a couple of steps, holding his gaze before turning to head in the direction of her mother's hospital room. The finals seconds of connection between them burned in her consciousness. But she hadn't had time to pursue the line of thinking and turned away to handle the priority at hand—her mother's recovery.

Cammie came out after speaking with the doctor, relieved now that Mom was out of the woods. She looked around for Grey and cursed herself for doing it. Mom was responding to the treatment and should make a full recovery after a few more days in the hospital with IV antibiotics, rest and continued recovery at home.

Maybe she would see Grey back at the house, or would call him later. Or maybe not.

≫≪

HOW COULD HE be so stupid to lose his head like that again—now, when Cammie was involved with someone else and lived a million miles away? He'd just stood there staring at her with great big, hound dog eyes right after she'd basically told him to eff-off.

His luck with women or lack thereof was legend. Too bad he wasn't the kind who was just out to get laid. With that he'd have no problem. Sex was easy. Love was a real bitch. He'd spent nine years married to a crazy person who'd raved he hadn't loved her as she'd held him hostage threatening self-harm if he abandoned her. And she'd finally had made good on her threat, whether she'd done it purposely or not, leaving their child motherless and broken. He should have left with Sam when she was a baby before Deb had the opportunity to damage her.

He'd just blown the attempt at simply making Cammie understand the depths of his regret at allowing himself to ruin both their lives for his gullibility, guilt, and overwhelming sense of responsibility. Able now to admit that he'd been no match for Deb's freight train-like combination of selfish and crazy was freeing. Except here he was standing glassy-eyed and love-struck once again.

Before Cammie had come back, he was simply a father trying to pick up the pieces for his child, not in the least concerned for the tamped-down part of himself that might wake up someday and experience something akin to emotional connection with another.

But now this wallop from the blue had him floundering in ways he'd never expected. At first he'd wanted her to understand why he'd done what he'd done. Maybe if she could forgive him, he could forgive himself. Now he wanted another chance with her. But she was in love with someone else and planned to marry him.

⋙⋘

MAEVE ARRIVED EARLY in the morning to cover Ben's shift at the hospital well-stocked to pass the time, it appeared.

"Did you bring a lamp, too?" He snickered, leaning in as she continued to unpack her bottomless tote bag of goodies. Spying the deck of playing cards, he couldn't resist. "I see you brought along the cards. You practicing for our next round, sister?"

"You wanna piece of me, little brother?" Her cobalt eyes sparkled. She really did have the prettiest eyes of them all. Not another of the siblings could claim them. Nor could their parents for that matter.

"Alright, you blue-eyed demon, give me your best shot!" The lifelong battle for bragging rights continued. Hearts was a cutthroat game best played with at least four of them, but two would do in a pinch. Too bad the others weren't around.

Ben was so involved in grinding his eldest sister to dust that he almost missed hearing the women ooh-ing and aah-ing over a huge bouquet of flowers at the nurse's station nearby. He glanced over just as one of the nurses waved the card toward them excitedly.

"These are for your mother. A handsome hottie just dropped them off and left."

Handsome hottie? He hadn't seen anyone come by. Wait, maybe he saw the flowers arrive, but that wasn't unusual in a hospital, so it hadn't caused him to look up.

"Wow. Who do think they're from, Ben? Should we read the card?" Maeve sniffed a lily.

"Let's take them down to Mom's room and let her read it," Ben said, not liking the hottie idea at all. He hefted the huge bouquet, careful not to upset the arrangement.

"Mom?" Maeve called softly as they entered the room in case she was still sleeping, seeing how early in the morning it was.

"Yes, dear? Come in, I'm awake."

"Someone dropped these flowers off for you. Thought you might want to have a look at the card," Ben said. Then, "How are you feeling?"

"Oooh, they're beautiful. Who are they from? Let me see the card, Maeve." Mom was a sucker for a fragrant bouquet.

Ben set the arrangement down on the hospital tray and Maeve handed their mother the card. "You two look like a couple of geese with your necks stretched out, craning to have a peek."

Immediately relaxing in posture, both tried to appear a bit less concerned with the sender's identity. Ben plopped down on the vacant bed on the other side of the room, while Maeve refilled her mother's water glass.

Ben kept his eyes peeled on his mother's face, wondering, still, who the hottie might be. Maureen's complexion seemed to lose color, and her fingers shook as she read the note. Her expression was not one of delight. "Mom, are you alright? Should I get a nurse?"

She closed her eyes, took a deep shaky breath, and smiled weakly, "No, Ben, I'm okay. Just—just a little surprised is all."

"You don't look happy surprised, Momma. Who sent the flowers?"

"Just an old friend, sweetheart." She sounded tired.

"The nurses referred to him as a hottie," Ben drawled.

"I can't imagine anyone his age falling into that category by today's standards." But her eyes drifted toward the ceiling as she clutched the small card with its envelope in her pale fingers.

"Should we sit with you for awhile? We hoped you were getting some rest."

"I would like to be alone for a bit, if you don't mind." She smiled in her loving way, but her eyes held unshed tears.

"Mom, I'm worried. Is there something wrong?" Maeve asked.

"No. I would like to collect my thoughts, is all. You can check on me later."

They both kissed her cheek and promised to be within shouting distance if she needed them. Ben's eye twitched, as it did when something wasn't right. He'd never seen his mother react so oddly and with such melancholy—certainly not to someone besides their father. Something about the sender of the flowers had really gotten to her. Mothers weren't supposed to have mysterious hotties in their pasts.

Once they were back out in the waiting area, Maeve turned on Ben, "What on God's green earth was that all about?"

"I don't have a clue. Mom's not the secretive type. I mean, she never has been as far as I've known." Ben observed people for a living, everyday. His mother's reaction to that card was fairly intense.

"She's—Mom. Of course she doesn't have secrets. Maybe secret recipes or a secret stash of chocolate somewhere, but a secret hottie? No freaking way."

"We'll ask her later what that was all about, but until then, let's not allow our imaginations to run amok, okay?"

MAUREEN SAT WIDE-EYED in her hospital bed clutching the small card in her shaking fingers. She might be in a hospital bed, but she wasn't hallucinating. This was plain crazy. How dared he show up here, of all places? And why now? It had been, what—forty years? Had it really? His clear, laughing blue eyes reflected in her mind every time she was in the company of her lovely eldest daughter, Maeve.

Maureen had lived and loved an entire lifetime with another man, the only other person in the world who'd borne her secret and stood by her side through it all. The very idea that *he'd* reappeared bearing gifts at this point was near laughable, but not funny in the least. She couldn't take the chance of his finding out her secret. It had died with Justin Laroux, her husband and father named on the birth certificates of all five of her children.

From what she knew, he'd only dropped the flowers and taken off. Hopefully, then scooted right out of town. But still, with the trouble he'd taken to track her down, it didn't seem likely. Maybe he was dying and wished to make amends. She'd lived long enough and experienced loss deeply to understand that motivation. She'd meant less to him than something or someone else had, obviously, or leaving her wouldn't have been an option forty years ago, no matter the circumstances.

How could his return even affect her emotions after all this time? It was fear, pure and simple; it had to be. If her children were to discover the buried lies and secrets, she would appear a phony. How could her hypocrisy not negatively impact and cause them to question everything they'd always believed true in their own lives?

Fortunately her fever was down, but her release from the hospital wouldn't be for several more days. There was no way to anticipate his next move. Sitting around within four walls and waiting for the antibiotics to slowly kill the infection might send her over the edge. And then, she still had several weeks of recovery from the initial surgery to contend with. Maybe she should head to Lake Burton with one of her daughters once the doctor okayed it—if he would. Then, she could rehab quietly at the cabin and hide out until *he* moseyed on out of town.

Hopefully Ben and Maeve would honor her request for privacy and leave well enough alone. Realizing it was likely too much to ask, she hid the small card with its unmistakable message inside her bible somewhere near a verse about the evils of fornication. Ben wouldn't have a clue where to find it there. Maeve wouldn't go digging without permission, being a typical rule-following first child.

Mothers shouldn't have pasts; certainly not deep, dark, secret ones. When a stranger rolled into Ministry, nearly everyone in town raised their brows to speculate on their identity and connection to the local residents. She'd already been connected to him by the flowers, with the nurses bearing witness. It wouldn't be long before word spread regarding the mysterious hottie.

Luckily, the events in question transpired two counties over and so long ago that witnesses would be very difficult to unearth—really most would be six feet under by now.

But his was the next move since she was trapped here and powerless.

Maybe not so powerless. She had a laptop, didn't she? She'd have Ben bring it over and she would do what she'd not allowed herself to all these years—she'd Google his lying ass and find out where he'd been all these years. Funny that she hadn't thought to do it before now. Of course, before now, she'd been perfectly content to let the sleeping dogs lie.

Maureen figured she'd better be prepared just in case he did show up again. Best to know what kind of man he'd become, how he'd made his living, if there was a wife and other children; that sort of thing.

Once she'd married Justin and given birth to Maeve, Maureen had forged ahead with life, never regretting. Evangeline House and her family filled her with joy and purpose. She'd been a good wife and mother, run a successful business, and never looked back. What had been the point? Howard had disappeared into thin air as far as she knew.

But sometimes late at night, while lying next to the most wonderful man to grace the planet, she'd missed something. More like she'd ached feverishly and burned for *him*, the bastard. Imagining his crooked smile in her mind's eye for a split second, or hearing his laughter in a crowd only to fall back in time for a sliver of a moment—to another life, one never truly lived.

He'd given no explanation as to why he hadn't shown up at the altar on their wedding day. Obviously he wasn't dead, since she received a note in his handwriting on that day simply stating, *"Sorry I couldn't go through with it. You'll always be my heart."* Today's note had been an echo of that very same one so many years ago.

So she'd certainly recognized Cammie's emotions where Grey was concerned. More than she'd been able to let on or outwardly empathize with her daughter. But then she couldn't have allowed or encouraged her to trust him completely. She'd never have forgiven herself if Grey had done to Cammie what had been done to her. It was different now. Now, Maureen believed Grey was different.

Maureen had hired Cammie's lost love to fix her beloved home weeks ago, not realizing at the time Cammie would be coming back, or even that she would be undergoing this blasted surgery. But Maureen also had to admit her part in keeping Grey's presence unknown to Cammie when encouraging her to come home.

Maureen understood her daughter's feelings toward Grey—recognized how she'd gone out of her way to avoid him these past years. But something about bringing the two face-to-face again before Cammie married seemed the right thing to do. Perhaps not having her own second chance factored into the decision. Maureen hadn't discussed hiring Grey with her other children until after the fact.

Chapter Seven

B EN AND MAEVE showed up just as Cammie was working her way through the spices in the kitchen. She'd taken them all out and was throwing away all the old ones, making lists to restock and alphabetizing them.

Their grave expressions put her instantly on alert. "What's wrong? Has Mom taken a bad turn?" She set down the crystallized ginger in her hand.

Ben's serious expression lightened, "No, Cam, they're talking about releasing her today or tomorrow. But we've just had a very weird experience over at the hospital."

"That's not unusual, given the locale." Cammie was dead serious.

"No joke, it was very strange." He and Maeve filled her in on the mystery man and the bouquet.

Cammie frowned, "That is odd. I've never known her to request privacy from her family to brood about something—or someone. Especially a man we don't know."

"We wanted to ask more questions, but she wasn't in the mood to answer."

"Did you see the card?" Cammie asked Maeve.

"No. She held it tight it in her hands the whole time. I don't think she was of a mind to share." Maeve said.

"I don't like it. The entire incident smacks of secrets. And secrets aren't good for anybody," Ben said.

"Brother dear, if we found out all your secrets, do you think anybody would ever speak to you again?" Maeve arched an eyebrow toward Ben.

"Oh, don't act all prissy over there. We all know you used to smoke weed out by the lake from time to time after church on Sundays when you were a teenager." Ben accused.

"Shut up," Maeve snapped.

"Well, so much for discussing this like mature adults," Cammie spoke softly, hoping not to draw fire.

"I could go and *clean* her room," Maeve suggested, rolling her eyes toward the ceiling innocently.

"No snooping," Cammie insisted.

"I guess we wait it out and ask her more about him when she gets home," Ben said.

"Has the doctor said for certain when she would be released?" Cammie asked, continuing to put things away in the kitchen.

"We should know later today," Maeve said.

"Seems like she's been in there a long time," Cammie hung the dish towel on the hook beside the sink and untied the apron she'd donned earlier. "Would the two of you like coffee?"

"About a gallon would be great," Ben said.

Grey picked that moment to enter the kitchen, all sexy

in his tool belt and jeans. They stared at him as if he had two heads.

"Oh, hey. Am I interrupting?" He stopped a few feet inside the door.

Maeve smiled at him. "No, you're fine. Just in time for coffee; right, Cammie?"

"Yeah, sure." Cammie wasn't really prepared yet this morning to see Grey. After yesterday's emotional weirdness at the hospital, she hadn't really known what to say to him. Maybe it was better this way, with her sister and brother here to run interference between them.

>>>×<<<

GREY HAD KNOWN he'd see her today at some point, Maeve and Ben's arrival had ensured she wouldn't bolt upstairs. After yesterday's jolting realization, he couldn't stay away. Besides his promise to handle the house problems, just knowing that Cammie could leave any time now that her mom's condition was improving made it seem that much more urgent that he—what? Do something. Maybe it was time to test her real feelings. He'd been getting vibes that her words weren't exactly coinciding with her body language.

He wasn't playing around here. She was still the woman he'd fallen for as a young man, and despite everything that had gone down, Cammie Laroux wasn't leaving here without a fight from Grey. If she went, it would be because she was truly in love with someone else and wanted to go. Right now, she didn't have a job calling her back, so it was now or never for them.

Ben took the steaming mug and stood. "I've got to get to the office. I'll let you know if I get any new information about Mom's discharge. We'll talk later, girls. Harrison."

"Later," Grey raised a hand.

Maeve also made to leave. "I've got a hair appointment, Cam, but I'll be back in a couple of hours. Call me on my cell or text if you need anything. Thanks for the coffee. Bye, Grey."

"Bye, Maeve." He smiled and waved.

Within thirty seconds they were alone in the kitchen, the old clock ticking loudly.

The house repairs were slow but coming along, so he figured he could pop in for a question just to get on her nerves, couldn't he? That had been the plan.

"How's your mom this morning?" Cammie was obviously in the middle of a project that had to do with all the hundred or so spices in the house. As always, she had a system going, and as usual, she was precise and efficient, but paid no mind to her appearance or what was happening around her.

She looked up, like she'd forgotten he was in the room. Right. Her hair was falling out of a once carefully-crafted ponytail. It was no longer centered with tendrils of the honeyed highlights drifting around her gorgeous face. She'd opted for jeans today, which meant she hadn't any planned meetings with clients.

"Mom is coming home from the hospital today or to-morrow. I'm planning to make her favorite cake before she gets here, but I need to organize the spices first.

"That's great. So glad she's on the mend." He grinned at her. "So, are there any plans for your boyfriend to visit while you're here?" He asked, curious why the guy hadn't met her family yet and why he hadn't bothered to come while she was here.

She shot him a curious glance. "I'm not sure, why?"

"Just wondered. I'm sure your family is dying to meet him."

She made a face. "Oh, they are; you bet they are. I'm not sure how that will go. He's awesome, but not exactly Alabama awesome, if you get my drift. More like New York City awesome."

"Does that suit you?"

"Jason suits me just fine. In fact, he suits me perfectly. I'm not sure why you're concerned about this."

"I just want you to be happy, Cammie. You deserve it. It just surprises me that you'd end up with a city slicker is all."

"Oh, and you think I should've stuck around here and ended up with what, a farmer or a handyman?"

"Ouch!"

"No, wait, I didn't even get that kind of choice in the matter, did I? I left town because my boyfriend got my best friend pregnant and married her *after* she had a miscarriage." Cammie's voice was getting shrill. But she wasn't finished. "Oh, wait, then the two of you named your child together the same name you and I had picked out for our own child someday."

He wondered when she would get around to that. He knew this had to happen, but now that it was happening, he wanted to be anywhere but here.

"What's the matter, Grey? You look a little uncomfortable. Too much to have to actually talk about it? 'Cause we never did you know?" Cammie challenged.

"No, we didn't because you left before we had the chance," he said.

"Really? I should have stuck around for more of your shit?"

"I—" he didn't even get a chance to speak.

"Would it have changed anything? Would Deb have been less pregnant? Would you both have been less deceitful? Would you have done anything different if I'd stuck around?"

"Cammie, I—" he tried again.

"No, I didn't think so. And just so you know, Grey, I'm good with marrying a city slicker. Nothing about him reminds me of you or this place. Coming back here wasn't such a mistake. I've been able to get closer to my family again and come to terms with all the awful stuff that you put me through back then."

This attack from her was long in coming and much deserved, and he knew it, but felt powerless defending it. "I hope you know I never meant to hurt you. And Samantha's name—" He floundered.

"But you did hurt me, didn't you? You ruined my life for a long time, made it impossible for me to trust anyone. And Samantha's name is just the icing on the whole thing."

Grey approached her then, unable to stand the raw hurt in her voice. She didn't move. So he put his arms around her from behind and buried his face in her neck. Her shoulders shook, but she didn't make a sound. They stood that way for a few precious moments, sharing her pain, his pain, then she broke away with a small sob. Grey heard her footfalls running up the stairs a moment later.

"Way to go, genius," he said aloud to the now empty kitchen.

⧽⧽⧽⧽⧺⧺⧺⧺

THINGS WERE SETTLING down to a dull roar now that Mom was home and truly on the mend. After a full two weeks in the hospital, she'd begun intensive physical therapy three days ago, her mule's constitution shining through, according to the doctor and therapist. Cammie could see the light at the end of the tunnel, as far as heading back to Virginia Beach. Since she'd stuck it out this long, another week or two wouldn't hurt. The Pecan Pie pageant was coming up, and with Mom's slight setback, she wasn't really ready to host that, so Cammie would stay and handle the pageant.

She'd been trying her best to dodge Grey while they went about their business, but lately, he seemed to be more in her space than not. He wasn't the easiest person to ignore within four walls, especially when certain situations required them to communicate or be together in the same room. His nearness caused blips in the radar of her day. She disliked blips.

Since her outburst at him the other day, neither of them brought up the elephant in the room. They both pretended like it hadn't happened and proceeded with awkward caution when they did come in contact.

Cammie forced herself to engage with residents when she ventured into town; she smiled, said hello, and put forth an effort at normal. Maybe it helped stifle some of the knowing glances and whispers behind her back. Now, it seemed, she was beginning to gain some sort of acceptance within her hometown again. Folks were now smiling and nodding instead of stealing sneaky looks her way when she passed.

Cammie, finally relenting to her sisters' ceaseless peer pressure, figured a little fun wouldn't hurt. So, she headed upstairs to try and find something to wear for the big night out.

She nearly cringed at the idea of heading to a bar alongside that bunch with the intention of letting loose. Hopefully they'd all be on their best behavior and not go out of their way to embarrass her. They'd dubbed her with the nickname, grandma, though Cammie believed she'd come down here more forward-thinking and slicker than all of them combined, but really, somebody had to behave like an adult.

As soon as she stepped foot in her bedroom and made to close the door, a stampede of high heels and boots within a cloud of Calvin Klein barreled up the stairs. "Cammie, honey, we're here!"

Oh, God. She had to give it a try, "I'll be down shortly."

The door burst open, "Are you kidding? We're here to make sure you don't go out looking like a granny tonight." Hands on her hips, Emma was a sight to behold. The term cougar just developed a capital C and an exclamation point at the end. She was stunning. Perfect hair, accessorized to the max, decked out in jeans, and high wedged heels, she all but growled. And she was gorgeous. A former Miss Alabama, she'd done them all proud. Clearly, she still had it.

The sisters chatted, giggled, and drank wine all while layering Cammie in makeup, clothing and local gossip. Her hesitation to survey their work was more a pitiable dread as the brutes dragged her before the full length mirror in the corner of the room. Her sisters were lovely women, she couldn't argue with that. Each had some crown or title of most this or that to claim from her glory days. Her style was typically more understated, that was all.

"Okay, honey, open your eyes."

Positioning her features in the most pleasantly surprised mask just before catching sight of herself would likely be her best bet. But when she finally did open her eyes, Cammie was really excited at the result. There was color on her eyelids, a shimmery cinnamon tone with liner and some miraculous mascara that made her nondescript eyes appear mysterious and heavy-lidded. "Wow."

They'd slid her into a pair of dark denim jeans so snug Cammie wondered she could still draw breath and a fitted tank of deep bronze with a silk overlay in the same color. The sleeves were capped, showing off her trim upper arms. Because the blouse was deceptively simple, they'd accessorized it by pairing a long string of tiny shimmering crystal stones with an updated carved, ivory cameo hanging below her breasts.

"This is gorgeous." The sisters all eyed one another knowingly.

"We missed your birthday this year. The outfit and the necklace are gifts from us all."

"Oh—I couldn't accept them." Cammie had some really great clothes, but Emma had an awesome sense of style that she didn't personally own. She'd never have chosen the ensemble herself, but boy did it work.

"Oh—you will accept them. None of us are skinny enough to squeeze our asses into those jeans, thank you very much," Emma replied for the group.

She hugged each one, hoping not to destroy the wonderful makeup job. "So, where are you wild things taking me this evening?"

"It's a secret. You just grab your handbag and come with us, sister dear."

Her nerves returned. Even though she was dressed for a big night out, she hoped she could hold up her end of the fun. When had she become such a stick in the mud?

Making certain Mom was comfortable before they left with the promise to call Junior two doors down if she had a problem, they kissed her and headed to the front door. As Cammie stepped outside onto the wide porch, she didn't have long to wonder at their mode of transportation. Ben was waiting in his black Range Rover to escort his sisters on their evening's adventure.

"Ladies," he bowed gallantly with a grin as he opened front passenger door for Cammie to climb into. The others piled in before he had a chance to get there.

"Thanks," she said just before he shut the door and made for the driver's seat.

"Everybody buckled up?" He turned toward his older sisters in the back and waggled his eyebrows in the way only he could since childhood, making them all shriek with laughter.

"Ben, I swear all you'd need is a cigar and we'd call you Groucho," Jo Jo dried her eyes, trying not to smudge her mascara.

"Ready to rock and roll, girls?"

"Somebody really should tell me where we're headed," Cammie laughed.

"Don't you dare, Ben. It's a surprise, remember?" Emma reminded him.

"Oh, come on. You know I hate surprises."

"A little Friday night trip down memory lane—a good one, don't worry," said Jo Jo.

Now she was worried. Memory lane around here usually involved Grey. But she kept her mouth shut. There weren't that many places to go in Ministry.

Dusk was settling as they arrived in Cheyneyville. She'd begun to suspect their destination not long into the journey. As teens, the cool place to go out was Cheyneyville, because it was the closest non-dry town in the next county bordering Okaloosa. Remaining such, it was also home to the nearest country and western bar. Shit Kickers, with a boot replacing both 'I's so as not to offend, boasted live music and a legendary dance floor. For a small town, it was big—stuff.

Cammie turned to her family members and said dubiously, "This frightens me."

"It damned well should." Ben laughed. "No worries, I'm to be your designated driver this evening, so feel free to enjoy yourselves however you see fit. But I draw the line at vomiting females in my car. I will put you out on the side of the road if anyone shows signs of a vomitous expression, understood?"

"Is vomitous a word?" Maeve asked.

"I'm certain you get my meaning. Oh, and no strange men. I promised the brothers-in-law that while they are caring for your offspring, you will behave in that respect."

"Woo-hoo, I haven't been out to a bar in a coon's age. I'm ready to get my drinkin' and dancin' on." Emma, having slickly exited the car, shimmied up to the entrance with a combination two-step and bootie-shake that had Cammie cringing with apprehension at what madness the next few hours might hold.

"There she goes. We can't stop her now that she's revved up and ready. Just gotta join her. C'mon girls." Cammie was grabbed in a vice grip by the two remaining sisters with no hope of escape.

"Fighting it is hopeless, you know, so you may as well shake the starch out of your panties and let loose. The Cammie we remember knew how to have a good time." Ben's parting shot rang in her ears as she was half-dragged in the wake of Emma.

Emma knew how to have fun. Weird how she'd never scratched the surface again relationship-wise though. Not even the most casual of dinner dates. But the men loved her.

>>><<<

GREY HADN'T PLANNED on going anywhere tonight. In fact, if his old buddy, Jake, hadn't stopped by this afternoon and given him a hand, hauling building materials and guilting Grey into accompanying him here, Grey wouldn't have considered stepping foot anywhere near this establishment. But Jake had other plans—the plans involved dragging Grey to a boot-scootin' dance hall.

Spotting the darkest, and farthest, stool from the music and mayhem, Grey parked himself in hopes time would pass quickly. Jake—being Jake, was snapped up and dragged out to dance by a lovely young female, not two steps inside the front door. Grey had waved him on his way reassuringly, despite weak protests on his own behalf.

As Grey's eyes adjusted to the dim lighting, and his half-full beer began to do its job, he took notice of the crowded bar area. The young crowd was out in force; a vast array of men and women in tight jeans, drinking beer and keeping a keen eye out for either a dance partner or someone to partner until morning. It appeared several lucky couples had already found success for the evening. Good for them.

>>><<<

"WHY, CAMMIE, CAN'T nobody say you forgot how to two-step, and that's a fact," her dance partner, Lloyd, a former high school classmate, remarked as they whirled around the scuffed wooden floor. He'd been one of several familiar faces she'd come across since they'd arrived.

She'd given up, and given in. "Thanks, Lloyd, I'd forgotten how much fun this is. I don't think anyone could forget how to two-step. It's so easy." The name of the dance itself should clue one in to the simplicity.

"Aw, Cammie, it's just 'cause you such a natural. Not everybody can do it like this, you know?"

She glanced around, realizing in about a second that, indeed, there were less than capable two-steppers all around. "I guess I'd never really thought about it."

The song ended much too quickly. Not because she couldn't bear to part company with Lloyd, though he was a handsome fellow and a good dancer, but because she was truly enjoying herself. Approaching the rather large table where her sisters and brother had taken on several others, she noticed a little ripple of shifting eyeballs. "What's going on?"

Ignoring her, Emma said, "You sure were cuttin' a rug out there with Lloyd, girl. Whoa, I haven't seen you dance like that in years." She smiled brightly.

Cammie crossed her arms and narrowed her eyes at them, then repeated, "What's going on?"

"Might as well tell her. She's bound to hear it in here or see for herself," Maeve said.

"Tell me what?"

Jo Jo stood, linked arms with her, and began leading her in the direction of the small bar over in a far corner. Just before they came too close, she pointed through the throng. Cammie followed her sister's line of vision and she spotted Grey sitting alone at the bar.

He was sipping a longneck and appeared to be brooding. Nothing like the hottest guy in the bar sitting there like he was waiting for her. *Well, hell.* She couldn't very well go back to having a good time with her people without at least saying hello, could she? It didn't seem very nice, especially since he appeared fairly miserable hanging there by himself. Maybe she would wait a little while and then come back—

At that moment, his head snapped up and he caught her staring through the crowd. Her feet instantly became blocks of cement, and utterly unmovable. *Crap.*

He smiled then and raised his beer in salute to her, slapped a bill on the bar, nodded to the bartender. Within a half a second he was closing the distance between them without breaking eye contact with Cammie. She tried again to move, feet still frozen, rooted to the floor.

She straightened her shoulders, realizing a getaway wasn't happening at this point. The intensity with which he bore down was intimidating, but maybe she'd asked for it with her surprised expression he'd caught her casting in his direction.

"Cammie," he murmured into her ear, his breath warm, his firm but gentle grip seared her bare upper arm, calloused fingers directed her to a less visible spot away from her family and interested onlookers.

What the hell was her problem, anyway? She had a fiancée. And she and Grey had been in near contact for these past weeks without major incident. Why should this moment be any different? She allowed herself to be maneuvered to a more private area.

He was only slightly manhandling her, but she wasn't sure she didn't like it—just a little.

Grey stopped as they reached a small area where a few couples danced in a darker corner, seemingly unaware of anyone else. The bar was laid out like an octopus with four arms, with several small bars and dance floors stretching out like appendages from the main area. Cammie and Grey stood toe-to-toe as an old, slow George Strait song began. Before she realized what was happening, she was wrapped in his muscular arms, breasts pressed against his chest, swaying softly to *their* song.

She'd consumed a couple of longnecks, resulting in a lovely tingly sensation. Combined with the soulful country ballad playing, reminiscent from their dating years, perhaps it was no wonder she was experiencing more than a little emotional and physical sizzle of electricity. Considering she'd always been wildly attracted to Grey, she might want to rein herself in. She inhaled the scent of him, closed her eyes, and fell back in time.

Dear Lord. Why did he make her feel like this? What was it about him that caused the young girl who'd loved and trusted him with her whole heart to take over without even a struggle from older, smarter her who'd thrown in the towel the moment they'd locked eyes?

At this particular moment, she couldn't think, only feel and remember what it'd been like with Grey.

≫≫⊱⊰≪≪

GREY'S DESIRE TO touch Cammie, to taste her, went beyond rational. It was the vital result of two adults who'd spent ten years craving what they'd missed: the scent, the taste, the feel of the other. But it was also a deep down visceral emotional remembrance as well. He'd loved her since he'd had his first pimple. God, he'd missed her.

The conflict of anger, desire, frustrated longing all presented in this full-body clash. Every one of his senses remembered. He couldn't control the emotions from rising to the surface once it began. Grey once again grabbed Cammie's arm and tugged her out the side door of the building.

Once outside, Grey pressed into Cammie against the cinderblock wall. He could feel her softer form yield to his harder, more demanding one.

Like ten years and a gigantic mistake had never happened, she was right there with him. She impatiently jerked up his shirttail and her hands slid underneath, burning his bare skin, kneading and touching him, driving him crazy.

Cammie moaned into his mouth as their bodies fused against the hard, cold wall. His need for her nearly sent him over the edge right then and there. Oh God, could this really finally be happening?

She felt so good, so hot. It was how things were between them a lifetime ago. They'd been young, but had waited until college before making love. So frustrating, but incredibly worth it. That was how he felt now. *So worth the wait.*

"Oh, Grey. I—" She kissed him again, with all the longing and enthusiasm he'd believed gone forever.

One hand cradled the back of her head, protecting it from the hard bricks behind her, his other thumb gently stroked her cheek as he went in for another soul-wrenching kiss. It wasn't enough. He placed a hand at the small of her back, pulling her hips forward, aching to feel all of her against him. His erection was such an obvious physical sign of his desire for her, not to be ignored.

"Aahh…" She leaned her head back and stared into his eyes, her expression perplexed, but so sexy. Her lips were swollen from their kisses, and he could see the desire there, too.

"You're so beautiful, Cammie. I've missed you—"

A car horn blared twice, causing Cammie to jump. Grey could cheerfully have shot whoever had interrupted them.

"Cammie, is that you out there? Yoo-hoo! You ready to head out? Ben says the bus is leavin'," Emma called from the corner of the building.

Cammie pulled away, seeming to gather her wits, "I'll be there in a sec."

"Grey, we can't—" she straightened her clothing, while not meeting his eyes.

"This wasn't a mistake, Cammie," he said, and blew out a deep breath and ran a hand through his hair.

"I don't know what this was, Grey. I have to go now."

He called after her, "Cammie—"

He was certain she'd heard him but pretended not to.

Chapter Eight

CAMMIE'S HEAD HURT. It was from beer. She hardly ever drank alcohol, like almost never. Making her way downstairs in her jammies, toward the pain relievers in the kitchen, she thought she heard a car door slam outside. Now wasn't the time for company. Nobody else was here except Mom, who was upstairs tucked in and not especially mobile yet.

Cammie decided to ignore the sounds and head straight toward pain relief.

But just as soon as she'd swallowed the pills, the doorbell rang. "Crap." She'd have to answer it in her pajamas. There weren't indecent, only very pajama-ish.

It was Grey. He was standing outside all clean and shaven, looking for all the world as if nothing untoward had gone down between them last night.

Right.

"Good morning," he said. He almost chirped.

"It's Saturday. Are you working here today?" She asked, her tone grudging, really hoping he wasn't planning to be underfoot.

"Nope. I'm here to see you." That didn't tell her much.

"Was I expecting you?" She asked. Her hair must look like vermin had crawled up and nested, and the remains of Emma's good work had been rearranged on her face during sleep and now she likely resembled a Picasso canvas.

"It's ten o'clock. I assumed you'd be up and dressed." He appeared amused at her really awful appearance. Amused, and something else. She could tell by his expression that he was remembering what'd happened between them last night. It was like a little seductive secret, but it wasn't a secret. Her sisters and brother had seen what they'd been up to. Or at least gotten the gist of it.

"I'm up. But I don't have any events until later in the evening, so I haven't dressed yet." She fought the very intense urge to dash upstairs and lock her bedroom door. The memories and sensations he'd triggered in both her body and emotions last night began rushing back as he continued to stare at her with such a knowing gleam.

"Would you like to go out to brunch with me?"

Wait, what? Did he think they were dating now because they'd made out?

Cammie looked down at her dishabille, glanced back up at him, and raised a brow. She really was in a crabby mood this morning. And she hadn't slept well after drinking and trying not to think about what had happened between them last night.

"Are you worried about what people might say?" He threw out the challenge.

"I've been talked about so much, it's a service I do by

putting myself out there for the entertainment of others. If you and I went out and had a meal in public, it would simply confirm the latest rumors. They already think you're shacking up here and using working on the house as an excuse; at least that's what I've heard is going around. It's likely you've been sneaking through the back gate every night under the cover of darkness."

A full, rich rumble of laughter burst from his chest. "I really hadn't thought of it." He wiggled his eyebrows suggestively. "But what a great idea."

"I can't go out with you this morning. I'm planning to hang upstairs with Mom. We're going to watch a Gunsmoke marathon in about half an hour."

"I was hoping we could talk—about what happened last night." Grey captured her hand in his.

It was all Cammie could do not to snatch it away and run screaming from the room. Literally. She took a deep breath. His hand was warm and strong. "Last night was a mistake. We got carried away."

"I've been waiting ten years to kiss you like that again. It was awesome, for both of us, and you can't lie to yourself or me about that. I won't believe you." The urgency in his words forced her to look at him. Big mistake. How could she say she hadn't felt something? He was right. It would be a big fat whopper.

But there couldn't be anything more than a steaming hot kiss between them now. It was impossible. "Grey, I won't deny that there's still chemistry between us—"

He reached for her other hand and pulled her toward

him, surprising her. "Chemistry? How about emotion? Heat? Passion? Are you so angry and out of touch with your feelings that you can't recognize what happened between us as so much more than a chemical attraction?" He let her go and turned away, running a hand through his hair, an outward sign of frustration. "You felt what I did last night."

"Grey, I'm engaged—"

He turned around and took a step toward her. "So you keep reminding me, Cammie. But so far, I haven't seen evidence of any huge emotional commitment to your boyfriend since you've been back here. What I have noticed is our dancing around one another trying to avoid the obvious."

"What obvious?" She really shouldn't ask, but the question was out.

"Us. We're not over. Yeah, I screwed us up when I married Deb, but here we are right now, together by whatever bizarre circumstances, and we're still connected, whether or not you want to admit it."

She tried to back away, shaking her head.

"We owe it to one another to find out what this could be."

She recoiled. "N-no, Grey. I can't." She could barely breathe. "I can't ever do that again with you. It's taken this long for me to be able to come back here and feel normal, and I'm not even that. Not really. And now you want me to throw away my solid future with someone who I know will make me happy to take another shot at it with you? Have you lost your mind?"

He really must have lost his mind; that was the only explanation for this conversation. The crazy hot kiss could be explained by physical desire. His suggesting they actually reconnect emotionally and work toward some sort of relationship went beyond the bounds of reality.

She stared at him, unspeaking. She could feel the pull pulsing between them right now, and it scared her to death. She was out of her mind to even listen to this, but, what if—*no*. She clamped down on that spark or hope. No not hope. Was she in some kind of alternate reality twilight zone?

"I get it. I do," he said. "But I can't watch you walk away again," he whispered.

"Me? Like I had a choice?"

"Cammie you never answered my…"

She held out her hand to ward him off, and the other one pressed hard against her mouth to hold something back, a scream, a sob, a kiss. She didn't know.

"Don't say anything," she finally spoke after what seemed like a forever amount of screaming tension.

"Please, Cammie. Tell me you don't think of me as that awful person anymore. We've both grown up and I've paid dearly for wrong choices within my own life. I'd like the chance to repair some of the damage those choices did to you. Think about it. That's all I ask." He turned away and walked out the door.

>>>×<<<

MAUREEN HAD RECEIVED another note. It read: *I would like*

to see you. I'll be in touch. My heart. Really, who was she supposed to tell? Did he think she would have a conversation with her family and let them know who he was? *My heart?* Really? That was a little dramatic considering how many years ago he'd left her at the altar, alone and pregnant.

In the meantime she'd done her research and figured out a few things: He'd entered the military academy almost immediately after leaving her. His parents had been killed in an automobile accident shortly after she'd married Justin Laroux. Howard had been severely wounded after his plane was shot down and was taken prisoner in Vietnam while flying a mission against the Viet Cong. He'd dropped off the radar after that.

The misery he'd endured after leaving her must have been staggering. He'd been extremely close with his parents. What a blow. They'd been foul to her, believing her socially beneath Howard's family, white trash. But this information didn't supply the answer to a question that still burned. *Why had he abandoned her on their wedding day?*

Her anxiety had risen hugely when she'd received that note. It had come in the mail with her name and address, written in bold, block letters, with no return address, and thankfully been delivered by Rose along with the other mail. The envelope had been white and nondescript so as not to raise any red flags, she supposed.

There'd been no phone number or contact information on the note. So, she'd have to wait until he was ready to show himself. This was all very mysterious, and if she'd admit it to herself, exciting for an old woman. But hurting her family was not on the table as far as Maureen was concerned. It was a tricky situation. He didn't know he had a daughter, but just might find out if he caught sight of Maeve and her blue eyes—his own eyes.

This was the sort of thing that tore families apart.

>>><<<

CAMMIE HADN'T SPOKEN with Jason in several days, and she wasn't sure whether it was her fault or his. Something didn't feel quite right lately. Of course, she now had to admit that plastering herself against Grey like a wanton woman on the cover of a romance novel wasn't exactly the behavior of a model fiancé. But an awkward sensation in the pit of her stomach made her question if the physical separation from Jason and their recent lack of communication was not just one-sided.

The estrangement of both time and distance blurred feelings that had seemed so certain and strong when she'd set out on her journey to Alabama. She dialed Jason's number now, wanting to reconnect with some of the emotion she'd felt only weeks ago. Her need to speak with him might have stemmed from Cammie's heavy burden of guilt that currently weighed like a giant boulder sitting on her shoulders. Her call went straight to his voicemail. She left a message.

Emotions in a tangle from the events of the past few days, she climbed the stairs to her mother's bedroom, carrying her breakfast tray. They'd spent time watching television together Saturday before the events that evening, the morning after her night out with the siblings. But Cammie hadn't confided all the conflicting emotions she'd been experiencing with Grey lately. Her mother, while on the mend, had seemed distracted and anxious. It was an unusual blend of qualities. Historically, Mom had been a steel magnolia of the most unflappable kind. For her to seem flustered was, well, unnerving for Cammie.

"Hello, darling," Mom said as Cammie entered the bedroom. She was sitting up with her laptop on her lap.

"How are you feeling this morning?" Cammie asked.

"A little sore, but nothing unusual about that." Her smile was bright, but again, Cammie noticed an edge of anxiety.

"Mom, is everything alright? You've seemed a little edgy since you've been home from the hospital."

Her mother's brows raised in innocence. "Why no, honey, everything's fine. What could possibly be wrong? Well, besides this darn house business, but Grey's got that handled for us, doesn't he?" She smiled radiantly, as if she had no cares in the world.

Before Cammie could make another comment, they were interrupted by female voices and footfalls on the stairs. Sounded like sisters to her.

The door burst open and Emma, followed closely by Maeve entered the room. "Hey Momma, how're you feeling this morning? Hey, Cammie." Emma wasn't the quiet type, and wouldn't ever get away with sneaking around, that was for sure.

"Hi, girls," her mother beamed at them all.

Emma winked slyly at Cammie and plopped down on the bed. "Momma, did Cammie tell you about her and Grey the other night?"

Cammie simultaneously was torn between the urge to tear her sister's hair out and dive under the bed in horror and shame. "Emma! Omigod, what would possess you to say such a thing?"

"We saw you licking his face off, you know." Emma's satisfied grin was so maddening that Cammie had to control the urge to rip her false eyelashes off, or maybe they weren't fake, but at the moment, she'd rip the real ones off if she could.

Instead, she took a deep, cleansing breath and said, "It was dark. You didn't see anything." That was her story, and she was sticking to it.

"Ha. There were lights shining behind the two of you, and believe me, not an inch separated any part of your bodies," Maeve said, grabbing Emma in a great big bear hug and squishing her sister against her while Emma squealed and giggled.

"The two of you are gross."

"We had to honk three times so you would hear us," Emma agreed.

"Sounds like quite an evening." Mom's eyes were wide.

"Don't listen to them. It was nothing."

"I want some of that nothing." Emma made kissing noises like a child.

"Shut up."

"Now, girls." Their mother stifled her laugh, so as not

to encourage the ribbing.

"Makes you wonder what might have happened if we hadn't shown up when we did," Emma said.

"You are all sworn to secrecy. I haven't told Jason details about Grey, and I certainly haven't told him that Grey's here working on the house or that we've, uh, had any contact."

Emma snorted and looked between them, then giggled. "Contact. That's a new one. I think I'll use it next time I refer to hot makey-outey."

"But you're still going to marry Jason, aren't you?" Maeve asked, as if that should suddenly put everything into complete perfect perspective.

Cammie was at a loss. Of course she was. Wasn't she? "I'm engaged. That means we're getting married."

"You don't have to just because you said you would. I mean, it's not too late to rethink this decision if it's not the right one," Maeve said.

Her mother, who had been watching and listening without comment, chimed in. "You know she's right, Cammie, dear. The time is now to raise any questions or voice doubts, not after you're married."

The way she'd said that had all three daughters swiveling their heads around toward their mother, who only shrugged. "What? I'm not talking about me; I'm pointing this out to Cammie. Marriage is forever, you know."

"Did you have doubts after you married Daddy?" Maeve asked.

"After I married your father, I knew I'd made the best

decision of my life," she smiled a watery smile that left none of them questioning her statement.

Their gazes all turned back to Cammie, as if to ask her the burning question.

"It was a kiss. That's all." Cammie defended.

They collectively hmmphed their disbelief, even Mom.

"We really thought you were done with Grey, and that nothing could've sparked up between the two of you again. But after what we saw the other night—" Maeve said.

"Yeah, it was hawt." Emma fanned her face. Another collective nod between the sisters.

"We were kids. He married my best friend. That part of my life ended ten years ago." Cammie was nearly yelling.

"She's over-protesting." They looked like a bunch of bobbleheads, damn them.

›››‹‹‹

EVERYONE IN THE room dissolved into fits of hysteria. Everyone that was, except Cammie.

"Might want to get up and take a shower before he arrives in the morning." her mother said.

"Mom! You, too?" Was her mother matchmaking? But Mom only smiled. The others giggled.

›››‹‹‹

THEY'D NOT HAD a conversation since he'd implored her to think about the two of them the other day. In fact, it was all she'd been thinking about.

"I'll be making quite a lot of noise today, some inside,

but mostly outside and wanted to let you know," Grey said, as he carried his equipment down the hallway, then set down a couple of power saws or something of the sort.

"Oh? What are you doing with those?" She asked, trying not to get close enough to him that she noticed things. Things like how good he smelled, or how the t-shirt he wore stretched over the very muscled torso, which led to the jeans that covered, well, she really didn't want to think about that. She'd been pressed up hard against all that the other night and really couldn't go there right now.

"Shoring up the floor here in the library. I've been working on the supports underneath, but the floor is sagging. I'll be working outside for the next few days, pouring concrete under a couple areas of the foundation with a small work crew. So, you might see a few extra guys around."

"Oh. Okay. Whatever you have to do to get things handled."

"We're going to have to replace the hardwoods in there, I'm sorry to say. There's water damage as well, so all the flooring will have to go."

That didn't sound good at all. "Was that expected?"

He nodded, a sympathetic expression in place. "It was one of the things that alerted your mother to some of the problems in the first place."

This was ridiculous, her reaction to him. She was having a difficult time keeping her breathing even, and her heart rate had escalated to what must be a dangerous level. So, she must sound like she was near panting.

"Are you alright?"

A flush stole over her cheeks. "I'm fine. Just in the middle of getting some things done for my mother." But she didn't move or look away, only continued to stare.

He grinned, knowingly. "Don't let me get in your way."

She wanted to climb him. Climb right up his gorgeous body and wrap her legs around his waist. Wonder what he'd do then. *Whoa, girl.*

He'd moved closer now, until they were toe-to-toe and nose-to-nose, because her thoughts must have been communicated to him through the hot gaze she couldn't break free from. "Cammie."

"What?" Her tone was breathy.

He must have picked up on her *discomfort*, because he placed his forehead against hers and closed his eyes, obviously struggling with his own desire. "I want this as much as you do, but I think I hear your sisters heading this way." He stepped back suddenly and turned toward his toolbox, bending over as if he was searching for something.

Sure enough, the two mother hens found them in the library looking for all the world to be discussing the flooring. With the weekend done, Cammie was up to her eyeballs in Evangeline House duties. Since very little catering had been done of late, Cammie spent time unloading serving pieces and going over recipes in the kitchen. She had a couple of mid-week meetings scheduled with clients as well.

The Chamber of Commerce's monthly luncheon was set to take place in one of the ballrooms as well as the Little

Miss Pecan Pie Princess Pageant committee meeting, Thursday evening in one of the smaller, less grand rooms. Cammie fell asleep that night contemplating a bunch of sticky little princesses with ginormous teased hair. She couldn't wait to meet their mamas. What she tried not to think about was Grey. And the two of them together.

One of Cammie's new duties, it seemed, was to care for Lucy if the school called while Maeve was at work. Normally that would have fallen to Mom, and so now it did to Cammie. Lucy called in a tizzy having forgotten her lunch. Apparently, Lucy was now a vegan, and such offerings weren't currently available at her school cafeteria. Cammie assured Lucy she would bring the food to her in time and made her way two doors down to Maeve's house. Using the key from the hook in her mother's laundry room, she found the prepared lunch in the refrigerator, and headed toward the same elementary school Cammie had attended eons ago.

It was nearly lunchtime by the time she arrived. To avoid the rigmarole in the school office, Cammie headed straight into the cafeteria. She could ask forgiveness from school administrators later if necessary. She was certain Mrs. Weed, the nasty old battle-ax, still sat at the front office, and would do her damnedest to give Cammie a demerit for disregarding procedure.

Scanning the utilitarian tables, partially filled with boys dressed in beaten up, baggy jeans and girls in tight clothing, and many wearing makeup far too early than they ought for such youngsters, she located her niece entering from a far door from the hallway with swarms of other hungry students. Most of them were headed toward the food lines. Lucy came further into the large room toward a group of tables. Cammie started toward her, hoping to hand off the lunch before the hormonally challenged crowd of children converged upon the space.

Just as she and Lucy made eye contact, a ruckus to the right drew both their attention. Samantha, obviously trying to make her way laden with a lunch tray, purse, and jacket was surrounded by three larger girls. They were taunting and pushing her within their circle. She appeared so frail and helpless within the tight ring of bullies. Cammie and Lucy both reacted immediately, heading as quickly as possible toward Samantha, but not before the precariously held lunch tray had been tipped down the front of her adorable top. Of course today's lunch would be spaghetti.

The bullies melted away before Cammie could reach Sam. Lucy bent down and picked up her purse and jacket. Samantha's head was bowed in utter humiliation and she was crouched low to the floor. Cammie looked around for a teacher, trying to process how something like this could occur while in a supervised area. It had happened so quickly. Someone must have notified a teacher on duty, because one was bearing down on the scene.

Cammie knew she wasn't Samantha's favorite person right now, but she must try and help if she could. "Honey, do you want me to call your dad?"

Sam looked up, quickly recognizing Cammie. Her furious green eyes blazed with anger, "This is all your fault! Stay away from my daddy!" she shrieked at Cammie. Her frail shoulders shook with rage. She'd obviously directed whatever emotions this incident had ignited using Cammie as the target of her angst.

Cammie blinked uncomprehendingly. Lucy looked horrified that her friend would attack her beloved aunt with such a vengeance. "Why are you yelling at Aunt Cammie? Sam?"

"You didn't know, did you? She's the reason my mom is dead. Now everybody's heard about it because their parents have been talking. Those girls were calling me a—a freak show because my mom wrecked her car into a pole. They said my mother was—was crazy." Samantha was sobbing in earnest now.

The school counselor appeared in moments and just happened to be a former classmate. She barely spared Cammie a glance though, focusing instead on Samantha's state of anguish. "Poor thing. She's been through so much. Look at you with spaghetti all over your pretty clothes."

"Is there anything I can do to help?" Cammie asked, trying to control her own tears.

"I think your being here is upsetting her. I'll take her to my office and call her father. You know, it's not the first time this sort of thing has happened since she's been back. Children can be very cruel."

"So can adults." Cammie took Lucy by the hand and walked toward the empty end of one of the tables. She appeared shaken.

"I don't understand, Aunt Cammie."

"It all happened a long time ago, honey. Samantha's dad

and I dated just before he married her mom. People sometimes say things they shouldn't, and I think Samantha must have overheard some gossip about her dad and me. She'll go home now and get her bearings, but don't let what happened between her father and me ruin your friendship. It will be hard, but she really needs you right now. Promise?"

"Uh, okay. But what did she mean that this is all your fault?"

"It's far too complicated to go into right now, but we will spend some time talking about it at home. Okay? It isn't like it sounds. I didn't have anything to do with her mother's death, so please don't think that I did. Everything that happened was before Samantha was born or Mr. Harrison married her mom."

Lucy stared at her and nodded slowly. "I'll go sit with my friends and eat. Thanks for bringing my food," she waved and walked off, a baffled expression on her young face.

By the time Cammie returned to her car, she noticed Grey's truck pulling in to the parking lot near her.

She rushed up to meet him. "Grey, I'm so sorry. Samantha overheard terrible things and believes Deb killed herself because of me. When she saw me, she really melted down." Cammie wanted more than anything to help. "If there's anything I can do?"

His expression was pure granite. "You're probably the last person she wants to see right now. It's best we stay away from one another for awhile." He turned on his heel and stalked toward the front office where Mrs. Weed was sure to be waiting.

Cammie stared after him in shocked silence as he stalked toward the school office entrance. Really? Did he think she was here to harass his daughter? She shook her head in bewilderment.

She thought about calling him later to try and make him understand why she'd gone to the school—that she'd was only delivering Lucy's lunch when the situation with Samantha had occurred, but she was stubborn enough to want him to think what he wanted. Still, she thought as got into the car, there'd been enough miscommunication between them to last a lifetime as far as she was concerned. She would give it some consideration. Maybe she just didn't want him to think ill of her?

If becoming a parent made a person behave the way Grey had earlier, she wanted none of it. Life was hard, and the way Cammie's heart hurt for his child was painful enough. It didn't seem to matter to her anymore that Samantha was also Deb's daughter.

Cammie returned home and tried to focus on returning a few calls and e-mails. How had things become so complicated in such a short amount of time? This trip thus far had been an extension of the hair-fire nightmare; beginning the morning she'd arrived to face Grey in her underwear. Things had pitched steeply downhill from there.

She wanted to return to her former life. The one that included a loving fiancé who didn't accuse her of foul intentions toward young children or hurt her beyond belief. The one where she called her mother once a week to check in. She would sort the career thing out sooner or later. She missed her beach house and her boyfriend. The sooner she got out of Misery, the better.

>>><<<

SAMANTHA HAD FINALLY worn herself down and was now sleeping. After watching her stare motionless for a long while at the wall in her bedroom, Grey had brought hot chocolate, and suggested they talk about what had happened at school today. She'd come unglued.

Following the temper tantrum, the tears, and the accusations, Grey was every bit the emotional wreck Sam appeared. They both had an appointment this Tuesday with a family counselor who was new on the edge of town. The necessity for Sam to see someone about her intense emotions was becoming dire, even before today. She seemed so—broken.

Maybe coming back here wasn't the right thing for either of them. It seemed an ideal solution at the time. His large restoration project had wrapped up, and he could take some time to help his father around the old house, and slow down his work pace. Grey's plan included spending more time with Samantha. He'd been at his wits end, grasping for a solution to ease the guilt and despair as he watched Samantha flounder day after day without her mom.

He would keep the appointment with the family therapist and go from there. No telling what can of worms it would open up, but if it helped them all find some sort of peace and closure in the long-term, he'd be willing to put forth the time and money necessary.

They both only had one life to live. Hers wasn't too late to rescue and rebuild. His—well; time would tell.

Grey quietly shut the door to Sam's room, then made his way to the kitchen in search of coffee. If he got lucky, he might avoid having to try and explain this afternoon's train wreck with his daughter.

Finding his dad sitting at the bar, reading the newspaper, felt right on par with the rest of the day. Norman raised his shaggy brows and inquired above his glasses at Grey. Shit. They were co-parenting now, he and his father. And his father was quite good at it, Grey was finding out. But he hadn't any issue with expressing his opinion when he felt the need. But his dad was also a wealth of support to Grey.

"Hey, Dad." He felt twelve again, and required to spill about the broken glass at the barn from the baseball incident.

"You mind sharing what was happening in there with my granddaughter? Sounded like an exorcism might be required."

"Closer to it than you realize." Grey explained about the incident at school with Cammie.

"Have you and Cammie had a conversation about this?"

"I told her we'd need to keep our distance from one another."

"How do you plan to do that while you're working for Maureen?"

"I'll do as much outside work as possible and take a week off until she leaves town. I can't be around her if it's going to hurt Sam." Grey knew it would kill him, but Cammie was not a good influence on his daughter right now. He still wondered what exactly had happened at school.

"Since when do kids get to say who you get to spend your time around?" His dad asked, and Grey felt the question like a punch. "I get it that she's upset, but she misunderstands the situation. She needs the facts. And." His gaze narrowed. "While you're at it. Samantha's built her mama up to be some kind of saint that she wasn't."

"That's an understatement."

"We all know Deb loved her daughter—kind of like a doll or a possession. But, son, you were the one who cooked her meals, helped her with her homework, and kissed her skinned knees—still do. Her mother put her on a pedestal and spoiled her something fierce when she wasn't shouting and throwing things. You're her anchor, don't forget that."

"It's a hard thing to communicate to a nine-year-old. She remembers things in her own way."

"Are you still planning to keep the appointment with the counselor?"

"Definitely. I don't see that I have a choice, especially now."

"Good. Years ago, I would have told you it was all non-sense. Now, I can see where this confusion has to be sorted out. I know these mind doctors train to help people make sense after such a shock to the system. Don't worry, Grey, we'll all be here to help her."

Grey ran his hand through his hair and rubbed his eyes.

What a damned mess all this was. In some ways, with Deb gone, it was over—the emotional manipulation and drama that had been so much a part of daily life. For now, the days could pass without that sort of upheaval. He knew his wife had been sick. Nevertheless, her illness had metastasized into all their lives. With her gone, he could hope for a cure.

Later that night, staring up at the ceiling in the dark, Grey remembered that awful night as if it was yesterday. The day he'd been released from his marriage and Samantha had lost her mother. Deb had gotten angry with him for another perceived slight, a small and insignificant thing that caused her to seek solace in her favorite pastime—drinking.

He'd assumed since it was getting late and Samantha was already asleep that he would avoid more conflict by leaving Deb to her bottle and heading up to bed. Deb typically had slept it off in the downstairs guest bedroom anyway. He'd not anticipated her decision to leave the house once she'd had too much to drink that night.

She'd only done that a couple times, and then, she'd driven just down the street to the convenience store for something. But that last time, they'd never discovered her intended destination, or if she'd even had one. The accident involved only Deb and an immovable electrical pole. No one called it suicide, only a tragic accident involving alcohol.

What a mess it all still was. If he thought for a moment Samantha's issues would simply resolve themselves, then waiting this out might be the path of least resistance. But this latest incident and her response really concerned him.

He would see what the counselor had to say. That meant seeing her himself as well as Samantha. Great. More analysis of the disaster he'd made of his life.

Chapter Nine

C AMMIE WOKE UP with a headache from lack of sleep. Lack of sleep and too much brooding, tossing and turning. She should call Jason down here and spill every bit of this to him right now. He would understand. And he would support her and help her deal with it all. But she hated emotional dumping. It was, after all, her mess.

One foot in front of the other. Right now, this instant, called for coffee and aspirin. Pulling on her robe and slippers, she stepped out into the still-darkened hallway and padded to the kitchen. Searching the cupboards for the aspirin, she didn't hear Jo enter. "Good morning, sunshine!"

"Oh, my God, Jo, you scared the crap out of me. What are you doing here so early?" Cammie put her hand to her throbbing head.

"I'm out of coffee. Easier to get it here than the store this early." She must have noticed Cammie's discomfort. "Honey, you okay? Are you dizzy or sick to your stomach?" Cammie felt her sister's touch beside her in an instant— sensed the concern in her voice.

"I'm fine. Just had a bad night."

"Yes, your eyes are puffy. Everything alright with Jason?"

"Who—oh, yes, things are fine with Jason." It took Cammie a moment to catch Jo's drift.

"What's going on then? Don't say nothing—it's obviously something enough that you're head is hurting from crying during the night." Jo's hand was on her hip and she wouldn't back down until Cammie cried 'uncle.'

Cammie told her what happened with Samantha at the school. She was surprised the whole family hadn't yet had a conference about it since it also involved Lucy.

Jo Jo looked as if she wanted to say something, but couldn't make up her mind.

"What is it you want to say?" Cammie demanded.

"Honey, we haven't really talked about Deb and how she was, really. We touched on it a few times, but never really got into it."

Cammie didn't know what that meant. "No. Obviously we've never really discussed Deb."

"I know she was your best friend growing up, but we all saw something disturbing in her that I don't think you ever did. Nobody ever said anything because you had such a soft heart and a blind spot where she was concerned."

"They were poor, but I didn't think my family held that against her," Cammie said.

"That's not what I'm talking about. One time Mom brought it up, but you got so stinkin' mad that she never did again."

"I remember Mom saying she was after Grey when we

were in high school." Realization dawned on Cammie. "Are you trying to tell me she was after him all along?

Jo Jo threw up her hands. "Cammie, that gal was no good. She was Looney Toons. I'm sorry to say she was just hangin' on to you because you were popular and could get her near the boys she wanted to screw."

"Josephine Laroux! What an awful thing to say about a dead woman." Cammie was appalled by her sister's lack of decorum.

"Are you upset that I said it, or that it's true?"

"Both!" That was true enough.

Cammie had known Deb was less—inhibited than most young girls when it came to guys when they'd been teens. But she'd been her dearest, most trusted friend.

When Deb had revealed how Grey had taken advantage of her in the barn after she'd been drinking heavily—after Cammie and Grey's big fight. It was as if a bright light had just been turned on. "Oh, my God. She lied to me." Funny how time and maturity brought clarity to a situation in a single instant when one took a moment to really re-examine. A ten year old irredeemable situation.

"Honey, had it never occurred to you that she'd made a play for your boyfriend when he was sad and upset?"

No, it hadn't. She'd blamed him a hundred percent. "No, I guess not. It—doesn't matter, does it? He married her even after she miscarried." Her head was really pounding now.

"No, it doesn't matter. But now you can understand how young and immature you all were and maybe just forgive him already."

Yes, maybe she should. "I guess I've been holding a grudge." Cammie knew deep down that she'd never have forgiven him for marrying Deb back then, so nothing could have worked out differently, except that she would have hated Deb all these years with a vengeance instead of only seeing her as an untrue friend and somewhat of a victim.

Chapter Ten

GREY HAD SPOKEN at length to the therapist with regards to Samantha's and his situation on the phone, leaving Cammie, specifically, out of the mix and focusing on Deb and her illness and its repercussions on Sam.

The counselor suggested they schedule sessions separately for each of them and then together to discuss ways to help improve communication within the home. He was all for that. In fact, the woman even suggested that his father come in periodically since he would be part of this fledgling puzzle. Grey figured it couldn't hurt to all be on the same page. Hell, nothing could hurt at this point.

Grey and Samantha went through the routine typical for a school morning; breakfast, bed making, and locating last minute items that had mysteriously disappeared from the backpack since Friday afternoon. He hadn't filled Sam in regarding their early-morning appointment with Dr. Sabine O'Connor, licensed clinical psychotherapist.

When they passed the turn for school without slowing, Samantha's head whipped around, "Hey, you missed the road—"

"We're not going to school just yet. We've got an appointment with a counselor."

"No way." Her tone was scathing, her arms crossed, and her posture became instantly rigid and defiant.

"Honey, are you happy with the way things are right now?" Grey tried to keep a neutral tone so as not to see her off.

"Of course I'm not happy—and I can't believe you would try and trick me into going to see another one of those stupid people who tries to make me talk about my feelings, Dad."

"Well, pumpkin, I want you to be happy. And my plan is to do whatever it takes to help us all get there, as crazy as it sounds." His knuckles were white with the anticipation of battle but his tone was pure honey.

He'd figured out over the years that when he quit revving up, she knew to back down. It was their way to stay in balance. Deb had been all over the map with moods and emotions. At times she'd been honey sweet and then turned to near abuse almost on a dime. Most of her anger had been directed at Grey, thank goodness.

But Samantha now was in such a confused state that he had to contain his obvious frustration with her until they set some real, solid ground rules. Hopefully the therapist would help with that. Having another adult in a position of authority might support his parental role. He could only hope.

Heat emanated from her angry glare. But she was his daughter and likely figured out by his manner that he'd drawn a line in the sand. This time she wouldn't win. She was headed to the stupid therapist's office to talk about those unhappy feelings or sit quietly for the requisite hour, whichever she chose. Either way, they would make the acquaintance of Ms. Sabine O'Connor this morning.

They traveled the remaining few miles in silence. Fortunately, Ms. O'Connor's office wasn't too far away from home, only about fifteen minutes on the quiet outskirts of Ministry. He often traveled that direction toward Cheneyville, since the town was larger than Ministry and supported big chain stores that sold items in bulk, like building supplies for their home renovation. The amount of materials necessary for the both the Evangeline House job and the renovation of his father's house—formerly his grandparent's place—would likely require several deliveries from building supply yards. Until the big jobs began, like the roof and wood for siding, Grey planned to pick things up along the way while he worked.

As they arrived, Sam began to squirm and fidget, her outward show of nerves hurt his heart, but he remained firm in his resolve to see this through.

He'd mapped out the address carefully and pulled into the small parking lot, then with a sigh, cut the engine. Turning to his angst-riddled daughter, he said, "You understand I'm insisting on this for all of us, don't you?" He searched her sweet face, splotchy now from where she'd carelessly swiped her fingers across her eyes and cheeks. Her green eyes, so like his, stared back at him with a mixture of wariness and defeat.

"I really don't have a choice, do I?" She said softly.

"No, you don't. But we will get through it together, like always, okay?"

Her shrug as she released the door handle was her response. He supposed it was better than an all-out refusal to leave the vehicle. Progress often came in very tiny measures.

The office was a renovated cottage, dating back to the turn of the century, from what Grey could tell from the architecture of the place. He enjoyed what he did and rarely missed details as they applied to older buildings. Whoever updated the home had done a nice job from what he could see so far. He rang the bell with one arm around Sam's stiff shoulders.

The door opened within seconds, as if their arrival had not only been expected but greatly anticipated. The woman who greeted them was nothing like the solemn therapist he'd expected—to put it mildly.

She was gorgeous. But almost before he registered her unexpected appearance, she began speaking directly to Samantha as if he wasn't there. "Hi there, you must be Samantha. You can call me Sabine. I love the name Samantha, always have. I'm so glad you're here this morning. Were you able to have breakfast before you left home? I baked blueberry muffins the minute I climbed out of bed. I had a craving during the night—maybe I had a dream about them, I don't remember. Anyway, there they are on the table if you'd like to have one. There's juice too, if you want a glass."

Finally, Sabine turned to Grey, "Oh, hi, you must be

Samantha's father, Grey. Samantha and I are going to get to know each other a little bit if that's all right with her." Then she fixed a questioning gaze toward his daughter. Samantha's expression was bemused, as if she wasn't quite certain what to make of this lovely steamroller of a woman.

"O-okay, I guess," Samantha replied to the part-inquiry, part-command.

"Great. I've left some additional paperwork for you to fill out on the coffee table in the waiting area. Make yourself comfortable and we'll see you in a little while." She fixed him with a gorgeous smile, all straight, white teeth and sparkling blue eyes. Combined with her mane of shiny, sable brown, wavy hair, long eyelashes, and lean-but-curvy body, the impact was nearly staggering. Grey figured it likely would be to any unsuspecting red-blooded man caught off guard the way he'd been.

He sat down on the sofa in the waiting area after locating the paperwork she'd mentioned. She would certainly know his whole life story if he answered all these questions honestly. He'd come this far, might as well go the distance.

As his pen scratched across the paper, he heard a familiar sound, it startled him almost enough to send him running toward the closed door across the hallway. He stilled and listened. Samantha was laughing. Not a soft or quiet giggle; no, this was an all-out, gut-busting, great big belly laugh. Like she'd just heard the funniest joke and couldn't contain herself. Whatever Sabine said had her hooting and howling with abandon.

He decided then and there he felt love toward Sabine

O'Connor for what she'd just done. A great big heart-full-of-gratitude kind of love. Whatever else happened during their therapy sessions from this day forward, he owed her big time for bringing back Sam's laughter.

For some reason, a picture of Cammie, looking guilty and miserable popped into his head just then. He'd treated her abysmally at the school. How could he believe that she would intentionally try and hurt Sam? He didn't really believe it, and he knew her well enough to understand that she harbored no bad intentions toward his daughter.

He had lashed out at her because she'd been there during the awful event in the lunchroom. And Samantha blamed her because she'd overheard the other kids and their moms gossiping. The old saying went, "You always hurt the ones you love the most." Boy that had certainly been the case where Cammie was concerned.

Hearing happy sounds coming from the room, Grey focused his attention to the paperwork in front of him. At least something was going right.

As he was just filling out the last line, the door opened and Sabine, with her arm casually slung around Samantha's shoulders, followed his smiling daughter out of the room. Not wanting to screw this up, he figured he'd best take his cues from them.

"Hi, daddy." Was it his imagination or had Samantha somehow snapped out of her funk in a matter of a half hour of so?

"We had a nice chat and some girl talk. I gave Samantha my personal e-mail address and told her to e-mail me one sentence every night to let me know how her day went. I will send a short reply and try to give a little helpful feedback. That way, she can try and begin the day with a simple strategy for positive progress every day."

"Sounds like a plan to me." Grey couldn't believe his good luck in finding this woman. Daily therapy for his struggling child—hallelujah. He barely stopped himself from gazing heavenward, arms outstretched.

"Grey, could I see you for a couple minutes privately? As I told Samantha, we should all be on the same page with our communication. Sam, could you begin that writing exercise we discussed? The paper's in the desk drawer." Sam nodded and smiled at Sabine, dimples showing.

Sabine motioned Grey to precede her into the office toward a very comfortable chair on the opposite side of her desk. She suddenly seemed very businesslike and far cooler than she'd been in Samantha's presence. "I know Samantha seems like a different child to you than when she came in, but don't be fooled."

Oh, God, what now? "What exactly do you mean?" He shifted uncomfortably in his seat.

"Her issues are extremely complex, and while on the surface she may seem to lighten up fairly quickly, her deeper feelings of abandonment by her mother will come out at unexpected times."

"She feels abandoned by Deb?" Grey knew she'd felt lonely and miserable without her, but abandoned?

"She wouldn't overtly blame her mother for leaving because it's tough for her to grasp how she could miss and love

Deb while holding deep anger and resentment simultane-ously. Such conflicting emotions wouldn't jive to a little girl. As we develop an environment of trust, hopefully she will begin to unload some of her locked up torment and begin to understand why she is so angry and that these are normal emotions."

"They are normal, right?" He asked.

"Perfectly. But you're not nearly out of the woods yet. So, suit up and get ready for displays of deep resentment at unexpected moments. She'll use you or anyone she identifies as a threat to her relationship with you as the outlet for her emotions."

"How should I handle the emotional outbursts?" Grey most wanted to know what to do when this happened.

"Let her vent to a point, but don't allow her to become abusive or disrespectful. She can express her feelings, but she can't mistreat anyone else in the process. The good news is that she's still capable of laughter and humor." Sabine leveled him with a radiant smile, and he wondered if she practiced the effect it must have on other humans.

"That's good news, I guess," he said.

"Yes. You've got a long way to go. But by seeking sup-port for Samantha, the road shouldn't be as long or hard. I've got another patient coming in a few minutes, but I would like to have a joint session with the two of you for half an hour next time and then see you each privately for fifteen minutes during the remainder of our time."

"That sounds like a good plan," he said as they made their way toward Samantha, who was busily writing something on a sheet of paper and barely glanced up as they approached.

"You ready to head to school?" She looked up then—and her body language changed immediately to a far more despairing droop.

"Remember what we discussed?" Sabine raised her brows in question to Sam, and Sam responded with a brisk nod and small semblance of a smile.

"I'll see the two of you next week," and to Sam, "I'll look for your e-mail this evening, all right?" Sam nodded again meeting Sabine's eyes in silent communication.

Sabine and Grey shook hands, hers firm and small in his much larger and rougher one.

This had been a really good idea for them both.

Hopefully, the strategies Sabine had suggested for Sam while in school would give her a little much-needed confidence to go about her day without fear and dread. He was curious about their private discussion, but decided Sam would see that as him butting in. As long as this was working, he would let things be.

At their next appointment with Sabine, he should get her opinion on how to go about questioning Sam about her school day, etc. He wasn't sure whether to allow her brooding and silence or insist on steady communication. She was still so young to not share things with her daddy.

Chapter Eleven

GREY HAD TO make Cammie understand that he didn't blame her for what had happened with Samantha at school. He'd lashed out instead of listening because she'd unfortunately crossed his path on his way inside while he'd been frantically trying to get to his daughter. He wasn't sure how to approach her with an apology.

Now that they'd seen Sabine, and he had real hope in healing for both he and Samantha, he was ready to forge ahead. Somehow he must communicate to Cammie how he felt and buy some time with her before she left town and walked out of his life permanently. Before she married another man and he'd lost any chance of figuring out what might still be between them.

He punched in her cell number quickly so he wouldn't chicken out. "Hello?" Just the sound of her voice created a mixture of nerves and joy within his entire being.

"Cammie? It's Grey."

The moment of silence seemed to stretch endlessly, then she responded, her voice guarded. "Oh, hi. I wasn't expecting your call." He could tell that her feelings were hurt.

"Could you meet me in the gazebo? I'd like to clear the air about what happened with Samantha at school the other day."

"It's really not a good time right now—" she began.

"Please, Cammie, just for a few minutes. I understand if you can't, but it's important. I took Samantha to a therapist after—after what happened, and well, we really do need to talk."

He sensed her continued hesitation. "I guess I could come out for a little while. Mom is down for the evening, but I don't want to be gone long in case she needs me. See you in a bit."

"Thanks. I really appreciate this." He realized he'd used slightly underhanded tactics to get her outside, but it was essential to their progress, both as friends and in healing the ten year rift that he apologize for his bad response to the situation.

Though his intentions were mostly pure, he couldn't help but experience a shot of adrenaline at meeting her in the gazebo out back. It had been the setting of countless make out sessions between them during their dating years. The idea of sneaking out after dark brought the thrill of anticipation back. Those cherished and unblemished memories with Cammie had gotten him through some of the darkest times with Deb. There was probably something really screwed up about that.

He found his father sitting in the small study where he watched television. "Hey, Dad, I'll be back in a few minutes. I need to speak with Cammie for a few minutes.

She's meeting me out back. If Samantha needs me, shoot me a text." Grey held up his phone.

His dad gave him a steady look. "Okay, son. I'll keep an ear out for her."

"Thanks."

Grey understood his father's concerns. No one understood the big picture about where he'd been to get where he was currently better than Dad, who thankfully kept his opinion to himself just then. Dad liked Cammie just fine, but likely thought Grey didn't need any more complications added to his life at the moment.

Grey was careful not to let the screen door slam, alerting Samantha to his leaving the house. He didn't want to have to explain where he was going and why. Lying to his child didn't rank high on his list of good parenting strategies, and he really didn't believe Samantha was ready to give Cammie the benefit of the doubt just yet.

As he reached the gazebo, he could see that she was already there, standing just inside against the railing, staring upward. His heart gave a hard thud. *He couldn't stand to let her go again.*

"Hi." He stepped up into the structure, the wooden steps creaking under his weight.

"Hi." She turned toward him, arms crossed over her chest protectively.

The white fairy lights were strung around the inside ceiling and down the sides, casting a glow all around them, just enough soft light to make out facial expressions but not bright or harsh.

He motioned for her to sit on the loveseat, and then dropped down across from her on the edge of the wicker chair. The seating was closely arranged, their knees nearly touching in the small space. It was an intimate setting, no doubt, but perfect for their situation.

"Cammie, I'm really sorry for lashing out at you at the school the other day. I know I hurt you."

She bowed her head for a second, then looked up. "It's alright. I know you were upset. It was a terrible situation. Those girls—they were awful to Samantha. I wanted to help her, I tried—"

He reached out and put a hand over hers. "I know you did. You wouldn't have done anything else; I know that. I knew it then, but was so upset that our past had hurt her. I wanted to blame someone. The only person to blame is myself. It's hard—to be the only one at fault all the time. I've carried that for a lot of years and lived with the consequences, as have you. I just didn't think Samantha would have to deal with those consequences in such an awful and new way. Sometimes I don't think I'll ever be able to get out from under making such a horrible mess of things all those years ago. It just keeps coming back in fresh ways to ruin my life and those I love." His eyes bore into hers then.

Cammie's cheeks had tears rolling down them. "Grey, I do forgive you. I hope you know that. I'm just so confused right now. Obviously, I can't deny how I felt back then, how much you hurt me, or that it's affected me in my trust and relationships with others."

He closed his eyes, her words like a body blow against

the pain he'd caused. "Again, my damned stupidity ruining lives."

It was her turn to squeeze his hand. "No. No more blame and guilt. It's over. We're adults now and we've all suffered enough. You focus on Samantha right now. I'm fine."

He opened his eyes and said, "But I want you in my life. Through everything, that's never changed.

"Jo Jo pointed out something to me that my grown-up self never really considered. You see, I've been stuck in the same thinking, the mindset of where I was back when all this happened. She made me take a look at Deb and how she really was from the outsider's perspective."

"You mean as the jealous friend who only wanted to get close to you to take what you had and she didn't?" He asked bitterly.

Cammie's eyes opened wide in surprise. "Y-yes. That's exactly what she said. That Deb hadn't been the friend I'd believed; that she'd actually been the worst kind of friend, one who never had my best interests at heart, and was resentful, no matter how much affection and respect I had for her."

"Knowing her the way I did until the end, Cammie, there wasn't anything anyone could have done to change her attitude or personality. It was a true disorder, fueled by borderline poverty, a broken home, and an incessant need for more. More love, more money, more things, and more of what you had that she didn't." Grey tried his best to verbalize what was the dark core of his late wife's soul.

"I had no idea it went so deep." Cammie shook her head sadly. "It sounds…" She hesitated. "Horrible."

She looked up at him, tears glittering on the ends of her lashes.

"It was horrible, Cammie. But you know what helped me get through the worst of it?"

She shrugged helplessly.

"You. Memories of how things were between us before I ruined everything with Deb. So, it was that much more awful to know I was at fault."

She smiled a watery smile then. "We had some pretty great times, didn't we?"

He moved beside her on the loveseat in a single motion. "We had the best times." They sat together for a while then, hands clasped, sides pressed together, but otherwise not touching. But it was enough. Sharing those memories and healing old hurts and misunderstandings had done more than a couple passionate kisses to repair their damaged past.

Grey's phone vibrated then, breaking the spell. It was a text from his dad, saying that Samantha had woken up and wondered where he was.

"Sorry, I have to go."

"No problem. Thanks for explaining—everything. I guess I'll see you tomorrow."

"Yep." He waved, and left her sitting there with a thoughtful expression on her lovely face.

❖

CAMMIE'S HEART WAS beating lighter by morning, which

made no sense whatsoever, considering how not engaged she'd been feeling lately. Not engaged, because she'd yet to speak with Jason since she'd tried to call him a couple days ago and he'd not yet returned the call. And she'd not made another attempt.

But still, the conversation last night with Grey had left her in a better state of the mind and heart. The process of forgiving, or at least understanding both Deb and Grey really was cathartic in helping her to dump some of the really acidic and damaging baggage she'd been carting around within her psyche for a really long time.

So, with this lighter attitude, she was able to think ahead a bit to something she'd seen in the local newspaper a few days ago. At the time, she hadn't really thought much about it, but now she allowed an idea to take root.

Cammie remembered that there was an entire festival surrounding the Little Miss Pecan Pie Pageant, and that included the Pecan Pie Bake-Off. It might have sounded like a small-town thing to someone out of the tri-state area, or the Southern region, but Southern Living Magazine was one of the major sponsors of the contest, and it drew some pretty big-name judges from national forums.

Cammie's future plan of opening her own "Southern cooking" seaside restaurant had begun to blossom somewhere in the back of her brain, underneath all the drama frustration that had been her life recently. Even before the hair fire, she'd gone so far as to make extensive notes and began working on a business proposal. Part of her strategy was to tout "award winning" recipes. Her pecan pie was kickass from the word go, and she'd been fine-tuning it for years. So, since there wasn't any rush to get back to her job, or apparently her fiancé, why not stay and help out with the pageant and enter the contest?

She would need to put some work into her efficiency and tweaking a couple things, but practice always made perfect in a competition like this. One wrong move, or spilled ingredient, could spell disaster—as she was well aware.

Putting herself out there again, even in such a small market, scared the pants off her, but what did she really have to lose? She'd already made the most ginormous spectacle of herself on national television. Plus, she had her family's support here, and hopefully some of her friends and local townspeople. Things really had changed in a few weeks, Cammie marveled.

⤜⤛⤜

ON THE OFF-HOURS in between his time at Evangeline House, Grey spent time working with his dad on the old section of his house. They worked side-by-side, installing the new subflooring upstairs. Next came the hardwoods he'd so meticulously searched the county for.

In keeping with the architectural integrity of the old place, only wide-planked, well-cured red oak boards could be considered an option in Grey's mind. The deep patina of old wood wasn't available new, either. He'd had to scour websites and ask around about construction sites where buildings had been either condemned and scheduled for demolition, or God forbid, remodeled—out with the old and in with new.

One morning, on the way back from a trip to the local builder's supply, he'd taken a back road due to some asphalt work and flag crews slowing things down on the main route. This led to his passing a great big old farmhouse and orchard, where he saw a hand-painted sign that read, *barn wood for sale.*

He couldn't stop thinking about the sign or the property. So, after he picked Samantha up from school, instead of her riding the bus, they headed out to the old house.

She was less sulky this afternoon, so hopefully she would enjoy their outing. As they passed the area in front of the farmhouse on the way home, Grey swung the truck into the long gravel drive leading toward the old orchard. Samantha's head swiveled toward him in question. "Why are we stopping here?"

"I passed by here a couple days ago and wondered about it. Grandpa needs some old wood boards for his floor, and I really love this old house. Just curious, I guess." He grinned at her.

"Just the way you felt about it—like it called to you or something?" She did suddenly seem to understand this thing he experienced with old houses. Their green gazes met, and hers shyly retreated.

"Yep. Just like that."

"It's pretty silly when you say it out loud, you know." She made a show of rolling her eyes, but not in nasty way.

"Then we don't have to tell anyone how houses speak to

me. You're right; it does sound silly out loud." He ruffled her hair. "You staying in or getting out?"

There were two pickups with the windows down parked outside the old farmhouse. Grey took a moment to admire the house's style and grace. The structure was wood and looked to be around a hundred or so years old, with a wide front porch running the length of the house and wrapping around. The paint was peeling, but there were carved cutwork accents running along under the front gutters and at the roof peaks. It was obvious to Grey that a lot of artistry went into this home during construction so many years ago.

He could see past the age and condition to appreciate the beauty beneath.

"Can I help y'all with something?" A squat fellow with yellow hair around mid-forties appeared from the front door, catching Grey off guard. Samantha jumped.

"Saw the house as I was passing by. She's a real beauty."

The yellow-haired gentleman let out a belly laugh. "Is that what you call it? I call it a plain mess."

"It's old and needs work, but has great bones." Grey surveyed the exterior again to verify his first impression and nodded.

The man extended his hand, "George Crawford."

"Grey Harrison," he replied, caught in a crushing hand-shake. After carefully extricating his hand, Grey asked, "You the owner?"

"My momma owns the place. Daddy passed last year and she won't set foot on the property anymore. She's living with my wife and me now. Roof got struck by lightning last week when that monster storm came through and now we got a big hole. Lucky it hasn't rained since."

"You looking to sell?" The words were out before Grey realized what he'd said.

George rubbed his head like he'd not thought of it until just now. "Might—just might. Have to talk to Momma and see what she's got on her mind about this place. She and Daddy lived here their whole married life, raised their kids here, just like her momma before her."

Grey pulled a business card from his wallet and said, "Give me a call if you want to discuss it further. It's a beautiful property."

"You want to see inside?"

Yes. Yes. Yes. "Love to." He checked with Sam and she preferred to wait outside.

"Watch your step. It's a little dusty and there's a few spider webs. We tried to cover everything, but nobody's been in here to clean for awhile."

Grey could hardly contain his enthusiasm. The fixtures were nearly as old as the house, and in excellent condition. The residents had loved this home, taken great care with it, and maintained it well over the years. Sure, it had seen some wear and tear, but it was a hundred years old. And it had a great gaping hole in the roof—up in the attic.

"You'll need to get a tarp over the roof until someone can fix it."

"The guys are on their way up with it now."

He wondered who was in the other truck. Must've just missed them.

"There are some real treasures here," Grey couldn't help but remarking on the household furnishings and fixtures.

"Momma doesn't want anything to do with it right now. We keep hoping she'll change her mind. She's heartbroken."

"Such a shame. Sorry for your loss." Grey couldn't help but put himself in this man's shoes with regards to losing his own mother. It was still a crushing emptiness at times.

"That old barn out back is chock full of stuff like what's in the house if you're in to that kind of thing. I noticed on your card that you renovate houses. Would you like to have a look? I've been told there's all means of materials and such out there. Be great to unload some of this stuff just sitting and gathering dust. My daddy was a collector, you see."

Grey felt his pulse quicken at the words, *materials* and *collector*. Judging by what he'd seen inside the house, visions of priceless antiquities popped into his head. "I've got my daughter out in the car."

"Might be something she'd be interested in out here, too. Lots of stuff."

"I saw the barn wood for sale sign."

"Yep. Got lots of old wood out there. Y'all go on a take a look."

The barn had been converted into a very large and quite organized workshop/storage facility. As George flipped on the double switch, light flooded the huge space. The stalls were organized and labeled with placards according to their contents. Samantha squealed as she discovered the doll and horse collection. Treasure trove, indeed.

There was so much to see that Grey hadn't a clue where to begin. He cautioned Sam to be careful picking around and to look for spiders. Then, he spied what looked to be piles of boards up in the loft. He asked George if he could have a look.

"Be my guest." George gestured him up the old ladder, which was impressively sturdy, given its age.

That was where he found the old floorboards. There was a mountain of them. Grey's heartbeat accelerated even faster than when he'd had his first glimpse inside the house and faster still than when the lights had burst on in here.

"Found something you're interested in up there?" George asked.

Deep breath. "How much for the old wood flooring?"

"Hundred bucks if you haul it away."

"Deal." Good thing Grey was pretty deep in the loft or the man would have thought he was a little kooky the way he was happy dancing around and fist-pumping.

"You alright up there?"

"Yes sir. Just figuring the square footage."

"Daddy!" Samantha called from below.

"Yes, pumpkin?" He peered over the edge.

"You won't believe what I've found—it's the horse that matches my other horse. Remember the one we looked for a couple years ago for my birthday and couldn't find? It's still in the box, Daddy."

"Sounds like you both found something you were looking for. Take the horse, hon. I'm sorry to say, my daddy wasn't just a collector, he had an online shopping, uh, habit."

"Have you considered selling some of this stuff on e-bay?"

"Naw, too much trouble. Might have a yard sale some-time. But so far, Momma won't let us. She doesn't care about any of the stuff, mind you, she just doesn't want to deal with it. So, here it sits, gathering dust."

"Well, if you don't think she'll mind my daughter tak-ing the horse, I want to pay you for it. I know it wasn't cheap." Grey pulled out bills to pay for both the flooring and the horse. But George only accepted enough for the wood.

"My daddy would have been tickled for your little girl to have that horse." His eyes shone. "We weren't blessed with children of our own, and it would make me proud for her to have it."

To Grey's shocked amazement, Sam shyly approached George and wrapped her thin arms around him in an awkward hug. He patted her back. "Now you enjoy that, you hear?"

"Thank you, Mr. George. She's beautiful," Sam said sweetly.

Pride surged through Grey and he swallowed a lump in his throat. "George, give me a call if you consider selling the place. It's been a pleasure."

"Will do. You can come by anytime to pick up your lumber. The side door here will be unlocked."

Grey couldn't help but think of Cammie when he'd en-tered the house. There'd been dried flowers hanging upside down on an iron pot rack. He remembered her drying flowers as a young girl. This was a home she would love; somehow he felt this to his core. She'd always found old items and made crafts or decorated with them. Even the most humble watering can would be painted and used in some creative way. Now they called that sort of thing 'country chic' or some such style. She'd always had the touch.

Chapter Twelve

MAUREEN DECIDED THE wisest thing to do would be draw the threat away from her family. No one here would begrudge her spending a few days at the lake cabin now that a bit more time had passed and she was on the road to a full recovery.

Rarely did she take time for herself. In fact, her children had been encouraging her to slow her pace before this blasted back injury. She had at least another week or two before resuming some of the daily duties around here, and this decision shouldn't raise too many eyebrows. But how to get someone to leave her there alone?

She could feel Howard on the periphery, ready to invade her world—more than he had already—at any moment. The cabin had belonged to her parents originally, and was the place where they'd met all those years ago. His note yesterday requested they meet down by the small park on the edge of town, about fifteen minutes away. Of course, the doctor hadn't cleared her to drive yet, and she wouldn't take the chance of hurting herself and winding up in the hospital again. She was all done with that nonsense.

There was one difference in this note. There was a phone number scrawled at the bottom of the page.

Her stomach roiled at the notion of speaking to him. The very idea of lifting the lid on the Pandora's box of her past promoted the urge to retch. But there was no getting around it. He'd come back here to settle something. But by God, they could settle it without a single one of her family members getting wind of it, if she played this right.

Dialing the number, she cleared her throat.

>>>><<<<

THEY HAD AN appointment with Sabine this afternoon, and Grey was relieved at the thought. He felt a sudden urge to really talk with her about some of his own emotions where Deb and Cammie were concerned.

Sabine was thrilled at his willingness to finally share his own situation and feelings, and said so.

"I hope you don't think I haven't discussed this because I don't trust you, it's just been difficult to put how I've felt into words, still hard to explain."

"That's progress, in my book." Sabine said.

He took a deep breath and briefly went back and described the role Cammie had played in his life prior to his marrying Deb, and how Deb had fixated her rage and jealousy against Cammie during their marriage.

"I totally get why hearing something with just enough of a child's perspective mixed with a good dose of weighted truth could give Samantha the idea that Cammie's mere existence drove Deb to such an extreme rage."

"Deb's rages knew no reason. Depending on the day, she would get something in her mind and act upon it. Occasionally, it was a reoccurring theme that came up from the past or more likely, whatever was happening in the moment. There wasn't a way to predict or explain it."

Sabine nodded. "You've described her unpredictable behavior, and I agree that anything at anytime could have sent her out the door that night. It's Samantha's perception we have to contend with."

"But I've also lost ten years of my life that I'd planned to spend with Cammie. She was the person I wanted to marry, that I'd planned to spend my life with. I've finally been able to see her again and realize the horrible choices I made, besides having Samantha, of course."

"Are you saying you want Cammie back in your life permanently?"

"I don't know if that's an option," Grey said. "But I still feel the same about her. I understand it's a mess, but there's still a lot between us."

Sabine was quiet, and Grey felt as if she were waiting for him to say more, but what? He'd already opened up more to Sabine about Cammie than he had to anyone in over ten years. Once he'd had no secrets. Cammie had always known how he'd felt about her. Everyone had known. Now he felt like he had to keep everything in to the point of choking on it. He didn't want to live that way anymore. He wouldn't live that way.

"Have you discussed your feelings with Cammie?"

He was quiet. Had he? Not exactly. She'd been rightly

focused on her mother's recovery. And he had Sam. Cammie had a fiancé. They had betrayal and guilt and hurt and anger to slog through before anything like a future could even begin to glimmer. The silence stretched. He'd never realized how much silence could be like a voice urging him on. The silences with Deb had pulsed with anger and blame. The silences with Cammie had been sweet with promise. He closed his eyes briefly.

"To some degree. I told her how I felt. I said I didn't want her to leave town before we settled things between us."

"There's a lot of guilt and hurt to work through."

"So you are looking for forgiveness and closure, but would like to see where it would take you."

"Hell yes."

"Sounds like you and Cammie have a complicated history."

Massive understatement.

"And Samantha has many complicated feelings of her own to work out."

Grey felt a spurt of anger along with pain.

"I've always put my daughter first."

He'd sacrificed to try to make Deb happy and had never come close. He'd endured. But he wanted more than that. Seeing Cammie again. Being home, being with her made him feel alive for the first time in a decade. But he was aware that if Sam blamed Cammie for anything Deb related it would be a huge hole to dig himself out of. That was why he was here. To help his daughter. To help himself.

"It is not unusual for children to resent a parent for

moving on emotionally," Sabine said slowly. "Samantha will need to learn how to sort through her feelings. Communicate and accept them. Trust is essential."

He nodded.

"It's important for her to build on her circle of friendships. And we'll need to work with Samantha on her immediate misunderstanding of the recent gossip and help her recognize the unintended consequences when people carelessly speak without thinking."

He nodded. Boy, wasn't that the truth?

Why was progress so confusing?

Sam was waiting out in Sabine's cozy waiting area working on her usual writing assignment. Her gaze sharpened when she saw them standing together, her expression suddenly wary. Sabine obviously took note of the change in her posture and awareness, stating as they approached, "Samantha, you do realize that some of your father's friends will be women, don't you? Just like at school. I bet some girls are friends with boys."

She nodded, still with a somewhat sullen stare, "Just as long as they aren't Lucy's Aunt Cammie."

Grey felt as if he'd been punched. It was hard to breathe.

"Really?" Sabine sounded faintly surprised. "Huh. Okay, honey, I want you to write down all the reasons you feel that Cammie wouldn't be a good friend for your dad."

Samantha's mouth pursed tightly.

"That's this week's assignment in addition to your daily email. So write down the things you know about Cammie from being around her, and then the things you've heard about her from other people—like the gossip stuff. That way, we can separate the things you know for sure from the things you've heard and aren't certain about."

Samantha looked confused.

"You must have heard things about her from other people. You live in a small town. People like to talk, but that doesn't mean that stuff is true." She shrugged. "Everyone deserves a fair shake, don't you think?"

Samantha rolled that around for a few seconds and then nodded solemnly. "I guess that's fair. But I have reasons I don't like her, true ones."

"Okay. Write them down," Sabine said then turned to Grey. "Why don't we meet later in the week? Sooner is better than later to get started with this dialogue, I think."

Grey still felt as if he was reeling from Sammie's dislike of Cammie, but he didn't regret sharing his feelings. He wanted his daughter happy and healthy, but he needed to finally take charge of his own life and not let Sam run it like Deb had. He knew from ten years experience that wasn't healthy. Sabine would help Sam release some of her anger toward Cammie. Help her make sense of her feelings. He wanted to try for a future with Cammie, make her see that she didn't need to leave Alabama, that Ministry didn't have to be her Misery, but he needed Sabine's reassurance and help guiding him so if he did have a shot with Cammie, he wouldn't do irreparable damage to Sam. Damn, this was all so complicated.

THE PAGEANT WAS coming up, and with it a million details to attend for Evangeline House. Cammie hadn't worked this hard in a very long time. She'd forgotten what a large event it was and how it eclipsed every other aspect of her life while the planning was happening. While she continued to be distracted by glimpses of Grey working, she hadn't even thought about Jason in days. She'd barely had time to go to the bathroom lately, she excused the lapse, but couldn't excuse the random walkabouts she made during her busy work day where she just happened to run into Grey.

Jason had finally returned her call, and when they'd spoken, he'd seemed loving and concerned, but something was missing. "Hey there. How's it going?" he'd asked.

"Pretty busy planning the Pecan Pie pageant for Mom. I feel like I haven't heard from you in a month, Jason. Is everything alright?" She asked.

"Sure, babe. I've been crazy busy. Things here have really picked up. We've got a big account and it's taken all my time lately. I really miss you." He sounded sincere, mostly.

"I miss you too, Jason." Maybe she should test him. "Our big family event is coming up next weekend. Did you want to fly down and join us?" *Say no, say no.*

There was a pause at the other end of the line. "Cammie, babe, I wish I could. I offered to come down a few weeks ago, but you turned me down. Now I can't. I'm so sorry. Things are too insane around here, and I've been working nonstop."

"It's okay, no worries. I'll be home soon, a couple weeks at the most," she paused a second then, "I think my mom is calling from upstairs. We'll talk soon. Bye." She hung up just as she heard him say her name.

She'd been sitting at her mother's desk while they'd spoken, and when she looked up from ending the call, Grey was standing there, a sheepish expression, getting busted eavesdropping.

"Ouch," he said.

"Excuse me?" she asked, trying to give him the stink eye for his rudeness, but finding herself ridiculously wanting to smile. "Did you need something or just intend to listen to my private conversation and sneak off?" She demanded, proud of how cool she sounded.

"Sorry, I was about to let you know I was here when things got a little awkward. So, lover boy can't make it down to the beauty pageant?"

"Don't you have work to finish?"

"Yeah, about that. I wanted to find out where you want me to store all these really nice books while we make a mess of the library shelving? I've got a couple dozen boxes, and we'll seal the contents, but I think we should put them someplace safe. I noticed that some are first editions and very old."

Cammie wished she could take back that conversation with Jason. It was embarrassing and yes, awkward that Grey overheard. She knew Grey wished she was free of her engagement to provide him some kind of shot, and this just put a dent in the armor in her ironclad defense against him. At least he would perceive it as such.

"You can put the books in the walk-in attic access at the

top of the stairs," she directed him.

He didn't leave immediately, but stood and held her gaze, his gorgeous green eyes narrowed and challenging.

"Did you need anything else?" She was acting bitchy, and she couldn't help it. A muscle twitched in his strong shaven jaw. He seemed to be making up his mind about something.

Cammie held her breath, not knowing what to expect. The house was empty except for her mother upstairs.

Before she could blink, Grey made his way around her mother's large, mahogany desk and hauled her up from the leather chair and into his very strong arms. Her pitiful whimper must've signaled consent, because she didn't struggle otherwise.

She allowed his lips to crush hers, then, surprising herself, her arms tightened around his neck and she became an equal, aggressive participant. She *wanted* him. Need flooded through her woman parts and she pressed closer, this scene reminiscent of that night outside the bar. He leaned her backward, torqueing her against the desk, one hand roaming through her hair, the other working its way down her spine, then slipping inside the back of her waistband. She whispered, "Yes," into his mouth, while trying to figure out how to climb him.

"Oh—" The one surprised syllable was like a bucket of ice water.

Cammie almost didn't register the sound, but thankfully, she could still hear beyond the blood pounding in her ears. Good Lord, how humiliating.

Dismounting Grey wasn't a graceful movement. He stepped in front of her, obviously trying to shield her from any possible loosened clothing. Her blouse was most certainly untucked and opened an extra button at the top. "Mom, uh—I—"

Her mother's expression appeared thoughtful, not as shocked as it might have, given the situation. "Okay, dear. I'll just be in the kitchen having a cup of tea. I had a couple things to discuss with you."

"Uh—okay. I'll be there in a minute."

After her mother eased out of earshot, she and Grey began laughing. "Wow, does that bring back high school or what?" How many times had they been busted by her mother making out in various places both in and out-of-doors during their teens? Mom had usually been a good sport, so long as they'd been fully dressed.

⋙✦⋘

GREY FOUND HIMSELF stopping by the old farmhouse again after he'd dropped Samantha off at school. It hadn't really been his intention to come back this soon, but the property already felt like home. Someday he would inherit his father's place, hopefully not within the next twenty years or so. He could hardly control the urge to have another look around here.

After clearing out the flooring from the barn's loft, Grey noticed what great potential the building had as a feasible workshop, should he have the opportunity to bid for it. It was large, airy, well-built and once cleaned out, would efficiently compartmentalize and store materials both large and small.

The open area in the center could be used as a workspace for refinishing custom woodwork or for any number of things. A large covered area came in handy so often in his line of work.

"Hey there, Grey. Did you get all the floor boards?" George Crawford appeared through the side door.

"Oh, hi, George. I'd like to say I came because I'd forgotten something. But I admit to trespassing just now."

"You're always welcome here, young man. Seems like this old place has gotten into your blood." George's shrewd smile let Grey know he understood his feelings.

"Something about it just fits."

"I've spoken with Momma some. She's pretty sure she's ready to downsize and sell the place. You interested?"

Grey's heart sped up. "You're serious?"

"Sad that it's come to this, but I'd rather it go to somebody who feels the same about it as we all do around the family."

"I hadn't really decided to stay in the area for certain, so I'll need to speak with my daughter and my father." Grey said.

"Take your time. There's no rush here."

"I've got your numbers. Thanks for letting me roam around."

"Look forward to hearing from you. You'll see yourself out?" George asked.

Grey nodded, letting this unexpected rightness seep into

his soul. He saw Cammie here with him and Samantha every time. While it was likely a fun daydream, he couldn't help but wonder and hope.

><<

THERE WAS AN art to making the perfect pecan pie. Cammie believed she'd finally mastered it. Pecan trees thrived in the south and were often the preferred nut over walnuts or most any other, for that matter. A whole pie full of them, well, that was dang Southern.

Winning against some of the competitors couldn't be accomplished by whipping up the recipe off the back of the Karo syrup bottle. Entrants far and wide sought this prestigious jewel in their baker's crown. Imagining the accolade in the front window of future her restaurant motivated Cammie to break new ground in the pecan pie arena.

The idea for a restaurant had begun as a tiny nagging seed, and had now taken root inside her brain to the point that she could envision nearly every detail; her menu, the ambience in the dining room, and the kitchen—that was the most exciting part. Her own loud, well run kitchen, filled with those who shared her passion for cooking.

"I believe I've died and gone to heaven." Sniffing appreciatively, Ben sauntered into the room. She shook off her daydream and brought herself back to her mother's kitchen, currently in shambles from her pecan pie experimentation.

"Hey, you." She gave him her cheek to kiss, as her hands were sticky with corn syrup and brown sugar.

"I've gone a little overboard, but figured out how to win

the contest." Cammie indicated the hurricane-like condition, and the number of test pies she'd constructed.

"Gonna give the reigning Shelia-Sue a run for her money?" He grinned.

"Shelia-Sue Gurtney? She's back? *Noooo…*" Even after all these years, Cammie remembered the legend of Shelia-Sue. She'd become the home economics teacher at their high school just after Mrs. Marshall retired and they'd all graduated. Ms. Gurtney's pies were iconic at the county fairs and had gone on to take top prizes at the state level. She and her predecessor, Mrs. Marshall, had had epic warfare over whose recipes should be taught to the students beyond Mrs. Marshall's thirty year reign.

"Yep. Got your work cut out for you, sister." Ben grinned.

"This may require further experimentation." But really, Cammie felt like she'd wrapped up this pie thing. The recipe was triple-encrypted in the stash of files on her laptop, as she had been making notes from the moment the idea had taken root.

"Well, you might want to hurry it up. Don't you have the big event cranking up in a couple of hours?" His eyebrows raised, he pointed to the clock on the wall.

"Oh, shi—" As she completed her expletive, Cammie realized that she'd gotten lost in her cooking once again. Fortunately, she hadn't blown it and still had time to prepare for the evening ahead. Most of the set up was being handled by the rental company, and Emma was supervising the various other particulars.

>>>«««

THE STAGE, COMPLETE with runway, was fully assembled. This was a large production requiring video and still photography, and advanced lighting. Audio and photography assistants bustled around, bumping into one another laying wiring for cameras and lighting. The producer rapidly ground out orders to minions rapid-fire, raising the level of tension to a fever pitch within the large ballroom.

Cammie'd learned from past experience to stay out of Emma's way whenever possible during this event. Nothing would be quite right, and since Cammie was running things behind the scenes, Emma, Queen Bee of the Miss Pecan Pie Princess Pageant would hunt her down regarding every single detail. It had been several years, but one did not forget the spectacle of her sister during this event. Once seen, it couldn't be unseen.

Cammie had dressed carefully, since this was one of the few black tie occasions in the community. Even though the pageant featured children, it was considered a major social event. Her sleeveless black dress fit like a second skin, though somehow the slightly stretchy fabric allowed for breathing and movement. It had a light shimmer, without being too shiny or flashy. When she'd seen it in the store last year, Cammie had splurged on the dress, placing it in the back of her closet, knowing the perfect event would present itself. She'd thrown it in while packing for this trip, never intending to be here this long, but just in case.

Cammie's breath whooshed out of her lungs, as she turned and met Grey's stare. It nearly melted her with its intensity. She went hot all over. He was hot all over in his black tux. The man had no right to come here to her place looking like that—at her like that. In fact, she'd not known he was coming this evening. Next to him were Samantha and his father. So sweet of him to bring his daughter here. Of course she'd want to come when everyone at school must be talking about it, and she imagined Samantha would meet up with Lucy. It was such a feminine thing, a beauty pageant. He was really a good daddy.

The lights went down, the curtain opened and the show began. She didn't see Grey again until afterward.

Emma sparkled when the spotlight shone on her. She commanded the attention of every eye in the ballroom, introducing her protégée, one by one, and the other entrants who'd been coached outside Emma's Jewels. Emma's company was a major sponsor of this pageant, and her logo, a sparkling diamond tiara sitting atop a cut emerald hung along the back of the stage with the other sponsor's banners. Emma's, of course, held the place of honor. Emma had really made something of her pageant coaching business and Cammie admired her for it. She knew her sister was a force to be reckoned with.

The judges had been invited from several different talent and modeling agencies by the pageant committee. Emma wasn't to have any say in who the judges were to keep things fair to the contestants coached by others. She was the emcee, but not part of the committee, preventing any possible conflict of interest.

When they'd gotten through to the last contestant and

everyone had filed out, the big shindig was finally over. "What a way to spend a Saturday night," Jo Jo flopped down in a kitchen chair.

"Oh, my God, did you see the mom who stood in front of the stage and mimed the entire dance routine, step-by-step and nearly blocked the judges from seeing her performance?" Ben had helped Cammie with crowd and overall damage control.

"They had to wipe the stage with 409 to clean up the puddle of makeup so the others wouldn't slip and fall." They all laughed good-naturedly as Ben regaled the drama.

And on it went. The tales from this year's pageant.

"As always, the one who didn't cry, fall down, wore the most makeup, had the biggest hair and smile won." Maeve said.

"Just as it should be." Jo Jo chimed in.

"All my girls, especially the older ones did a great job. I'm so glad to see they did me proud tonight." Emma had taken off her shoes and appeared relaxed and satisfied. The older contingent of the pageant was taken more seriously, complete with a talent component in the competition.

"Jacy Johnson has an incredible voice," Grey said, and the others agreed. Somehow he'd ended up back here with them. His father had taken Samantha home as it was getting late. Grey had stayed to help with the clean up.

"Things went off without a hitch, thanks to everyone," Mom said. She'd sneaked down just as the show began.

This post-pageant gathering in the kitchen was an annual tradition. Cammie hadn't been here for it in a very long time. She'd seen photos, videotape, and heard the retelling of it, but hadn't physically been here in several years. It was like being wrapped in a warm blanket. Except, somehow Grey had gotten in on the mix, too. He stood in the corner of the kitchen, his bowtie loosened and his hair disheveled as if he'd run his hand through it a time or two. So hot. He appeared relaxed and right at home with the rest.

A loud clanging noise from outside got their attention. Ben jumped to his feet and opened the side kitchen door, trying to make out the source of the racket.

A woman shrieked and yelled, and the loud clank sounded again, like metal hitting metal. An angry female shout responded to the first. Uh-oh.

"Sounds like a brawl," Ben said, and made a face. It wasn't his first catfight, and they all knew it. Fortunately for Ben, he wasn't the reason for the clash this time around.

As he started to head out, Grey was on his heels, "You might need help."

Everyone spilled out the door, except Mom, who stood inside the threshold. Cammie pulled out her cell phone, should they need to call the police, or worse.

It was dark as pitch, and hard to see across the yard, but easy enough to make out where the action was from the sounds. The screeching continued, and the conflict seemed to revolve around tonight's contest judging. Oh Lord. Not this again. More than a few of these pageants had ended in near fistfights between angry parents whose little darlings hadn't brought home the big trophy.

Ben and Grey had made it to the far edge of the parking

area along the creek, under one of the largest oak trees on the property. Rumor had it; duels were fought on this very spot, back in the day. How fitting, Cammie thought unkindly.

The group moved a bit closer to hear what the commotion was about.

The women became aware of their encroachment.

"She hit my truck with a damned tire iron; did you see that? I'm gonna sue you!"

"I'm gonna hit *you* with it if you talk about my baby girl like that again!"

"Are you kiddin' me? Your…" Ben leapt quickly to wrestle the tire iron out of red, manicured nails, while Grey stood between the other and her target.

"Ladies, the pageant is over, and there's no need for this kind of violent behavior or trash talking." Grey soothed them with his honeyed voice.

Cammie recognized that persuasive tone.

"Think of the example you set for your children," Ben suggested carefully to the women.

Both men positioned themselves in case the women decided to have a go at one another. They were circling in a slow, catlike way that made Cammie very nervous.

Ben and Grey managed to call the husbands of the women and keep any physical blows from landing; these two had had words at the luncheon last week, though it had been minor and pretty typical pageant mom stuff. The little girls had gone on home after the pageant with their daddies, and the women stayed to gather up the remains of the fray.

That was when the trash talk had begun, and apparently continued outside as they'd loaded up.

Cammie walked Grey out to his car after all the hubbub ended. "Thanks for stepping in to break up the ruckus," Cammie said.

He grinned. "At your service, though it got pretty hairy there for a little while. Those ladies don't play."

"Yeah, well, it was a good thing you and Ben broke it up when you did. The last thing we needed was a pageant mommy murder on the property to make national headlines and put Evangeline House on the map."

"I thought you already did that," he joked.

"Funny. You're funny." She shoved at his chest, playfully. They hadn't discussed that hot kiss they'd shared in Mom's office the other day. There hadn't really been an opportunity since then.

"So, Cammie, I was hoping we could get together before you leave to go back to Virginia. Maybe for dinner?" Grey suggested.

Was he suggesting a date? He'd overheard her awkward conversation with Jason, whom she'd also not had a chance to speak with since that day and was overdue.

She heard herself suggesting, "How about I cook dinner for you one evening next week? I need to try my hand at Papa Bean's gumbo recipe."

A satisfied smile lit his handsome features. "That'll do."

⟫⟫⟪⟪

"MY DEARS, I'M planning to spend a few days up at the

cabin," Maureen announced to her children as soon as Cammie returned from seeing Grey out.

They erupted in a cacophony of protests. Maureen held up her well-worn hand as a signal to cease their objections.

"Don't worry. I've already worked out the details. Anna will drive up and stay with me. She will assist with my medications and meals—not that I require this type of nursing care anymore, mind you."

"Mom, we know you're getting better; it's just that having you here while you're still under a doctor's care is a good idea," Ben said.

"I'm fine. I already spoke to my doctor, and he says as long as someone is within shouting distance, there shouldn't be an issue. All the infection is gone, and thank goodness it wasn't that awful staph business, so my healing is progressing. It's only for a few days, and I will continue the physical therapy when I return. I have exercises to do every day on my own, too."

"Mom, are you sure about this? Why don't you let one of us drive you up?" Maeve suggested.

"Thank you, honey, for offering, but my plans are set. I simply knew you all would not want me to leave your sight. So, my decision is made, and I'm leaving tomorrow at noon. I expect you will all find a moment to say goodbye. I haven't gone to the cabin in ages, and it will do me good. The leaves are changing, and you know how I love fall in the mountains. It reminds me of your father." They all fell silent whenever she mentioned their dad, which she rarely did. It made everyone too sad.

"The cabin reminds us all of Dad," Ben said with a small smile. The others nodded.

Changing the subject, she said, "Thank you all again for such a wonderful job tonight. Besides the catfight outside, things went off without a hitch." Maureen moved toward the door and bid her children goodnight.

As she slowly made her way upstairs, Maureen let out a relieved sigh. It was the first step in removing the threat of Howard's return and the potential damage his coming back could inflict on this family. They must speak to one another—alone. She'd called the number he'd left for her on the last note. There was no answer. Part of her had been relieved, but she'd heard an older man's voice on the recording, but it had been *his* voice. She'd simply said, "I'll be at the cabin soon. Wait for my call."

Shutting her door firmly, she continued her packing for tomorrow's journey to the mountain lake. She couldn't let herself go back in time and fall into the memories with Howard. He'd been her first love—her first lover. It had been magical. And it felt like what it was—another lifetime.

Her children's remembrances of the cabin on Lake Burton held treasured memories with their dear father. Each time they went there as a family, she was conflicted with special memories of a man who stole her heart and left her alone with a secret. Justin understood to some degree that she had a past and it got the better of her occasionally. Maureen believed he liked to think she tortured herself for her mistakes instead of pining for another.

Rosie's daughter, Anna, was like one of her own. She'd

played in the house with her kids as Rosie worked alongside Maureen all these years. Anna came to Maureen when she felt at odds with her own mother during the difficult teen years, just as her girls had gone to Rose for mothering when they'd needed her. Anna would do as Maureen asked when the time came to give her some space up at the lake.

It might be a gamble, but it was worth taking to handle this situation once and for all. Maureen climbed into bed after taking her medications. Goodness, when had she gotten so old that she took this many pills? After all the surgery business was far behind her, maybe there wouldn't be so many things to remember. A good night's rest was essential to prepare for the coming days. Tomorrow was Sunday, which for most folks around here was a day of rest. For her, who knew what tomorrow would bring? Maureen had the sense it might be the first day of the rest of her life somehow.

Chapter Thirteen

THE CAR RIDE up to Lake Burton launched Maureen back in time. As they passed the many landmarks, so familiar, memories of family weekends and summer getaways played in her head like movies on a reel—the laughter, fights, and pranks the children shared as they squeezed together seat beltless in the old station wagon telling jokes, playing card games, and eye spy while their parents absorbed their laughter and shenanigans from up front. She wouldn't trade a moment.

But earlier flashbacks snagged her consciousness as well; before the children and Justin Laroux, she'd made this same trek with her parents. They'd driven a different car, she'd fought with her own siblings, but the memories were just as dear. As a young teen, Maureen looked forward to entire summers at the cabin. Her parents had both been educators in the local school system; her father was the principal at the high school, and her mother a kindergarten teacher in the district. Memorial Day weekend marked the end of work and school for the family and the beginning of idyllic summers on the lake.

Rope swings ending with a splash, devouring books snuggled into shaded hammocks, and the unlimited supply of homemade lemonade and cookies available all hours of the day created a sense of rightness with the world she hadn't quite managed to recapture in the many years since.

Those endless days of innocence were long gone but never forgotten, framed in a kind of faded sepia within Maureen's mental files, enjoyed privately; perhaps on a rainy morning with a hot cup of tea on the veranda before the flurry of the day's activity began. These were treasured moments, ones she'd not trade for anything in tangible form.

Certainly, the memories made with her own children were just as special and treasured, but Maureen's parents were no longer of this earth, nor were her siblings, God rest their precious souls. So, the times they'd shared were all the more guarded in mind's box of memories, lest she forget as time and age took their toll. That was a real fear, having lost her mother to the wickedest Alzheimer's. The very notion that her own children might watch her lose her cognizance of who they were and their personal history together made her sick in her gut.

"Miss Maureen, you alright?" Anna broke into her depressing train of thought.

"Yes, Anna, I'm alright," Maureen patted Anna's arm and smiled. "I'm just woolgathering, I guess. Lots of memories making this trip, you know. Even some with you in the car when you were a little girl."

"Yes, ma'am. I love it up here. Nobody needs me for

anything, and I can put my feet up and relax." Then Anna appeared a bit uncomfortable. "Oh—I mean, I'm here to help you as much as you need me to—"

"Anna, here's what I need…" Their situation would work out perfectly. Anna so obviously hoped for some time off, and Maureen wanted some privacy.

>>>><<<<

THE BEAN FAMILY reunion was the most fun Cammie could remember in a long while. Her entire family pitched in to assist with the event, and they all ended up making new friends in the process.

The Beans were a great big mixed-raced Creole family originally from Southern Louisiana. They'd opted for a huge, Lowcountry boil as the catering option, along with Papa Bean's seafood gumbo.

"Cammie, did you see the contraption Papa Bean brought with him?" Ben pointed to the edge of the property where the elderly man had unhitched a small flatbed trailer and set up an enormous cook pot and portable countertop on which he proceeded to chop vegetables and meats for his famous gumbo. He danced in time to the music rocking on a sound system provided by DJ Juicy Jimmy Bean, known to most as Jelly Bean.

"Yes. Mom told me about this reunion, and how they wanted to use our facilities, but include some of their own catering as well. She okayed it because it wasn't something she could provide to their satisfaction. Plus, at the time she was planning to have someone else cater the food," Cammie said and shrugged as she looked across the grass at Papa Bean in action.

She planned to mosey over and watch him work his magic in a few minutes. She knew how to put together a gumbo, but loved to learn cooking secrets and tips from old hands of any heritage. They were the masters.

There were stations set up for the children's games; the hula-hoop competition was fierce, the jump-ropers, better than any Cammie had ever seen, and the tetherball was swinging around the pole so fast she thought someone might lose a head. The Bean adults competed at corn hole, ladder ball, and had tables set up for checkers and chess. There was some adult/child overlap on all the games, and she believed they were all dancing with Jelly Bean as they played.

Papa Bean hailed Cammie, and she seized the opportunity to learn more about the gumbo. She had placed her own large pot filled with water its gas burner and propane tank nearby and set it to boil with Old Bay seasoning, halved lemons, and cloves of garlic. A pile of new potatoes and shucked ears of fresh corn were ready to throw into the pot with the jumbo heads-on Gulf shrimp. Cammie had perfected the Lowcountry boil from working so closely with Jessica Greene, the Queen of Southern Cuisine. Some good things had come from her association with the woman. She was an awesome cook—just not a stellar person.

As she reached Papa Bean, he grinned a great big white smile. "It's so good to finally meet you, honey. I saw you on television, but I never believed anything that woman said."

Instead of shaking her hand, he stepped around the table and pulled Cammie in a giant bear hug.

Papa Bean hung onto both her hands as soon the hug was over, but before he let her go, looked deep in her eyes and said, "Now girl, don't you ever allow anybody take you down again the way that woman managed to. Anybody with two eyes could tell you didn't set her on fire. She got too damned close to the flame is all. When you're cookin,' you can't lean in over your flambé as soon as it catches. That's just plain good sense." His dark eyes twinkled as he grinned and released her hands.

Papa Bean did make good sense. In fact, after all the mud-slinging, his words made more sense than she'd heard up 'til now. Maybe the flashpoint temperature of the specific butter hadn't had a thing to do with the fire on Jess' head. Could it really be so simple a thing as she'd put her head too close to an open flame while wearing loads of flammable hair product? Cammie wanted to hug Papa Bean again for the sheer genius of his reasoning.

"I've thought of about a hundred ways I could or should have prevented the whole thing from happening, but it never occurred to me that she might have been the cause all by herself." Cammie said.

"Sometimes when it's staring you right in the face, it's easy to miss the real way of things," Papa Bean nodded.

"Oh, but I really shouldn't discuss any of this because of my contract verbiage. She could sue me if I speak in public about the incident."

"Let me get this straight. The crazy woman lights herself

on fire, goes on every talk show in our great nation making fun of her idiot sous chef for bringing her the wrong butter, then makes sure you can't defend yourself because of how your contract is worded?" Papa Bean appeared angry enough to spit fire.

Cammie just shrugged.

"Honey, I look forward to that day. You deserve a halo, that's all I'm gonna say."

"I do have a favor to ask."

"Name it, dahlin'" She recognized the slight New Orleans accent coming through.

"I'd like to get a few tips on making this famous gumbo you've got going here, if you don't mind sharing a few of your secrets."

"There's no secret to a good gumbo; just like anything else that works—it takes practice." He motioned her over to have a look. "You start by making a dark roux almost the color of chocolate…"

⤚⤚⤚⧓⧓⧓⧫

BEN REGALED THE family with stories of the day during cleanup after the Beans' departure. "Uncle Joe Bean says there are black Beans and white Beans, but when the white Beans get sunburned, they call 'em red Beans."

Jo chimed in, "The double-dutchers called themselves the jumping Beans."

Maeve wasn't to be outdone. It seemed the entire family loved to share their family jokes. "Judy Bean told me that the branch of the family with freckles call themselves the speckled butter Beans."

"Okay, that's just wrong." Ben laughed and shook his head as he tied up a trash bag.

"Hey, did anybody hear from Mom and Anna?" Maeve asked of the group.

"I called them earlier, and they'd stopped for lunch at Batesville General Store," Ben said.

"Of course they did," Emma nodded. The establishment was a combination old-time convenience store and lunch grill that served home-cooked specials on the menu. It had been a tradition to stop either on the way up or back home for a family meal.

"I have dreams of that apple pie," Ben sighed, eyes closed.

They all laughed, as they collectively remembered the pie he referenced so worshipfully. It had been lovingly paired with a generous scoop of homemade, vanilla ice cream. Someday they would all have to return to the cabin together. "We should go back and have some, and maybe check on Mom. What do you all think? Just for fun."

"I haven't been back there in ages," Jo said.

"We could go for the day," Maeve agreed.

"Wait, when are you all thinking of going?" Cammie tried to slow this train down. "I don't think I can leave—"

"Tomorrow is Monday, and we know that next weekend is booked with a couple of events, so, let's all give it some thought and talk tomorrow night at dinner. We'll order pizza and discuss it. Should we bring the kids and husbands?" Maeve was making plans.

"If everyone can get away for pizza tomorrow, let's just the five of us decide what we're going to do. Then, we can bring everyone else in on things if we want to do husbands, kids, and dogs." Jo said.

"Looks like we're all done here. I've gotta go on home and put some time in with little Joe and his history project now. I'll see everyone tomorrow. This is going to be so much fun. Won't Mom be so surprised when all her children show up together at the cabin just like old times?" Emma's enthusiasm was a reflection of everyone's happiness at the idea of returning to their special childhood getaway.

"I think Mom might have gone there for some peace and quiet, don't you think?" Cammie hated to throw cold water on such a fun idea, but their mother had obviously wanted to get away.

"She just needed a change of scenery, is all. Plus, we'll only go for a day," Maeve said.

The others all nodded. Well, it looked as if that was that. Deep down, Cammie loved the idea. It would be like running away and embracing the past—the past before all the angst. Except that her father wouldn't be with them.

If everything else fell to pieces, they had each other. After all these years, she was just now realizing the vital role of family in her life, thanks in part to the jumping Beans, Jelly Bean, speckled butter Beans, white, black and red Beans, and not least of all, Papa Bean.

Tomorrow was the pie contest. Cammie had butterflies and hoped she'd be able to sleep tonight. It would be an early morning and long day. This was the kind of environment she thrived in and the anticipation of creating something wonderful sent a thrill of excitement coursing through her.

Oh, how she'd missed real cooking and baking. The kind that turned heads and won awards. The judges' names had been kept under wraps, but this was a highly publicized contest, and drew some impressive names both in entrants and judging. Despite her own notoriety, she was determined to rise above and compete.

⟫⟫⟩⟨⟨⟨

CAMMIE DREAMT OF pecans. Of winning the blue ribbon and the expression of horror on Sheila Sue's face when Cammie accepted her prize. She'd had nightmares as well. That she'd gone on stage to accept the coveted trophy and been laughed back down to the pavement. Then there was the fear of an errant sliver of shell missed in the cleaning process which could ruin a perfectly crafted pecan confection. So many pitfalls to pie heaven.

Finally, at five in the morning, Cammie couldn't lie in bed imagining the worst any longer. She showered for the day, dressed in her bakers' attire, black flat-front chino pants, a white, well-fitted t-shirt, and a white cotton blouse buttoned over the t-shirt with the sleeves rolled to just below her elbows. They would be working in a large craft/market area, not well-climate controlled, and if she did get warm, she could shed the outer layer on top.

She then pulled back her hair into a tight pony tail and made certain no strands fell forward. Cammie slid a thin hair band over the front, just in case. It was likely they would be given hairnets as precaution, but she didn't want to take any chances.

This was no ordinary pie bake-off. One didn't bring in the pies already prepared and ready for judging. This particular contest was a day long festival unto itself, with games, food booths, and local craft makers set up, hoping to sell their wares during the event. The contestants would make the pies for all to see, set up at individual tables in makeshift stalls with individual ovens set up for the event. Cammie's entry was the final one they'd accepted, according to the contest coordinator. In fact, she'd been a late entry, therefore lucky, as they'd had someone drop out at the last minute.

Not just anyone was accepted into the contest. One must have credentials for this esteemed bake-off. Not like in other counties, where every housewife and keeper of the family recipes could throw their pie into the fray. This particular contest had risen in pie bake-off status through-out the nation, well at least a tri-state area or more. Cammie should consider herself fortunate indeed, the woman had preened, that she'd been accepted as a contestant.

Cammie had just entered the area and was beginning setup in her workspace, when a familiar voice cut into her efforts, "Hey there. Aren't you a busy little bee?"

Cammie didn't have time for this. "Oh, hey, Jenna. How's it going?" She looked up with a patient and pleasant expression she'd dubbed her 'television face'. Having had much practice by necessity, Cammie had this expression down pat.

Jenna had her daughter, Lilah, by the hand, and they were decked out in what looked like pageant gear. Cammie hid her surprise at Lilah's large hairstyle and glittery gown with the sash.

"We're guests of honor during the pie judging since Lilah placed honorable mention in the pageant. Jazzy-Lou, the second runner-up couldn't make it on account of her getting Hand, Foot, and Mouth Disease at the tumble gym." Sympathy oozed from Jenna like molasses.

"Oh, how—tragic. Sounds like an opportunity for Lilah." Cammie turned and addressed the little girl, who appeared as if she'd rather be on a playground with friends rather than gunked up and smiling pretty. "Have fun, honey, and after the contest is over, stop and have a piece of pie." Lilah grinned at Cammie. Had Jenna bleached Lilah's tiny teeth?

"Oh, Cammie, we just saw a big hubbub out back. I mean, lots of cameras and a big black limousine. You'll never believe who's here to judge the contest—" Jenna broke off, then leaned in dramatically toward Cammie as if she was telling a huge secret, "Jessica Greene."

Jenna was cheated out of witnessing Cammie's response, because at that moment, Lilah broke away from her mother's grasp and ran shrieking toward a woman dressed down the aisle in sparkling princess attire. Thank the Lord for Cinderella.

Cammie blinked, then blinked again. She swallowed, and thought she might actually vomit, so vile was the nausea that rose up and threatened. She sank down on the metal folding chair provided for approximately thirty seconds while struggling to process this information.

Deciding now was as good a time as any to make a quick escape to the ladies room, Cammie slipped away while Jenna was still distracted by Cinderella and company. She eased out the rear of the cooking booth making her getaway less obvious, and hopefully clean.

The restroom was surprisingly empty as she dashed cold water on her heated cheeks. Wearing makeup while she cooked was an exercise in futility on a normal day, so she chose not to bother with anything other than a bit of waterproof mascara and lip-gloss. The televised shows had been another matter entirely. Makeup was an obstacle that steam, heated ovens, and perspiration from within the kitchen often obliterated. Appearing fresh and well groomed throughout an entire taping was a challenge, even with the aid of trained makeup artists.

How in the holy hell was she going to handle a face-to-face meeting with Jessica Greene? There were no lawyers here to intervene and advise them what they could and could not say to one another. Jess hadn't ever looked her in the eye since the incident with her hair.

The executive producer had called her in the next day to let her know she would be paid through the terms of her contract, but she had to leave and not set foot near Jessica nor the set again. Also, she couldn't speak about the event or malign the network or Jessica in any way. Jessica had no such restrictions to Cammie, it seemed.

Of course, she'd been in shock and had no idea how The Southern Queen would lay blame on her in the media or make cutting jokes about her "blunder." That was putting it mildly. It was more like character assassination, especially since it hadn't been true.

As she made her way back to her pie booth, Sheila-Sue flagged her down as she passed, "Hey, Cammie, long time, no see." The woman looked like a porcelain doll, with big blinkie eyes in human form, and considering she'd been Miss Gurtney, well, it was a little weird to be addressed like a peer.

But she'd make nice when it was offered around here these days. "Hi, Sheila-Sue. It's good to see you again. Good luck today," Cammie said.

"Oh, I'm good. I've got this pie recipe down, honey. Did you hear who's judging?" Then, as if it just occurred to her what she'd said, her head swiveled like a dolly and she grinned, "Oh, that's right, you and Miz Greene aren't the best of friends. Ouch! I heard her talking about you on TV. I almost hadn't put two and two together. Well, good luck anyway." Her dolly eyes blinked and she turned her attention to her own pie preparations.

"Yeah, see you later." Cammie had no idea if the woman was out of her mind, or a malicious bitch. Either way, she was stiff competition and bore watching.

Gathering all the courage and backbone she could muster, Cammie put her head down and marched to the cubicle, determined to focus on her main goal—beating the pants off these amateurs. Not stopping to reassess the unfair mental reference to her competitors, Cammie pushed forward. She couldn't get bogged down worrying about the rest of it right now. She had to make some dang pecan pies.

The rules stated that the baker must use her own recipe, not referenced, copy written, or printed in any cookbook or online site. The paperwork included a sworn affidavit she'd had to sign and submit. Cammie planned to use a secret ingredient that, so far, hadn't appeared anywhere that she'd read in a recipe for this particular type of pie. Luckily, they'd not had to surrender their recipes to the judges unless there was a question of thievery. It had happened before.

Because this was her own recipe, all tucked away on her hard drive, and she hoped to include it in her restaurant menu, Cammie had no intention of sharing it with anyone. People often preferred to keep recipes secret for various reasons, mostly so no cousin could show up at the family reunion with their own casserole and claim it, but certainly there were other motives.

Cammie had done quite a bit of pre-preparation to ensure things went smoothly. She'd chopped a load of fresh pecans, bagged them in pre-measured quantities along with all the other ingredients. She now turned the large ball of piecrust dough onto the floured surface straight from her cooler bag, careful to maintain a uniform thickness as she gently worked it into the right size and shape. Less was more when it came to pie crust. Not overworking the dough and keeping it cool really mattered.

She laid the pie pan upside down onto of the large circle and cut the crust with pastry scissors an inch larger around the pan's perimeter. Removing the pan, she gently folded the crust in quarters, loosening the bottom with a thin spatula coated with flour, then lifted the rounded triangle to the inside of her pie pan. She repeated the process without incident. Cammie heard a few moans and groans here and there as some of the other bakers struggled with their piecrusts. The dough was notorious for sticking or developing holes during the folding and removing process.

The public was prohibited from watching preparations, due to the necessity for concentration during this process. She could only imagine a bunch of kiddos running around, bumping into the tables as the bakers tried to finesse their crusts.

Timing and a backup candy thermometer were vital, so having everything at the ready to make the filling while the crust baked was essential. They'd all been provided a two-burner electric cooker. Not very high-tech, but the only heat besides the oven necessary was enough to bring things to a boil so that the brown and white sugars could merge with the butter, etc. She would add the eggs and a couple other important ingredients after things cooled down a bit, but before the pies went into the oven.

As Cammie shut the oven door, after double-checking the temperature on the gauge, and the interior thermometer she'd placed inside as backup, she could cool her heels for the next half hour while she cleaned up her area. Scraping the flour into the large trashcan provided, she froze as a pair of gorgeous, red Western boots appeared in her line of vision. She'd seen the boots, or a variation of them, countless times and dreaded raising her eyes to their wearer's face.

"Well, lookie here, it's my little Cammie, baking pies at the county fair in Alabama." Jessica Greene's bleached blonde wig was now her signature, along with the red cowboy boots.

"Hi there, Jess. It's good to see you." Cammie decided to take the high road here since she wasn't in a position to do anything else at the moment.

"Aren't you sweet? I'm doing just fine, thanks for asking, honey. Good luck with your little pies."

Um, no she hadn't asked, thank you very much. Jess hadn't made eye contact as she'd spoken at Cammie, then dismissed her as she turned away, leaving Cammie to stare at her retreating ample backside.

Thank goodness the judging would be anonymous. Their pies would be lined up with the bakers' assigned numbers—the name correlation not available to the judges—taped facing inward on the bottom of the pans before the judges were brought in to taste them.

The pitfalls of such a cutthroat competition were accusations of personal bias. Past such drama had led to the board of directors employing security officers to protect the integrity of the contest. Cammie, for one, was extremely thankful for the overkill, just now.

Even Jessica Greene and her entourage wouldn't be able to take this from her if she were the legitimate winner.

Cammie wondered if Jessica realized the lengths carried out to protect this contest. She hoped there wouldn't be trouble on her account, but hadn't liked the look in Jess's eye. It was like she'd had an axe to grind with Cammie, the way she'd gone off on her so publically. While they'd worked together, Jessica had never overtly been horrible to Cammie, but there had been signs of insecurity and jealousy. She couldn't imagine why someone with such status and fame in her realm would behave like that, but some of the most talented and beautiful people she'd ever known were eaten up with it.

A loud bell signaled that all contestants' pies should be inside the ovens baking at this time. Cammie's peace of mind was so totally shot that she dug her smartphone from her bag and cranked up some classical music. Pulling out a bottle of water and a food magazine, she settled on her folding chair to wait out the timer. It beat pacing and went a little ways to soothe her frazzled nerves.

➤➤➤◄◄◄

GREY GOT UNINTENTIONALLY caught up in the hubbub while picking Samantha up from school. Wondering what the traffic tie-up was all about, he turned on the local radio station and was instantly informed by the enthusiastic female deejay that this last minute announcement of Jess Greene's arrival in town was just the greatest thing *ever*, though it was causing a bit of chaos within the city limits and beyond.

Great. Not because he would sit for a while in a bumper-to-bumper mess, but that Cammie would likely find herself face-to-face with that awful eyebrowless woman again, during the pie contest. Grey wondered what the odds were of Jessica Greene showing up here almost unannounced with Cammie a contender for the prize. Something sticky other than pecan pie was most definitely afoot.

"Dad, what's going on?" Samantha was wearing headphones and missed the radio announcement.

"Sounds like Jessica Greene is in town, judging the big pecan pie baking contest, and it's causing some traffic backup." He glanced over at her and smiled.

She wrinkled her nose, "Oh. Isn't that the woman whose hair caught on fire or something?" Then, she giggled, remembering the clip.

"Did you know that was Lucy's Aunt Cammie that threw the water and flour on her head to put out the fire?"

Sam gave him a dubious look, "Really? Why didn't Lucy tell me that?"

"I don't think the family is talking about it. It's been a little embarrassing for Cammie because Ms. Greene hasn't been very nice when she talks about her on television."

"Was it Cammie's fault?"

"I don't think so. I believe she was trying to help her."

"Then why would Ms. Greene be mean about it on TV?"

"When we're embarrassed, it's pretty normal to react badly, and not always toward the person who caused it—sometimes just whoever's there in front of us at the time gives us somebody to yell at and blame things on."

That got her attention, and Grey could tell she was thinking about what he'd just said, how unfair it seemed, and he realized this was a learning opportunity for Samantha. She'd lashed out at Cammie in the lunchroom during her humiliating moment; just as Cammie had tried to help. And even though Sam believed Cammie a root cause of her problems, he knew she hadn't really believed her the reason for the spaghetti incident. She'd carried guilt around for her reaction to Cammie's compassion because she had a conscience.

"You know I don't really like her that much," Samantha said.

"I know you've heard things about her that upset you, and I don't blame you for your reaction to those things." Grey reasoned.

"But I don't think people should be mean just because they get embarrassed and blame the wrong person. It's not fair. Things should be fair when they can be." Samantha said, brows knit.

"When they can be, they should," Grey agreed with that logic wholeheartedly.

"But it wasn't fair for Mom to die. I mean, it wasn't fair for me."

Grey didn't move a muscle. She hadn't had an outburst in quite a while, and he wasn't certain where this thread of conversation might lead. "No, Sam, it wasn't fair to you. None of the bad things you've gone through were fair. And none of them were your fault." He gently reached over and lifted her chin with two fingers, peering into his daughter's eyes. It was vitally important she comprehend this.

She nodded, "No, Daddy, none of it was fair. And it wasn't your fault either. Was it Cammie's fault? Did Mom think she was the reason you didn't love her?" She hadn't burst into tears—yet.

The question hovered. It was a question no child should ever have to ask, but Deb had never been private about her fears or insecurities. How to answer this very pivotal question honestly?

"Mom thought she knew about my feelings, but she just believed something and wouldn't listen. No, pumpkin, there's really no one to blame. It's sad and awful, but it's nobody's fault."

She heaved a big sigh, "I know sometimes Mom was hard to understand."

He nodded. "Sometimes she was," he agreed.

"Okay." Then, she put her headphones back into her ears and transferred her attention to her phone, where she shuffled through her playlist.

Subject closed.

Chapter Fourteen

MAUREEN HAD ALLOWED Anna to fuss over her, help unload the car, stock the refrigerator, and check to make certain the bed linens were fresh before shooing her away to visit her cousin across the lake when they'd arrived. "You sure you're gonna be alright over here all by yourself, Miss Maureen?"

"I've got your cell number programmed in, along with Daisy Mae's written right here next to the microwave. You go on; I don't like the idea of your driving on these winding roads this close to dark. It makes me think of my poor Cammie when she had her accident a few weeks ago." Maureen tried to control the small shudder, but when she pictured her daughter's near miss, it made her shaky all over.

"I know. I think about it too sometimes, how scary that must have been for her. But you don't worry for me. I'll be fine except for worrying about you." Anna leaned over and hugged Maureen. "And thank you for allowing me this little bit of a vacation. My momma would have my hide should she find out."

"I've got this covered, honey. It's our secret. The doctor

said the only things I can't do are lift heavy objects and drive. I won't be doing either, I promise." She smiled as she waved Anna out the door and down the front steps. Standing on the porch, watching her drive away, Maureen suddenly realized a couple of things: At some point a man would arrive, and she would finally get answers to one of the great mysteries of her past. She could only hope his arrival didn't open up the can of backwash she'd just as soon forget entirely.

Making her way back inside, Maureen stopped a moment to admire the interior of the cabin. The structure was somewhat enormous, truth be told, and intended to house two or three families vacationing together at any given time. It was crafted of solid Pine logs, and had been updated throughout the years. So, even though it was aging, it didn't seem outdated. There were scars on the beams left behind marking the families who'd come and gone, which added character to this old lady, who still maintained a cozy, welcoming presence no matter how long one stayed away.

Catching herself in the mirror, Maureen wondered how she'd become such an old woman. She knew, obviously that years passed and changes occurred, but marveled to still *be* the same deep down, but see such a different reflection. Tires on gravel wrenched her out of her musings. Dear Lord, he was here.

Not certain what to do, Maureen began straightening pillows, she smoothed her hair, then she heard the knock. Her stomach flipped, heart pounded.

Bang. Bang. Bang. "Maureen, you in there? It's me,

Howard." He called though the screen. She'd left the heavy door open, allowing air to flow even though it was a bit chilly.

Yes, it was Howard. He sounded the same, almost. Deeper, gruffer, but she recognized the tone of his voice. *He really was here.*

"Hello? Anyone there?"

She found her voice, somehow, and managed to answer, "I—I'm coming. Just a moment."

She caught her own eye in the mirror as she made for the door, but recognized that expression. It was one that Maureen thought long gone from her facial arrangements.

He was still tall, from what she could see through the screen door. Her hand faltered.

"You gonna let me in?" Howard flashed her a smile through the metal mesh. His face was weathered, but those eyes were still dark, cobalt blue like a midnight sky. He'd always had a magnificent head of hair, thick and dark, now steel grey, and just as thick. How had he kept his hair? She figured him to be around sixty-five.

"I'm not sure that I should." She replied, while carefully cataloguing him through the barrier. This was a good way to begin, Maureen decided. Slow and easy.

"Fair enough." They both stared at the other for a moment. It had been such a long time. She wondered what his thoughts were about her.

"Where are you staying?" She asked.

"Just outside of Ministry," he answered.

"I'm surprised you remembered how to get here." It was

something to say. And it was a challenging drive, to say the least.

"Like I could forget." His voice became smooth as silk, remembering.

"I mean, there are lots of small roads and turns and such—" She began.

"Like I was just here yesterday." His words said one thing but his eyes, even through the screen door, conveyed another message.

"Would you like to come inside?" Maureen was moved to action by her discomfort.

"Thought you'd never ask." He stepped inside as she pushed the door open. He lightly skimmed her body with his as he moved past. She tingled from head to toe, little spikes of energy igniting her pulses. This wasn't a sensation grandmothers experienced. It must be a sin. He had been her sin, always.

Once inside, she motioned for him to sit on the large chair and a half, while she perched on the edge of the sofa. He nodded and sat, but his eyes never left her face for a moment.

"Why are you here?" There, she'd said it.

"I had to see you." His eyes caressed her face, as if he was remembering everything.

"Again, why?" She tried to ignore his unnerving stare.

"I've missed you." That was really enough. His words tore through her, while she fought the emotions.

"We were kids about to get married and you left me at the altar with a note. I spent my life with another man. I have grandchildren. Why are you here now?" Maureen still wanted and needed his explanation.

"I wanted to marry you, Maureen, to spend my life with you. You were the love of my life."

"It doesn't matter now, but why didn't you marry me, if you cared so much?" She worked to maintain her reasonable, detached tone.

"My mother was ill, had been having heart scares, and told me that if I went through with the wedding, it would kill her."

"How did she find out? We were marrying in secret." She asked.

"The judge who signed the license was a friend of Daddy's." He hung his head.

"So, you chose your mother over me." Maureen couldn't imagine a mother placing a child in the position to choose her happiness over his, but certainly understood hard choices when it came down to taking steps to ensure your child's future. In fact, she had done a few things on behalf of her offspring she wasn't particularly proud of.

"I was young and her only child; we were very close. She used my guilt to control me."

"Desperation often causes mothers to take less than honorable actions." It wasn't an absolution, but she hated to hear that kind of dejection and regret in anyone's soul. "I heard about their accident. I'm sorry."

"Yes, it broke my heart all over again. I was grief stricken after losing you, and then their deaths nearly sent me over the edge. I went back for you, but found out you'd already married and were expecting. So, I joined the military and was sent overseas to fight. It seemed the thing to do."

She didn't want him to know that she'd researched his military career. If he wanted her to know about his torture and captivity, he could enlighten her.

"I realize your choices put into effect a terrible set of consequences, but I've had a good life. My husband was a wonderful man. My family means everything to me."

"I envy you that." She could tell he really did.

"Do you have a family?"

"No. I never married."

How sad.

"What did you do after the military?"

"I healed for a long while, then I worked for the government for many years—unfortunately, I can't share details of my employment, sufficed to say, I traveled extensively and I'm now retired with a pension." And that, clearly, was all to be said about that.

"I hope you've found some happiness along the way."

"Some, here and there, I suppose. But I've never forgotten about you."

"But I'm an old lady now."

"You're beautiful. Just as I remember. It breaks my heart to look at you and what I've missed all these years." His eyes were suspiciously moist.

"What could you possibly want? Here? Now?"

"I want another chance." He wanted her.

She only shook her head, realizing that even if she entertained the idea of allowing him into her life, he would never forgive her for not telling him about his daughter. He'd missed a lifetime of being a father, loving her; watching her grow. And how would Maeve ever forgive her? He had a granddaughter.

It was better to grant him his absolution and send him on his way, none the wiser for all their sakes, or maybe, just for her sake. This could send the world, as she'd constructed it, tumbling down around them. And she was far too old to rebuild both a house and her life.

❯❯❯❯❮❮❮❮

THERE WAS WINNING, and there was winning. Cammie was awarded the Alabama State Pecan Pie Festival's Best Pecan Pie award this year. This was no small accomplishment, considering her competition had been finessing their recipes for years, hoping to bring home the trophy. Aside from Shelia Sue, none had ever won twice. Several were well known chefs from fine restaurants all over several states. So, it was a very big deal.

"She stole my recipe, y'all! You know she did," Jessica Greene stood up from her seat among the judges as soon as Cammie's name was announced as the grand prize winner.

Cammie's gut had been warning her all day that the woman was up to no good. What could Jessica possibly have to gain by this outlandish lie? The other judges turned very serious and questioning glances toward Cammie. The crowd's gasp of horror let Cammie know she was instantly guilty in the public's opinion, no matter how strongly she might contest her innocence. Plus, they had no idea what lengths the contest board went to ensure the integrity of the contest.

The contest director moved forward and whispered into Jessica's ear, but the woman wasn't to be silenced. "I want everybody here to know that she's a cheater and a phony." She wagged her pudgy finger toward Cammie. "You have some gall to steal my recipe and enter it in such an *esteemed* competition? You've made a mockery of me, yet again. I won't have it!"

The other judges and board of directors were horrified at such a display. The famous Jessica Greene was surrounded by the group, much to her protestations, but not before the crowd began to buzz with this most enticing bit of juicy news.

The director insisted on continuing with the scheduled proceedings and celebrations.

Mayor Tad Beaumont announced, "Ladies and gentlemen, we're going to get this all sorted out. Our contest is pretty foolproof when it comes to this type situation. I'm certain there's been a misunderstanding. Please feel free to visit our local vendor booths and enjoy the festival."

Cammie knew she was covered, because she'd typed her recipe on her computer as soon as she'd settled on the final details, which showed her exact ingredients and amounts. This proved her conceptual copyright to the recipe, unless Jess could come up with an exact duplicate of the recipe from Cammie's brain, which she could not. Cammie smelled justice heading her way, in the form of pecan pie. But first, a quick visit with Jessica Greene.

But what about the restraining order? Well, it wasn't exactly a restraining order, more a clause in her contract they'd written in upon her hasty exit from the network. They'd added that little tidbit after the incident, notarized it within about thirty seconds and she'd signed it on her way out the door. It had been the only way to retain her full pay and benefits through the term of her contract when they'd let her go. Because who knew where'd she'd land, or when?

It stated that she not seek Jessica out. But Jessica had most definitely sought her, of that Cammie now had no doubt. After Cammie had slunk away in shame following the televised debacle, Jessica kept taunting her on every talk show and venue possible. Now, she'd turned up here, in Cammie's home town. The coincidence was simply too much.

Cammie turned and nearly butted heads with Jessica, who now stood not two inches from her face. It was a little too late to pray for peace, and after the foul woman had just accused her of cheating in public on her own home turf, well, enough was enough. But making a nasty scene wasn't Cammie's style, so she'd try to avert one if possible.

She took a deep breath. "Jessica, I'm not sure why you've come here, but you are about to ruin your career by accusing me of cheating and stealing your recipe. Because you know I didn't."

"Well, of course you did. How else could *you* have come up with something so wonderful on your own?"

"So that's it. You're threatened by me?" Cammie was incredulous.

"How preposterous. Me? Honey, they call me the queen."

"How many of your messes did I fix while we worked together?"

"I can't imagine what you mean." But Cammie could see by her expression that she was correct.

"Listen well, Queen. I've got that recipe on my hard drive. The original. If you have a copy, you'll have to produce it simultaneously to prove anything—which you can't. And *honey*, I know you're dying to figure what that ingredient is you can't identify. You will look the fool, and when my contract expires, I plan to write an expose about our time together. Wouldn't that be illuminating?"

Jessica opened her puffy lips to speak, but no sound emerged. Then, she tried again, her Southern accent a bit less brash. "Fine. I won't say you cheated again if you won't rat me out to my fans." She sighed, a great heavy puff of breath.

Cammie narrowed her eyes at the pathetic woman. "For now, retract your accusation, and say you were wrong. And I don't mean that you made a mistake. Admit you were wrong about me for setting your stupid hair on fire, which you know I didn't, and for stealing your recipe." Cammie stared, waiting.

She could tell that Jessica would rather set Cammie's hair on fire than admit to any such thing, but being ridiculous wasn't the same as stupid. The woman wasn't stupid. "Alright, but you have to promise not to write a book about me and tell everybody what a bad person I've been to you."

Cammie considered that. "I'll sign off on that, but you've got to knock off the talk shows. You've had your ten minutes of blazing fame; can't you just be satisfied with your television show, cookbooks, and all the rest?"

"I said I wouldn't call you a cheater. I've got a couple more shows already booked. What am I supposed to do about that?"

"Use the opportunity to say that you've had a change of heart, and that you realize your mistake in believing that I caused your accident—because we both know I didn't. And people will find out eventually, and you'll look the fool. Show your graceful side and do some good for once. It will help us both."

Jessica fisted her hands at her side, clearly bested. "Alright. But you'd better not write that book if you know what's good for you. You're a nobody and I'm the Queen."

"Thing is, you've made me a somebody. Who knows what I might do with it? So, thanks for that." Cammie smiled and held out a hand to shake on their semi-agreement.

"Well, we'll go back out there now, I guess. For now, we'll say, "No comment until things die down.""

"No. You'll say that we've made up and that you made an egregious mistake, and you'd like to apologize to me and to the planning committee."

"Fine."

It was a fine, fine ending to the whole scenario. To her whole awful year.

IT WAS DECIDED. The siblings, sans children and spouses would surprise mom at the cabin by driving up early Friday morning. Evangeline House was hosting a couple events during the day Saturday, so they would return late Friday evening. They all wanted to check on Mom, and it had been far too long since they'd all been together at the cabin. It would be great fun.

They would drag out old photo albums and spend time remembering favorite tales for retelling. Sneaking this little slice of family history might be good for everyone, considering the connection of the cabin with their Dad's death. It hadn't ever been the same there since. The bad memories had mixed with the good from then on. This might be a healing experience for all. Emotional, but healing.

Anticipating the likelihood of sadness mixed with fun, each sibling had agreed this particular road trip would be best taken without the children. Once the ice was broken, and they'd trudged through the emotions, their next visit would be a purely joyous family vacation. Hopefully, Mom would be up for this invasion. Cammie had voiced the loudest concern on this topic, but was overruled by her siblings.

Mom had never spent a lot of time discussing her feelings where their father's death was concerned. They'd seen her grieve after his passing, but it was a quiet sadness that penetrated throughout the walls of their family home. Each of them had felt a special bond with Dad. He was a hands-on father before it had been cool. He'd laughed and played and parented with love and joy. His children were his life.

Losing him was akin to having the background sound-track of their lives silenced. No more booming laughter or deep, lively conversations about Alabama's offense on Saturdays; life became quieter, less—fun. And as lively as her siblings now were, it had taken a long while for them all to get back to that. The accident had taken more than a beloved father and husband, but a vital life force, especially from Mom.

Coming together again, where the tragedy occurred might just be what her family needed. Cammie prayed this was a good idea.

She missed Grey, even though she didn't want to.

>>><<<

"Hi Grey, come on in."

"Thanks. Hey, congrats on winning the pie contest. I heard Heat Miser called you a cheater."

She nearly burst out laughing at the image that appeared in her mind's eye of the cartoon character whose hair was perpetually on fire. "Good one."

"So, what brought about the change of heart in accusing you?" He asked.

"I did. I told her I'd write an exposé when my contract was up and tell the world what a hag she was."

He laughed then. "I'm surprised your contract didn't include a lifetime gag order."

"If they'd had more than ten minutes to think about it, I'm certain they'd have penciled it in. As it was, I think they got off with a pretty sweet deal in not letting me defend myself and tell the truth of how it all went down, at least for the next year."

"Better than sweet. Especially when they were telling you not to let the door hit you in the ass on your way out." He shook his head as he said that, clearly angry at the network's treatment and firing of her.

"I had my moment yesterday, and it was especially sweet telling Jessica Greene how the cow eats cabbage. Can you believe she was threatened by me, with all her fame and fortune?"

"Yes. I can. It was clear you were a rising star, and she's a fading one."

She smiled at him then. "Thanks for that. Too bad that's not the case anymore. She took that away from me. But at least she's agreed to make a public statement exonerating me from any wrongdoing."

"Because of your threats. But who knows how that might help your career moving forward."

Cammie shrugged. "I wouldn't have been able to make those threats had she not stalked me and not the other way around. So, it's really her fault that she's in this new and less than flattering position."

"That's just awesome." He smiled, all tool-belted male.

She sighed. It was going to be a long day, knowing he was just down the hall.

While cutting her losses might be the only way to avoid throwing herself at Grey and begging him to do what he would with her willing body, she hoped once she arrived back up north, she would be satisfied with her life as it was.

Not that she hadn't already been a wreck from the number done on her life by Jessica, but once things settled into a normal routine—would it be enough?

This trip home admittedly had come at a crossroads for her. She was hiding, in a sense, from the world up there, hoping to find success and contentment as an outcast from her former life. Since she hadn't yet decided what direction her life might take, how could she really know that Jason, with his unruffled manner, and non-hugging family, would fulfill her in a forever way?

The truth was, she was hoping; hoping for the best and taking steps toward a goal instead of wallowing in self-pity, which was a positive and healthy way to live, right? It beat the hell out of living alone with fifteen cats the rest of her life.

But how would she ever know what the end result of this hot, deep longing for Grey was like if she didn't give it and him another chance. Could she do that? Let go of all her hurt and trust him? Was she that brave? Or would that be stupid? And what about his daughter? The questions flew around her brain like birds. But she didn't have an answer for any of them.

She did feel that Jason had been pulling away while she'd been here in Alabama, and what had become even clearer to her the more time she spent home was that she didn't really mind at all. That in itself was an answer.

Certainly, Jason couldn't know about Grey, could he? He wasn't a dumb guy, and she hadn't behaved as a fiancé of another man should. Jason had tried in the past to get her to discuss her romantic past, but she'd always blown off his efforts by telling him he was the only one who mattered. He'd replied that everyone had a past, but never filled her in on his own. Now, that was curious, wasn't it? Not only that had he not shared, but that she hadn't bothered to ask.

Lost in her musings, she worked on her mushroom pate. She considered her mother, up at the lake house, and wondered what had made her decide to go there alone, after all these years. This time of year was a veritable treasure trove of roadside fruit and vegetable stands headed through the North Georgia Mountains. This little road trip with her siblings would also afford Cammie the opportunity to pick up several other items she could use for her menus.

Lost in her plans for fresh fruit tarts and cobblers, she suddenly spotted Grey standing just inside the kitchen doorway. "Oh, I didn't hear you. Can I help you with something?"

"I'm just going to grab some water."

"Oh. Sure. Bottles are in the fridge, and glasses are in the cabinet," she said. How long had he been working here now? Of course he knew this. He did look a little hot, as in, sweaty.

"Thanks." He reached up into the cabinet, his t-shirt stretching over his back in what seemed like a pre-porn movie scene minus the cheesy music.

"No problem."

She watched as his long fingers held the glass and drained it. His neck was glistening with a mist of perspiration. Since when was a sweaty neck sexy? Maybe because every single thing about Grey Harrison was sexy. She held out her hand and reached for his empty glass. Their fingers brushed, just for a fraction of a second, causing more havoc upon Cammie's insides. What was wrong with her? She was ready to jump on him right here in her mother's kitchen.

Grey cleared his throat, "I'll head back to the library. I've got about another hours' work left in there. Should I lock the front door on my way out after I've finished for today if you're not around, or do you want me to call you before I leave?"

"Just plan to turn the lock on the knob if you don't see me on your way out. I can deadbolt it later. Mom's gone to the lake, so I'm here alone." Why the hell did she say that?

"Got it. I'll see you later. Or, I guess maybe, I'll just see you tomorrow."

"Okay." She tore her eyes away from his, and turned her back on him, diving back in to the mushroom paste. It could use a bit more parsley, she supposed.

⫸⫷

HE'D BEEN DISMISSED. Okay, but she was bothered. He'd made her uncomfortable, physically. He wanted him. The realization dawned as he pieced together bits of conversation and Cammie's odd behavior. This wasn't about the past any longer. Well, she still wasn't satisfied with how their relationship had ended, but her discomfort around him wasn't related to that any longer, he was sure of it.

Making a move to test his new theory might end up with his looking like an ass again. He realized all her bluster was about her trying to deny her feelings. Of course, they may only be physical, but it was a start.

Grinning, he shimmed the two-by-four that would add temporary support to the doorframe in the library. He planned to enjoy this job and whatever else came of it. Grey planned as he worked. His intentions were not to lead her to do something she would regret, but for them to push through all the old emotions and figure out if there was anything valid left on her part. For Grey, she was the real deal.

He'd learned the hard way that true love wasn't something you took for granted, rather he planned on fighting tooth and nail, no matter what it took until either Cammie saw things his way, or it was clear that things would never work out between them. He saw a helluva fight ahead, but was prepared.

He truly believed she wasn't sure what she wanted or where she belonged. He hoped to persuade her that home is where her heart still belonged—with him.

⤜⤜⤜⤜⤜

CAMMIE WAS CLEANING up the last of the mess from the kitchen countertop, and figured she would go up and take a hot bath in her room, possibly read for a while, then watch the news and turn in early. Maybe she should call Jason. So far, she hadn't heard the front door, which meant Grey was still inside the house. Instead of heading upstairs, she waited in the kitchen with a cup of hot tea, not wanting to take a chance of running into him between here and the stairs. She didn't think she would survive one more encounter with his person without jumping him. It was a sad state of affairs.

So, she waited. The front door slammed. Thank goodness; she'd made it through the day. Now she could relax. Shedding her top blouse from over the tank top, she dropped it into the washing machine in the laundry room, which left her in jeans. The house was completely empty now with Mom up at the lake. Kicking off her shoes next to the utility room door, she padded back into the kitchen to make certain the door was locked.

Cammie pulled her hair out of its cooking knot and let it fall, then massaged her scalp as she continued her door-checking, "Ahhh…."

"Oh, sorry."

She shrieked, startled. But then, she realized that Grey was still in the house. "You scared the crap out of me. I thought you'd gone home. I heard the door shut."

"I was loading up." The man was shirtless.

"Where is your shirt?" Dear God, he was trying to kill her. She couldn't seem to avert her eyes, no matter that her brain told her to do so.

"I was hot. It's a small room. Next time I'll wear a t-shirt." She knew she should answer or make eye contact just now.

"You okay?" He sounded amused. That got her attention. She pulled her head up and looked at him—his face. Didn't help her much, damn.

"Yep. I'm fine." She became aware of her thin tank top, and that the peaks of her nipples were likely staring at him as hard as she was.

He closed the space between them as he reached out and touched her face. She flinched. "Easy, you got a little something on your forehead." If either took a deep breath, they'd be touching, head to toe, so close had he moved.

"It's from the cream puffs, most likely," She babbled, her fingers itching to touch his muscled, chest. Who was she kidding? She wanted to rip every scrap off him and have a heyday.

He swiped it off and licked his finger, "Hmm, my favorite." A scathing remark about how cliché that sounded didn't make it off her lips as she leaned in just as he wrapped her up in his big strong arms.

The heat of his chest burned through her scant clothing as if it were nonexistent. One great big arm wrapped around the lower part of her back, pulling her hips against his, igniting sensations in her that she'd barely held in check all day. The other wrapped up in her hair at the base of her neck, massaging as he kissed her, devouring her lips, somehow fusing them as one. She inhaled his soapy, male scent. Dear God, she had to have him, now.

Cammie didn't recognize the kiss of this wildly passionate man as the same boy he'd been. But her soul recognized him.

"Take me upstairs, please. Now." She breathed the words, hardly able to contain her control.

⟫⟫⟫✳⟪⟪⟪

GREY HOPED HE could make it upstairs with Cammie. He

was ready to explode from a single kiss. He caught her under the knees and took the stairs two at a time, "Your room?"

"Yes. Please."

He continued to kiss her somehow as they entered the bedroom and he kicked the door shut. Good thing this house was built so well. Her big four poster was the most welcome sight he could remember, besides Cammie in that tank top a few minutes ago.

He laid her on the bed, and employing all his self-control, stepped back to simply look at her, hair unbound, lips swollen from kissing him, and those amber eyes from his dreams darkened with passion. "God, you're gorgeous."

She reached out her arms, and he fell into them. She became the aggressor then, working to unbuckle his belt and divest him of his jeans, which he was only too happy to assist with. Once she had him completely naked, she took her time undressing. Had she suddenly become shy?

"Is something wrong?" He asked.

"No, I'm just looking at you, thinking that if I'd done this ten years ago, things might be a whole lot different now." She continued to slide her jeans down her thighs, which threatened Grey's control.

"We can't go back, you know," he said.

"But I think we both owe this to each other." She was only in her tiny lacy bra and panties now.

"Don't know about that, but I'm thankful for the opportunity." He pulled her over toward him on the bed, taking his time and settling into a less-hurried, deeply sensual full-bodied embrace, leaving her with no doubt as to the effect she was having on his body.

"Can we—I mean, I need to—" She was breathing hard and pressing herself against him in an age-old mating rhythm that left no doubt as to what she wanted from him.

"Oh yes, we can." He helped her divest of her underthings until they were both completely naked.

"I'll get a condom."

He hadn't even thought of that. Everything had happened so naturally, it just hadn't occurred to him.

She was back in a flash.

Grey couldn't wait to get his hands on her skin again, and immediately Cammie's urgency took over, and she really didn't seem to be able to wait any longer, which suited Grey, because he was in a considerable amount of distress.

As she rolled atop him, her gorgeous breasts begging for his touch, she glided him slowly inside her very slick and swollen perfection, their eyes met and caught, and then she leaned down and whispered, "I've waited so long for this."

He joined their mouths and when she came it was sudden and very intense, her cries escalating while his deep, rhythmic movements increased her satisfaction while building to his own soul-shattering climax. It had never been that way with anyone else, ever.

>>><<<

THE SECOND THEY'D burst through her bedroom door, Cammie had been beyond the point of no return, like an animal with its mate.

When she'd seen his naked body spread out for her enjoyment, she'd thought she'd gone to heaven. She'd had to take a moment and slow things down, lest she make a complete fool of herself. Sex in her past had been a relatively calm undertaking, until Grey came back into her life. Now it was primitive.

Imagining her life without this kind of passion again wasn't an option. Now she knew why lives were ruined and people killed one another for this kind of experience. Because it was worth it. But she feared it was more than that with Grey. Much more.

>>>×<<<

AS THEY LAY there together, covered with only a sheet, Cammie's head resting on Grey's bicep, neither spoke for a few minutes. What happened next could affect the course of the rest of their lives, so the words really mattered. Grey had no idea what was going on in Cammie's mind. What had just happened only solidified his feelings for her. He only hoped this hadn't confused her further.

She stretched her length against him and turned to look at him. She smiled a misty and very satisfied smile. Well, that boded well. She hadn't jumped up, gathered clothing, and demanded he get the hell out. So far, so good.

"I don't know what to do about this, you," she said softly.

He knew what he wanted to do, but he didn't want to spook or push her, although what they'd just done had been far beyond a push he thought ruefully.

"We don't have to do anything right now," he said. "It was incredible—I mean, indescribable would be a better word." He felt himself getting hard again just remembering what had just occurred.

She must have seen the sheet rise from where she lay. "Oh. Look at that. I can tell you aren't lying." She giggled.

"Obviously, my body cannot lie."

She rubbed against him suggestively, "Might I interest you in figuring out our current quandary by another attempt at problem solving?"

"You want to solve my problem?"

"It does seem to be a growing one."

He glanced down toward the tented sheet, "Indeed, a problem solver could be in order."

"I volunteer."

This time, their lovemaking took on a playful, sensuous, and less urgent nature. They explored one another, tasted, and drew out the experience in ways he hadn't experienced with anyone else. It was an extremely intimate undertaking for Grey. And very appropriate, as he adored her and wanted her for the rest of his life.

⇛⇚

CAMMIE WAS SO confused by the time Grey left, she couldn't even string together a complete thought. What the hell was she doing involving herself emotionally with Grey now? She'd just experienced the kind of satisfaction and closeness with him that she'd never even dreamed existed.

Now what? There wasn't a clear answer.

She couldn't stay here for an extended period to see where this went. She had a life and a home in a state several hundred miles away. Her career, while currently nonexistent, kept her away shooting on location for extended periods, not to mention her incomplete relationship with someone else that she now realized must end. Not because she didn't care about Jason, but because she now knew what had been missing between them.

It wasn't something she felt comfortable doing over the phone, but keeping Jason in limbo wasn't fair either. They'd been good together, but suddenly, good wasn't enough.

She and Grey had left things exactly as they were—uncertain what their next step would be. He had no idea of her definitive decision to end things with Jason. No matter the outcome with Grey, Jason wasn't her future. Heading to the lake with her siblings looked more and more appealing to Cammie now. She needed to get away and clear her head. But all she really wanted was to drag Grey back here and hold him captive in her bed.

She was pulled from her steamy thoughts by her phone's vibrating. She noticed Jason's number on the display. Her stomach clenched, and guilt overwhelmed her. "Hello?"

"Hey there, stranger. How are you?" His voice was warm, but different.

"I'm doing well, you?" This was so awkward.

"Do you think it's time we talk about our situation?" He asked.

Relief and dread in equal parts flooded in. "Yes, Jason, I

do."

"You know, I'm not as naïve as you seem to think."

"What does that mean?" She was hedging and knew it.

"What's his name? You stopped being mine the minute you landed there. He must have been waiting for you the day you arrived." He sounded a little bitter.

That definitely caught her off guard. "What does that mean?"

"The guy from your past. Has he been there the whole time? He's the reason you couldn't commit to me or set a wedding date isn't he?"

She was busted. "His name is Grey Harrison. How did you know?" She'd never said anything specifically.

"He was the one who hurt you back then, wasn't he?"

"Yes; he married my best friend, they had a daughter and she died awhile back."

He whistled softly.

"He and I have quite a past."

"I'll say. Do you trust him now?" He asked.

"Yes. He's not the issue. I'm the one with all the screwy problems." She ran a hand through her hair.

"Because of him?" His tone lacked heat as he pointed out the obvious.

"It's complicated."

"Sounds like a reality television show." He said.

"You're right, it does. But we were all really young and stupid. Deb worked him over. Not that I don't blame him for some of what happened, but I understand things better now than I did then."

He let it drop. "Are you keeping your house here?"

"I'm not sure, yet." Jason lived only minutes away down the beach. He was her neighbor, which is how they met originally.

"So, what are your plans with Grey?"

"I really don't know."

"I've met someone, Cammie."

This surprised her. "Oh? I—I guess congratulations are in order."

"Not yet. We're taking it very slow. For now, we're friends, and I didn't want to lead her on if you and I had anything left dangling between us." He sounded sad.

"I'm sorry, Jason. I really wanted it to work out between us. My past has had me strangled for too many years. I've got to see this through, whether it works out with Grey or I end up alone. At least I'll be free of the awful anger and regret."

Jason sighed. "Good luck, Cammie. I've missed you. I want you to be happy. Let me know what you plan to do with the house. I might have a buyer if you decide to sell."

She smiled into the phone. "Thanks, Jason. Take care of yourself."

They hung up. No matter where she went from here, at least she knew Jason was okay.

⤜⤛

GREY WAS GREETED at the door by Samantha and his father when he arrived home. "Hey, what's up?"

Both Samantha and his father's expressions were quite

comical and dramatic, but Samantha said, "Grandma called."

He'd planned to set up a supervised visit soon, but hadn't gotten around to it. Truth be told, he'd been avoiding Deb's mother like the plague.

A couple weeks after they'd arrived back in town, Grey had given in and stopped by with Samantha at Trudy's house for a short visit. It hadn't gone especially well. Trudy had chained smoked the entire time and barreled through three neat scotches. He really hadn't meant for this much time to go by without another visit, but no time had seemed like a good time.

Norman asked, "What do you think about having her over?"

Grey watched his father make a face as he said this. She was one of the few people he'd like to push off a cliff. Grey stifled a smile.

Trudy believed they'd intentionally kept her from Samantha.

It was true she'd called repeatedly and Grey had found a multitude of reasons for not returning her call or setting up a visit. He just hadn't been ready for Trudy and her over imposing accusations and unpredictable behavior.

He supposed he'd have to break down and have her over. "It's your call, Sam. We'll do what you're okay with."

This woman had caused unnamed issues and exacerbated conflict at every turn between him and Deb during their marriage, especially after Samantha was born. That was specifically what she thrived on—conflict.

He wouldn't allow her to get under his skin any longer. And he knew she set Samantha on edge, but there wasn't any way around their spending small amounts of time together.

"I guess we could have her over soon," Sam said. She really was a good sport. Or maybe she wanted her grandmother's company. Either way, it was unfair to keep Trudy away indefinitely.

"That sounds like a good plan. You can give her a call back and invite her to dinner this weekend."

"What if she wants me to go someplace with her or go to her house? I don't think I want to do that," Sam said.

"You only have to do what you're ready to do. If she asks for something else, I'll get on the phone and work out the details so you don't have to have any conflict with Grandma Trudy."

Sam appeared relieved. "Okay. I'll call her back."

Grey's parent radar warned him that Trudy was bound to upset their tentative balance if allowed.

Sabine might have some good advice in dealing with Trudy. The sad truth was that she was Samantha's only living grandmother and she was part of Sam's life, like it or not.

Grey poked his head inside Samantha's room after a quick knock.

"You okay?"

She was sitting on her bed with schoolbooks spread around.

"I guess. She said she could come over Saturday night

and that she wants Grandpa's chicken and dumplings. Why is Grandma Trudy so strange?" She asked.

Grey didn't want to impose his own prejudices on her, so he tried to appear nonchalant. "I think she's still sad from losing your Mom, so to her, you're the next best thing. Spending time with you makes her feel closer to her own daughter. Plus, she loves you, sweetheart. You're her only granddaughter." He cleared a space just large enough to sit beside her.

"I guess. But I don't feel normal around her. She said she wants to take me shopping. Do I have to go?"

"No, you don't. You don't have to do anything you're uncomfortable doing. I would prefer she visit you here as well. And you should always tell me if anything she says or does confuses or upsets you, okay?" He laid his arm across her slim shoulders.

"Okay, I promise." Sam leaned her head on his chest and he gave her a squeeze and kissed the top of her head.

"I love you, kiddo, and I won't let anything bad happen to you."

"I know, Daddy."

"You need any help in here?" He stood and motioned to the books.

"No, I've got it." But she yawned as she said it.

"Don't stay up too late, you hear?"

"I won't. I didn't have quite as much to finish tonight as I told Grandma. I just didn't feel like having a long talk on the phone. I'm sorry for lying."

"You know I don't like dishonesty, but I understand

why you stretched the truth just this once. Goodnight, honey."

He shut her door, glad they were communicating so well again, and hoping like everything she was back on the road to healthy and positive emotional development.

He just wanted her to grow up to be a happy, well-adjusted child despite all the bad things she'd been dealt.

Grey double-checked all the locks throughout the old house, making certain even the windows were secure.

He showered quickly, and then climbed into his bed, realizing he hadn't had a moment to reflect on what had happened earlier with Cammie. All the emotions and sensations flooded back the instant he began to relax and allow himself to remember. It was like a dream, one he hadn't dared allow himself to believe would ever come true.

He fell asleep with a hard-on and a smile.

Chapter Fifteen

⸻

MAUREEN SENT HOWARD away after they'd spent a couple hours reminiscing, both lost in shared memories. They'd laughed, and even cried just a little. It had been such a long time ago. But his coming here had erased the years, bringing back poignant reminders of what might have been. Difficult as it was, she had to reject his loving offer of spending time together and, maybe, just maybe, the possibility of rediscovering someone with whom to share the rest of her years. Yet, she'd made the right decision for everyone else.

He'd been hurt, and hadn't quite understood why she wouldn't even entertain the idea. She'd told him a partial truth; that she hadn't wanted her family to figure out the nature of their past relationship, and somehow change their opinion of her at this stage in their lives—in her life.

Hopefully, he would take her at her word and not try again. She'd gone for closure with their meeting, but she was left feeling guilty, deeply guilty. She envisioned the kind of loneliness he must live every day, and couldn't imagine it. No family, none. If she were to expose her secrets and open her heart to him, his world would expand exponentially. Hers would implode.

She must spend her time soul-searching, praying, and hoping for divine guidance in this matter. Never had she been so conflicted. Well, almost never.

And she simply couldn't allow herself another opportunity for that kind of pain. Which made her think of Cammie's current situation. She realized there might have been a possibility of a different ending with Grey had Maureen turned over the letter that he'd left for Cammie during all the mess with Deb.

Maureen still held the letter—and the guilt. She'd never given it to Cammie, and even now Maureen believed that, at the time, it had been best for her daughter. Maureen also realized her decision had been colored by her own fear of abandonment after what she'd experienced with Howard. But that was water under the bridge, and Cammie was all good now—well, she seemed to be.

➤➤➤✦◄◄◄

CAMMIE AND GREY avoided each other until the end of his workday, but when she showed up, hair unbound with a cold beer in her hand, in a robe without a stitch on underneath, Grey forgot all about his tools and the beer.

"You are driving me crazy, woman," he was nearly wild with lust by the time they reached her bedroom. He could hardly take the time to wrestle himself out of his jeans and boots before they were tangled together and sweat-slickened, making passionate love on her big bed.

She couldn't seem to get enough of him, which thrilled his ego and his heart equally. At some point they would sit down and talk about feelings, but right now he planned to enjoy the ride—literally.

>>><<<

ANOTHER DAY PASSED like the last; only yesterday, neither of them had managed to accomplish much. How long had this been going on now? Two, three days? She'd waited as long as possible before heading in where Grey was working. What the hell was wrong with her? She was like a female dog in heat. He was all she could think about. Correction—having sex with him was all she could think about. Maybe they were making up for the ten years of not having each other. It was like the movies. The naughty ones.

She'd vowed after their first encounter to stay away from him and work at sorting out her emotions. Screw that. Maybe working him out of her system physically first would clear her head so she could think a single rational thought.

Thank goodness she was heading to the lake tomorrow with her siblings. They'd been like animals for three days straight.

"You know I'm leaving for the cabin with my sisters and brother tomorrow morning for the day." She traced the curve of his shoulder with her forefinger.

"Uh-huh." His eyes were closed, their foreheads touching.

"Maybe you'll miss me?"

He kissed the top of her head; "I've missed you since I

was twenty-one years old, Cammie Laroux. The past three days have been like nonstop Christmas to a little kid for me."

"Why *did* you sleep with Deb all those years ago?" The question crossed her lips before she could retract it.

He stiffened. "You want to do this now?"

"Why not?" Yes, why not? Now was as good a time as any.

"Okay, I guess this is long overdue," he agreed, without enthusiasm. "I'd hoped my letter would have helped back then."

"What letter?" Curious, Cammie pulled away and sat back against the pillows.

"The letter I left for you. My feeble attempt at an explanation of everything that had happened. I gave it to your mother and got her word that she would make sure she gave it to you as soon as she saw you."

Cammie frowned. "There was no letter. I asked over and over when I spoke with her if you'd tried to contact me, and she said you hadn't." Shocked and angry at the time, she'd run as far and as fast as she could the moment she'd heard about Deb's pregnancy. But then she'd returned and wanted answers. By then, it had been too late. They'd already gotten married.

"I can't believe that. Your mother wouldn't have broken her word."

"No. I can't imagine she would." Cammie shook head.

Grey snorted. "It was the night you called the fraternity house at Auburn and heard that silly, drunk girl in the background. You broke up with me because I wanted to stay for the big game and you thought it was because I was cheating on you."

"I did think that. I was so young and jealous that you would rather do something besides be with me." It had been an awful gut-ripping feeling, believing he stayed at school to be with another girl.

"Well, as soon as you hung up, I grabbed my things and drove like a maniac back to Ministry. Your mom told me you didn't want to see me. So I went out to my dad's barn with a couple bottles of Boone's Farm and figured you'd cool down by the next morning. But I was pretty torn up, and angry."

"I never knew you were there. Mom must have thought I wouldn't want you around after she'd overheard our argument."

"I'm assuming you called your good friend, Deb, and poured your heart out?" He cocked up an eyebrow.

"Yes. I was so upset and I needed a sympathetic ear."

"She must have tried to call me at the frat house, or driven by my house and seen my truck, because she came out to the barn bent on seduction and I was ripe for some tender lovin' that night." Grey's expression of self-loathing made her sad.

Cammie could picture a despondent, young Grey drinking in his daddy's barn approached by a sexy, sweetly accommodating Deb. And young Deb knew how to work it.

"The two of you were not fifty yards away in the barn

while I was up here crying my eyes out." She teared up for a moment, and then shook her head to clear it. "I don't blame you, Grey, I really don't. Deb was a vixen when she set her mind to something or someone." Cammie took a breath, trying to remain calm. She couldn't be angry at a dead person.

"How could you say that? I loved you—I was weak and frustrated, but it wasn't an excuse for betraying your trust. I hated myself afterward. You were right; Deb wasn't one of my favorite people. She sensed it, I think, and it motivated her even more." He tried to smile, but was unsuccessful.

She moved closer to him. "Deb figured out how to accomplish her goal and took the opportunity she'd been waiting for. I see that now. It was a jealousy thing. My family had more money, more respectability. I had the football quarterback. She wanted what I had."

"She got it, too. But she wasn't sane, Cammie. As truly mean-spirited as it all sounds, she was mentally ill. I married her because she threatened suicide, and she accused me of ruining her life. Looking back, I see it wasn't completely my fault, but at twenty-one, I played right in to it."

"Oh, Grey, I'm sorry you had to sacrifice so much time to someone who made you so miserable." Cammie had spent years nurturing hurt, angry feelings, but now, she was beginning to understand what a difficult position he'd been in at the time.

"I wasn't blameless, so don't think I believe it. It's been a tough road, but I have my daughter." He sighed deeply, "Deb approached me about six weeks after—the barn, after you and I were back together. I kept silent about what had happened between the two us in the barn until she told me about the baby and demanded we get married right away. I should have told you about sleeping with her, but I was so scared you'd never forgive me."

"I really don't know what I'd have done back then if you'd confessed to sleeping with her. I likely would have broken up with you; maybe I'd never have trusted you again. I guess the ending could have been the same, except you wouldn't have married her and you wouldn't have had Samantha." This was part of why she was so confused right now.

"I tried to find you before you heard about the baby. I wanted you to understand how everything had gone so wrong, what had led up to it. But she'd gotten to you first— even before she came to me. Then she had a miscarriage before we married. I thought I was home free."

Cammie sat up. "Deb came to me and told me the two of you had slept together, that you'd taken advantage of her when she was drunk one night, and she was pregnant with your baby. But, why *did* you marry her after the miscarriage?" Cammie wouldn't ever forget Deb's tearful dramatic performance. She'd twisted things like she'd done Cammie a favor for discovering his true colors.

"Because she refused to believe the baby was gone, and then became legitimately suicidal. I didn't know what else to do. I was scared, pressured by her and her mother, so married her. I'd left you the letter, but hadn't been able to speak to you. Since I didn't hear anything back from you, I assumed you wouldn't forgive me, and I didn't want to be responsible for Deb's death—I didn't think I could live with that. I felt like I'd made such a mess of everything."

"When did you leave the letter with my mother?" This was a biggie for Cammie. Her mother had some serious explaining to do here.

"Just before I married Deb, I stopped by your house to try and see you—to try and make you understand. Your mom said she hadn't heard from you, but that I could leave a message. I had already written the letter in case you weren't there. I was about to be married and realized it was my last chance."

Cammie felt sick. "I was hiding out at the cabin on Lake Burton. I couldn't face any of it; that you'd slept with Deb, or you would be her baby's father. We'd made so many plans together." A tear rolled down her cheek. It still hurt after all these years, yet she wondered how it could.

He pulled her close, but continued, "I needed you to understand how it all had happened, and why I'd done what I had. I knew it wouldn't fix things, but I held out hope that if Deb's mental condition improved that I might somehow have the marriage annulled and come back to you. I know that sounds crazy—but then, she got pregnant again."

"It's hard to believe with her so nuts that you were having sex." She hadn't meant to sound judgmental. Or, maybe just a little.

"I wasn't an altar boy, and she insisted that we were married and should make love. Honestly, I mostly went along to keep peace at all costs. I didn't realize she was trying to have a baby. I thought she was on birth control."

"It was all such a long time ago." She said, turning to look at him.

"Not so long that it doesn't matter," he answered, his expression sad and intense.

"No, it still matters. I haven't been able to trust another man since," she told him, because he should understand how losing him that way had affected her other relationships with men.

"I'm so sorry I did that to you." He wiped her remaining tears.

"I'm sorry about all of it." And she was sorry, not angry anymore because now she understood his actions. She was sorry Deb had been so ill and wired the way she had been. It had been costly for them all.

"How's Samantha doing now?" Cammie asked, thinking of Deb's main casualty.

"She's handling things much better these days. We've been going to a psychologist regularly who's been a godsend." He sounded very relieved and far more positive as he spoke about his daughter compared to recent conversations.

"I'm so glad for you both."

"Unfortunately, Deb's mother has reentered the picture."

"Trudy? I haven't seen her in years. Is she still—the same?" Cammie didn't want to speak ill of his mother-in-law, but Deb's mom had always made her uneasy, her manner was very abrupt and confrontational. She was always just a little—rough around the edges and over the top, for lack of a better description. Cammie really hated to cast someone into a mold, but Trudy'd made the mold, with her smoking, heavy makeup, and bawdy behavior. Even Deb had been embarrassed by her.

"She's the same, only more of everything. More in your face, more insistent on having her way, more sure than ever that I'm trying to keep her from Samantha, which I hate to do, but want to shield Sam from anything hurtful she might say."

"She's always been a bit of a handful. I remember my mother not wanting me to spend time at Deb's house because she didn't think being around Trudy was good for me. I didn't like going over there because she smoked and the house always reeked of stale cigarettes and ashes." Cammie shuddered, remembering that smell. "Do you think she poses some kind of threat to Sam?"

"I really don't think so. She's just brokenhearted and angry that Deb's gone. And of course, she blames me. Right now, I'm insisting that she only visit at our house with either Dad or me in the room. I have no idea what she might say to Samantha based on some of the things she spewed right after Deb died. She blamed me for her daughter's unhappiness and suggested she would still be alive if she hadn't been so miserable."

"Wow. That's not very subtle. Didn't she realize that Deb had some very serious mental issues?"

"I guess Deb had persuaded her that I controlled her time with Sam, and I married her as a second choice and never really loved her."

"Oh, my God, Grey. You were in an impossible position—and she had guilted you there. How could she expect to be the love of your life?"

"She wasn't stable, like I said. But the facts were the facts. Everything she told her mother was true. I did shield Sam from Deb when she was in a rage, deep depression, or crying jag. She wanted Samantha to lay with her in bed while she suffered. I wouldn't allow it. So, she accused me of keeping her daughter from her when she needed her most."

"But she was just a baby. How damaging would that kind of emotional dumping have been to a young child? Poor little thing. Poor you. You couldn't win, no matter what you did."

"I did what I thought was best for my daughter. Trudy believes the skewed version of perspective Deb fed her for years. She didn't want to believe Deb was ill—only desperate."

"Well, I don't blame you for being concerned about what she might tell Samantha when you're not looking. She's been through so much already; it would be dreadful for her own grandmother to plant poisonous ideas in her head."

"She's coming over Saturday and I'm not looking forward to it. She wanted to take Sam shopping and have a girls' night at her house."

Cammie made a face at the thought. "What does Sam think?"

"Sam asked me to have Trudy over to our house for now."

"At least you're on the same page with this, then. Hopefully Trudy'll be polite and you all can get through her visit without a scene."

"I don't see any way around it, so I guess we'll just have to gut it out," he agreed.

She became aware of a buzzing sound in the corner of the room. "Do you hear that?"

"It must be my phone. It's set on vibrate." He eased out from under her and quickly retrieved his phone, naked as a jaybird. He was a fine looking man.

Looking down at the screen, he said, "I missed a call from my dad. I'd better see what's up at home. He picked up Samantha from the bus today. They're likely trying to figure out dinner and what's keeping me."

Cammie gathered up her clothing, and glanced at the clock, "We've been up here for over two hours, wow, I had no idea." She smiled over at him.

He pulled her against him, "Do you have any regrets about what's happened between us?"

"No. I don't think so. I mean, I understand everything better now, and I do forgive you. I only wished I'd known the whole story years ago."

"I still can't believe your mother didn't give you my letter." His expression was puzzled.

It mirrored her thoughts. "I can't, either. She and I apparently have matters to discuss."

❧❧❧

CAMMIE'S CELL PHONE began to ring as she heard the front

door shut behind Grey. She recognized the New York area code, but it wasn't a number she typically received calls from.

Curious, she answered, "Hello?"

"Is this Cammie Laroux?"

"Yes?"

"It's Bruce Bernard from the studio. I'm so glad I was able to track you down."

Bruce Bernard was the last person she wanted to speak with. In fact, the only information she'd like to share with him were her deepest thoughts on the creative ways she'd dreamed up to cause him agonizing pain without leaving a mark; just so they were clear.

"Have you come up with another way to humiliate me?" She rarely used this nasty tone on anyone, but Bruce deserved it after taking Jessica Green's side.

"Wait, what? No, Cammie, I've called to offer you your own show. There's been a resurgence of social media in your favor. That video of your cat fight with Jessica at the pie contest is blowing up on YouTube. I know you saw the photos splashed on the front of the tabloids of the, um, incident."

"I'd heard about them, but tried to ignore the gossip." Her voice sounded remarkably calm, which surprised her since her heart began to race at the thought of her own show.

"In any case, the fans want to see you back on the air. Apparently, you're why lots of people watched the show to begin with. They loved Southern charm with a touch of class. We'd love for you to fly up to New York and meet with us as soon as possible."

Cammie stood there, rooted to the spot where Grey'd left her, mouth wide open, completely unable to believe what had just occurred. Somehow she managed to respond that she'd give Bruce's proposition serious thought and call him back in the morning. Until Jessica Green's hair had gone ablaze, Cammie's career had unfailingly been the one thing she could count on.

Jason was the other. Then, she'd thrown caution to the wind by losing her focus and rushing into mad-dog sex with Grey; for what eventual outcome? What in the world had she been thinking? That they'd get married and live happily ever after in Ministry, Alabama? That she would make pecan pies at the county fair and it would be enough for her?

Yes, she forgave Grey. They were all good now. Could be, that was what this was about—the might-have beens taken from them both by Deb. To struggle in her industry and achieve what she had these last ten years and throw away her future here seemed really shortsighted, especially considering this new offer on the table.

But what did this momentary lapse with Grey steal from her current life? Maybe everything.

»»»«««

MAUREEN TENSED WHEN she heard the light squeal of brakes and crunch on the rocks of the driveway. She wasn't expecting a visitor this evening. In fact, she'd not anticipated anyone invading her solitude the rest of the week through the weekend. Maybe Annie had decided to check on her and forgotten to call. It was just after dark.

She'd already bathed and changed into a soft flannel gown, with plans to watch an old black and white Carey Grant movie after she'd warmed up a bowl of Annie's potato soup with cheese toast. The kindling she'd lit under the stack of logs had just taken and was crackling in the large fireplace. She'd planned the perfect evening—for an old, single lady.

Heavy footfalls on the porch alerted her that her visitor wasn't Annie, but a male caller. Alarm and excitement mixed, as she eased over toward the locked front door to peer through the small peephole. The front porch light was on, thank goodness, so she would be able to see who stood on the other side of her door.

Heart pounding, she dared a glance. Relief and panic flooded through every cell in her body. He'd come back. She'd told him to stay away, and he'd come back anyway. His firm knock nearly sent her two feet in the air.

"Maureen, it's Howard. I need to see you," he called through the door.

She couldn't move a muscle. If she opened the door now, she wouldn't just let in the man, physically, she'd be consciously opening herself and her family up to what she'd sent packing two days ago. Dared she unlock the past and wake sleeping dogs?

"Maureen, I heard your reasons for keeping me away, but you should reconsider yourself in all of this. We don't have to be alone. I don't want to be alone for the rest of my life." He said this softly, but the words somehow permeated through the door and her heart.

She slid back the bolt and opened the heavy door. Lord, what was she doing?

His black blue gaze was thunderous with emotion. "I couldn't take no for answer. Not after I'd seen you again."

All the years somehow didn't matter at that moment. She fell into his strong, waiting arms. How could two men both feel like home? She'd been home with Justin for all those wonderful years, but this, this was like finding something necessary for survival after searching in the dark for a lifetime. His scent, his warmth and strength. She wept at the safety and rightness.

"Ahh, my love. I never thought—never dreamed—" He nearly crushed her heart with his intensity.

"Shhh…let's just stay like this for now. I can't think about anything yet." So they held each other, Maureen absorbing his strength and security. She'd forgotten what this felt like, this leaning in to another person both physically and emotionally. It had been such a long time.

The change in their embrace was subtle, two bodies merged together for comfort, relaxed and content evolved into something less content, more tense and demanding.

Maureen first noticed his obvious physical response, while wondering at her own increase in heartbeat and the hardening of her nipples under the thin nightgown separating them from his flannel shirt. She wondered if he felt them.

This hadn't happened to her in so many years, she couldn't even venture a guess as to how long it'd been. She shifted her position to make things less noticeable on her part. He momentarily released her when he felt her squirming, but somehow the readjustment had them falling back on the sofa, which was thankfully and strategically behind them, her half on top of him—and his full arousal. Oh, my.

Their eyes met, his dark and stormy, hers lost in his. "Maureen, I—you're still the sexiest woman I've ever—" She couldn't have said who made the first move, but the flurry of clothing removal was quite impressive, and would likely be downright teen-like looking back. He'd stopped for a second, asking if she was recovered enough from her surgery yet and she'd nodded, assuring him she was. He'd taken special care with his weight, she could tell, but it had been heavenly.

They made love like before—a lifetime ago, before she'd ever known another. He'd been her first, and certainly her last. She wasn't sure how this would work, but if this was her final night on earth, she would die a happy woman.

"You're smiling." He lay beside her under the soft blanket she'd kept across the back of the sofa.

"So are you, you wicked man." She blushed. How embarrassing.

"You're beautiful, Maureen. And I'm the luckiest bastard alive." Howard did appear content and thrilled to be exactly where he was; naked under a blanket in a cabin at the lake in front of a roaring fire with her.

She had to admit, tonight had been a most unexpectedly

blissful and life-changing turn of events for them both. Sighing, she relaxed and fell asleep, content that no matter what tomorrow threw her way, she would always treasure tonight's wonderful memories.

"How did your husband pass away?" Howard asked.

"Trying to save Ben's friend, Scott, from drowning." Maureen still had a very difficult time speaking of it. In fact, had never spoken of it to anyone.

"Did the boy survive?"

Maureen shook her head, allowing the tears to flow. She'd never discussed the accident beyond the trial that nearly ruined her family.

"I'm so sorry, honey. What a senseless tragedy." She took comfort from his gently stroking her arm.

"It was—the worse thing that's ever happened to any of us. The boy, Scott, was our neighbor, and Ben's best friend. They'd gone out tubing, and Scott was thrown off the back of the boat by a large wave. It was Fourth of July weekend, and a busy time on the lake. Our rule was that everyone on the boat had to wear a life vest, but Scott must have slipped his off after he'd had his turn."

Howard moved closer and puller her to him, but she had to verbalize what she'd kept in for so many years.

"Justin pulled off his life vest so he could dive down into the water and search for Scott. The last time he came up, he was hit by a jet ski. He'd gone a ways from the boat, and everyone was calling for Scott and didn't see where Justin had surfaced until it was too late." Tears streamed for her husband who'd been such a good man, who'd loved their children, and searched for a missing child.

"Were your kids on the boat during the accident?" Howard asked.

"Maeve, Jo Jo, and Ben saw it. They tried to get to him before he went under, but were too far away, and Scott never resurfaced. He was a strong swimmer, too." She shook her head, reliving the scene of seventeen-year-old Ben pulling up to the dock in their boat, with his hysterical sisters, escorted by the harbor patrol, yelling for her to come outside.

"I imagine you lived your worst nightmare that day," he said.

"It could only have been worse had it been one of my own children. But Scott's death has haunted us all. It's hard to come here as a family anymore. It took a couple of years before we even attempted it after the accidents." She'd stopped crying now, and she was surprised at what a relief it had been to finally tell the story.

"I'm surprised you didn't sell the place,"

"It was my parent's home. I couldn't part with it, even after everything that happened. You and I met here." She watched him carefully and wondered if her own face displayed such raw emotion.

"Yes, we did. It will always be special for that reason and because this is where I found you again."

"Yes. I only hope my children will feel that way in time."

"I'm betting they'll want to see you happy. It likely won't happen overnight, but I'll do my damnedest to show them how much I care about you." He seemed so confident.

Chapter Sixteen

M AUREEN AWOKE SLOWLY, realizing a couple of things right away: The first was that she was stark naked next to an equally stark naked man. Second, they weren't sleeping in a bed, but on the floor on the rug in front of the last embers of last night's fire. Sometime during the early hours, Howard had gone into her bedroom and gathered pillows, sheets, and comforter for their pallet in front of the fireplace. They'd made slow, tender love again before falling into a deep sleep from which he'd still not awakened.

Stretching luxuriously, and surprised she wasn't terribly sore from her recent activities and sleeping on the floor, Maureen cuddled against Howard, content to lie here. The doctor had said, the firmer the surface, the better. He'd also winked and given her the go-ahead to carefully resume sexual activity—nothing too vigorous, he said. She'd assumed he knew her sexual activity was nonexistent. But now she was glad to know it was alright.

More relaxed than she could remember, she almost didn't hear the noise at the front door. It wasn't a knock, it was a key slipping into the lock and the knob turning. Dear

God, she was cold busted.

"Surprise, Mom!" the chorus of her children's voices died out the moment they spotted her hiding behind Howard, who had come awake the instant the door swung open. Being ex-military, his reflexes were excellent, and he had no care for modesty, none at all.

So the scene her children witnessed must have resembled something between a horror movie and a dark comedy. But no one laughed.

She'd have to err on the side of horror. "Oh, my dears, this is a surprise." On the one hand she wished she'd had a still shot of her kids' expressions at that moment. But mortification got the better of her.

Howard, realizing his state of undress, grabbed the sheet she offered and covered himself immediately. "Hello, everyone, I'm Howard Jessup. Your mother and I go way back." He smiled at them. "Sorry to meet you all under such—uncomfortable circumstances."

"Mom?" Maeve was eyeballing Howard as if he was a ghost. Damn, she'd seen his eyes—her eyes.

They'd all made silly comments to her over the years about where her eyes had come from. She also had the same very specific chin dimple. Right now, staring at one another, their resemblance was nearly unmistakable. When she'd spoken, she'd caught Howard's attention, which gave him the opportunity to make direct eye contact with her. Even naked, wrapped in a sheet, he took a step closer, peering into an identical gaze.

"Maureen? Is there something I should know?"

"Mom? Who is he? What is going on?" Ben piped up.

Maureen's courage nearly fled. She hadn't gotten this far to allow everything to come crashing down around them all. None of this was anyone's fault. She just hadn't informed them, that was all.

"How long have you all known me?" Silent shocked stares. "Yes, your whole lives. It gives me the right to insist you wait a minute while I get dressed so we can all sit down and discuss this like the adults we are." She breezed out of the room, hoping not to lose her cool before clearing the door.

Howard must have followed, because she felt him nearby. "Maureen, am I correct to assume that beautiful girl out there is my daughter?"

"Yes. Howard, I was only a couple of weeks pregnant when you left. I didn't even know about the baby yet." Her lip quivered, but she couldn't look him in the eye.

"You never told me. How could you keep her from me?"

"You left me at the altar. I was pregnant and jilted. Should I have hunted you down? That's why I married Justin so quickly. He'd been my steady boyfriend before I met you and he agreed to marry me and raise Maeve as his own. He'd loved me since we were kids. I was so lucky."

"I was a fool," he said, simply.

"You were a fool," she agreed.

"I can't believe you didn't tell me I had a daughter. There's no statute of limitations on letting someone know they have a child."

"Yes, but when that child was parented and loved by a man who was a model father, why would I chance the damage to her? She loved Justin with all her heart. Now she sees me as a liar. Her own mother, a liar," Maureen cried.

"Do I have grandchildren?" He was incredulous at the idea of having a family.

The cat was out of the bag and, despite everything, she couldn't deny him this, "Yes, her name is Lucy, and she's almost ten."

His eyes teared up almost immediately. "I have a grand-daughter."

She wasn't certain how he felt about her now, so she said, "Howard, I was young and terrified. Justin offered security after you'd left. I didn't even know where to find you. Please understand why I didn't try to hunt you down to tell you."

His expression was one of complete awe. "I can't believe I have a family. I've had no one in my life to love for so many years. I thought it my penance for leaving you behind. Can't you see, Maureen? It's not too late."

He wrapped his arms around her, his entire body racked with sobs. She forgot everything and gave over to his raw emotion, weeping with him, for him. She'd given him family, and he'd saved her from being alone the rest of her life.

After they'd spent some time drying each other's tears, Maureen took a quick shower while Howard dressed. Good thing he'd thought to grab his clothing on the way in to her room.

Now she had to go and approach the very delicate task of explaining all of this to her children, Maeve especially.

⇒⇒⇒≪≪≪

THEY'D BEEN STUNNED into several minutes of speechlessness. Catching their mother in her birthday suit with a strange man in the living room was the very last scenario any of them would've imagined bursting into. But recognizing the man was, without a doubt Maeve's biological father was beyond anything they could have dreamed up. Poor Maeve was sitting, staring sightlessly, and likely trying to process what had just occurred.

"Wow. Just wow," Ben said.

"I really don't have any words for this, either," agreed Jo.

"Shit fire, and burn my hair, I'll go to my grave with that image in my mind." Emma had a few more words than the other two, apparently.

Maeve continued to stare silently into space, so Cammie eased over beside her and simply took her hand, stroking it, "This is going to be alright, Maeve. I know it's crazy and a huge shock, but something really big must have happened a long time ago with Mom that we didn't know about."

"Ya think?" snorted Emma.

"He has my eyes—I mean, I have his eyes. I always wondered where my eyes came from." She still had that blank, shocky look, but at least she was processing thoughts and words again.

"It's really almost funny that mom would have had a

mystery man before Dad. You'd never have thought she would have something this big in her boring old history." Cammie said, but was thinking about her own not-so-boring history.

"Must not have been so boring if I have a different father—Oh, God, he's my father! That means my daddy isn't my daddy. That your daddy isn't my daddy. That we're—" She looked around at her siblings in panic. "Only half siblings"

Ben came over to the other side of Maeve, placing his arm around her shoulders, "Hold it, sister. This doesn't change anything, you hear? You couldn't ever be any less our sister. And Dad will always be your dad. He loved you and raised you your whole life. Nothing will change with any of us."

"He looked pretty stunned when he saw you. Mom must not have told him he had a daughter," Jo Jo said, "So, you might go easy on the poor man. He's in just as much shock as you are."

"I can't believe Mom has lied to us all our whole lives," Emma snapped, obviously very angry and upset at being kept in the dark about something this important.

Cammie didn't blame her, she was miffed that Maeve had been blindsided like this too, but she hadn't wanted to add fuel to the fire that would most certainly erupt before things died down. This whole situation smelled like a big long-term mess in the making. How they reacted here today would no doubt set the tone for keeping their family together or splintering them into factions and taking sides.

"Hey, guys, no matter how upset and angry we are at how this all went down today, we have to remember that we barged in on Mom without a warning. She's a grown woman with a right to privacy—" She saw Emma ready to breathe fire at her and held up a hand. "Please let me finish. Whatever this man is—besides Maeve's father—to Mom, we have to remember that Dad wouldn't have wanted her to live the rest of her life alone. Now that we're all grown, we can't want that for her either. She's not so old that it's unthinkable for her to want to share the rest of her life with someone."

"She's happy. She's always been happy. I'll bet he's a fortune hunter after her money," Emma said.

"I believe everyone should get a fair trial," said Ben.

"I just wish she would come back in here so we can get this over with," Maeve sniffed.

Just then, Mom and the man, Howard, reentered the room. Mom appeared a bit haggard, but freshly showered and dressed. "Let's go into the dining room, shall we?" Mom suggested, and motioned toward the next room.

"I know you all have so many questions, and truth be known, I'm glad this has finally all come to light. It's been a strain keeping this secret all these years. Your father and I discussed many times sharing this with you, but never decided on a good time."

"Dad knew?" Ben asked, clearly shocked that his father was in the secret as well.

"Of course he knew, dear. I married him when I was three months along with your sister. He and I were high school sweethearts."

"Why didn't the two of you get married? Did you love each other?" Maeve addressed both Howard and Mom.

"Because I was a coward," Howard answered with feeling.

"You knew she was pregnant and refused to marry her?" Ben demanded.

"No, son, if I had known about Maeve, nothing in the world would have kept me from marrying your mother and raising my daughter." He stared into Maeve's eyes as he said the words.

⋙⋘

AFTER THE DAY they'd had, Grey's letter had slipped Cammie's mind. She'd planned to ask her mother about it when the opportunity presented. Funny how things changed from most important to least important in the blink of an eye, depending on perspective.

Today'd really rocked all their worlds and the ride home was unusually silent, each of them working out this new information on their own. To say finding out about Howard's relationship with their mother was a confusing turn of events was an understatement. Mom had always been unerringly solid—emotionally, in business decisions, and during crises throughout their lives. She wasn't a flaky, hippy who slept with men naked on the floor in front of a fireplace.

Maybe he was her Grey, her first true love she'd never really forgotten, even after all these years. The thought both soothed and terrified Cammie.

This was comforting because it meant her mother hadn't lost her mind. But on the other hand, when thinking in terms of her own life, could there be no peace for Cammie beyond Grey if a second chance wasn't in the cards; throughout a lifetime married to someone else, children, and grandchildren? Would she never be truly fulfilled and content with another?

Now, with this new offer from the studio on the table, Cammie felt more confused than ever about what her next step should be. She'd called Bruce early this morning before they'd left for the lake and agreed to fly to New York for a day to discuss the offer. She'd be a fool to shut the door on this kind of opportunity after she'd believed her career over.

"Cammie, you awake?" Maeve asked, jabbing Cammie in the ribs, assuring the correct answer.

She turned toward her eldest sister, noting Maeve's red, swollen eyes. "Yes, I'm awake."

"I don't know how I'm supposed to feel about all of this," Maeve sniffed.

Cammie leaned in toward Maeve and laid her head on her big sister's shoulder. "There's no right way to feel. You know Mom never meant to hurt you. She loves you and understands how close you were with Dad. I guess she never saw a reason to upset your life by making a big confession if she didn't have to." Cammie said in a low voice, attempting to keep their conversation private.

"I just can't believe there was someone before Dad—I mean, right before Dad. Does that mean she didn't love

Dad as much as Howard? Did she ever really love Dad?" Maeve asked.

"We grew up in their household. I've never seen anyone more devoted to each other than Mom and Dad. Honestly, Maeve, have you?" She hoped the imprint of their parents' ease and closeness was as well defined for Maeve as it was for Cammie.

"No, I haven't. I have a husband and a child and I understand what it means to live with a man day after day. They couldn't have created such a happy and loving home for us unless they loved each other."

"They did love each other. It was so obvious," Cammie said.

"Thanks for reminding me. You're pretty smart for a little kid, you know that?" Maeve ruffled her hair like she'd done as kids. Maybe her big sis would be okay, after all.

"What about Howard? He seemed pretty excited to meet an unexpected daughter." Cammie realized this was pushing things, but life was short and took extreme turns.

"How will you all feel now that I have a father again, even though he's not Dad?" They were still keeping their voices low, trying to whisper below the hearing of the others.

"From the looks of the two of them, we may all end up with a new father." She'd said that a little too loud. Crap.

"You're so bad," Maeve laughed. Good, at least she'd found a bit of humor in the situation.

"I heard that and I object to it," Emma snapped. She was evidently handling this in her usual fashion.

The music in the car went away suddenly and the fray began in earnest. "Lord, what have I started?" Cammie whispered to Maeve, who only rolled her eyes in the dimly lit car.

❯❯❯❮❮❮

CAMMIE HAD RETURNED with her siblings around nine p.m. from the cabin, and decided it was too late to do anything to prepare for their events. Fortunately, she and Jo Jo could handle things at the crack of dawn. An early night and a really early start made the most sense after their day. Today had been a whopper.

She noticed that Grey had tried to call several times. She really wanted to talk to him, but hesitated. After the emotional and confusing fiasco with her mother, her vulnerability might lead her right back into his arms. And she hadn't shared the news about the fantastic offer from the studio with anyone yet. That omission pricked her conscience. What did it mean?

If she called Grey, he'd want to come over. She might let him; and then where would she be? Even more confused. Maybe less frustrated, but more confused emotionally, and it wasn't fair to him. He clearly wanted to take up where they'd left off, like ten years hadn't happened, and it scared her how easy that seemed at the moment. But what would she want a month from now? A year?

Somehow, the situation with Mom seemed tied to her own history with Grey, like a reconnection with the past and a move backwards. Now, with this new career opportunity, Cammie could move ahead. Grey wasn't a fit with this plan. He couldn't be, could he? She didn't envision him in New York City any more than she could imagine herself giving up this kind of offer and remaining here in small town Alabama, abandoning her childhood dreams of escape. She might resent him for the rest of her life.

She'd lived for too long with might-have-beens where he was concerned to take such a risk. Plus, his daughter still held some serious resentment toward her. That wasn't something that would be resolved anytime soon. Still the pull to him was strong. Cammie shook her head as if she could get rid of him that way. What she needed, she decided, was to travel to New York for a couple days, and hopefully determine the course of her immediate future with a clear head.

She had a couple of events scheduled later this week, but she could make this flight to New York work if she got cracking with some serious cooking tomorrow morning first thing. Her sisters would cover the phones while she was gone forty-eight hours, as long as they believed she'd been called away to handle something besides a permanent move to NYC.

The key would be to keep the job offer on the down low. If her family caught wind of her plans, they might thwart her at every turn, for her own good. Ben wouldn't stand in her way, so she would reach out to him for help in escaping Alabama for a few days. She needed a smoke screen.

Maybe what she required was a stop along the way to

legitimize this trip. It was something that must be done, no matter how much she dreaded facing it.

➤➤➤❖◄◄◄

COMING TO WORK GAVE Grey a natural excuse to see Cammie without seeming over-eager by continuing to blow up her phone with unreturned calls.

He forced himself to wait until a decent hour before heading over. He knocked on the door around eight o'clock, just as soon as Samantha was safely headed to school on the bus.

He grinned at her, beautiful as always. "Good morning," He said. Cammie had already begun her day in the kitchen, as evidenced by the ingredients smeared on her apron.

"Hi." She smiled, but it didn't sparkle as it had the other night. Something definitely was off.

"Is everything alright?" He searched her face, trying to get a read on what had happened.

"Uh, yeah. Just trying to get a jump on the week. Come on in." She moved aside, allowing him to enter with his tools and the few items he'd brought for today's project.

He brushed past her and heard her quick intake of breath. Shutting the door behind him, she said, "I'll be in the kitchen if you need anything."

She hadn't asked about their dinner with Trudy or mentioned her trip to the lake to visit her mother. How very odd.

"How's your mom?" He would make her talk to him.

"She seems fine." Her words were quick and tight.

"Did something happen at the cabin?" He asked.

Cammie's eyes welled, and she burst out, "We-caught-her-naked-with-a-man-named-Howard-who-has-the-same-dark-blue-eyes-as-Maeve-and-he's-her-dad-and-now-Maeve's   only-our-half-sister-and-Howard's-Lucy's-grandfather—"

"Whoa!" He dropped the items in his hands and grabbed her into his arms while she sobbed. "That's quite a lot to deal with all at once. Let's sit down a minute and you can give me the blow-by-blow."

He kept his arm firmly around her shoulders as led her to the sofa in the main sitting area.

"I didn't realize how much this whole thing has upset me. I've been worried more about Maeve and Emma. They've taken it so hard."

"Sounds like they've taken it hard out loud. You've just been quiet about it as usual and supported them without dealing with your own feelings." He felt he knew her better than she did at times.

Cammie filled him in on as many details as she knew about the situation regarding Maureen and Howard's past. What a doozy. No wonder she was reeling with emotions.

"Mom's explanation about how it all happened makes perfect sense, and I really do understand hers and Howard's sort of tragic star-crossed lovers thing. It's actually very romantic. But it really screws around with our whole family foundation, you know?"

"It might take more time for Maeve, especially, to get

used to. Does Howard seem like a good man?"

"My gut instinct is that he is a very good man and is thrilled to finally reconnect with mom, and he's beside himself to discover that he has both a daughter and a granddaughter."

"Having a child fills a man with a whole new perspective." He understood how overwhelmed Howard must be right now.

"I want to understand that kind of fulfillment someday." Cammie said in a wistful tone.

"You will," he said comforting her. "You're going to be a terrific mother."

Cammie stood suddenly, as if she'd snapped out of a trance. She looked nervous, and Grey found himself confused again.

"I hope the evening with Trudy wasn't too painful for Samantha."

"Not too bad. Thanks for asking." He searched her face. Something was missing between the two of them that he'd believed they were starting to get back, and it hurt, like a hole in his heart, a hole that had begun to fill each moment he could spend with her.

"Are you sure there's nothing else bothering you?" He asked again, softly.

"Grey." Her eyes were drenched with unshed tears, but she held up her hand when he stepped forward to hold her. "I've got some things to work out," she said quickly. "I'm heading up to New York for a couple days."

"New York?" He echoed.

"I really need to reevaluate my goals—where my life is headed."

He could barely breathe, but he had to ask the question. No more silences between them.

"After what's happened between us, how can you doubt where you belong?"

"Where I belong? Seriously?" She dashed the few tears that fell away with the back of her hand in a jerky motion. "It took almost five years after you married Deb before I would go on a second date with a guy. I didn't trust anyone not to annihilate my heart before I met Jason. He was so patient and kind."

She was crying again. And it was his fault. He'd had no idea how deeply he'd damaged her. He'd believed she'd simply moved on after a while. It was easier to think like that, especially when he'd been so irrevocably trapped in his marriage, missing her every day, even though he tried not to think about her.

"You know I never meant to hurt you like that. I wanted to spend my life with you, not Deb." He paused a moment, knowing his words meant everything—or nothing at this point. "I can't change the past or get back what either of us has lost, but I can spend the rest of my life making it up to you, Cammie."

He got down on one knee in front of her. "Cammie Laroux, you are the love of my life, and I don't know how or when, but I want to marry you. Please give me a chance to prove how much I love you."

He'd never seen her look quite so sad as she did at this

moment, shaking her head as if there was no hope, and he felt as if all the light and warmth got sucked out of the room. "Grey, I wish it was that simple. For years, I didn't let myself think about you because it hurt so much. I forgive you for what happened. I think I really do now, but the consequences were so disastrous that I don't know if I can change the course of my life for you again. I'm a chef. I have career dreams of a restaurant. I have a house," she broke off.

"What do you want to do?" He hated to ask. "Why are you going to New York? You're not a big city girl, Cammie. You aren't."

"I have a job offer in New York City—my own show." She said.

It was strange how he could be so proud and happy for her, yet feel destroyed at the same time. New York. It was far away. Alien. And he couldn't relocate Samantha again, especially there.

"That's great!" he said slowly, meaning it. "I'd never want to hold you back; you know that. New York City." The words were like a drum beat of doom in his skull.

"Exactly," Cammie said, sounding quick and angry and defensive. "We can't do this between New York and Alabama. It would never work."

"Please don't say never." He couldn't bear it.

"I have to cook now. I'm leaving tomorrow."

No, don't go. He wanted to beg her to stay, to turn down the job offer, to want nothing more than to stay with him here in Ministry. To start over. But her jaw was set, and she could hardly meet his gaze that was probably filled with desperate longing. She was going. And he couldn't stop her. What else could he do? He'd cut his heart open and poured out his emotions.

"You know how I feel and what I want," he said, wanting nothing ever again left ambiguous between them. "The offer to be with me, to marry me stands—no matter what." He kissed her cheek and wiped away a tear that had rolled down to the corner of her mouth.

She stood, shoulders hunched and walked slowly toward the kitchen.

>>>><<<<

"IT DOESN'T MATTER. I'm not hungry." Grey slammed the cabinet harder than he'd intended.

"So what's gotten you all worked up, son?" His father asked, brow raised in concern.

"Sorry, dad. It's not your fault. I'm just frustrated and not sure what to think about things right now."

"About what? Or should I ask, whom?" His father wasn't an idiot.

"I thought that Cammie and I had come to an understanding of sorts."

"What kind of, ah, *understanding*?" He asked.

"Yes, that kind, too. But it was way more than that. I told her I loved her and wanted to marry her."

His father let out a low whistle. "Son, I knew you still cared, but that's a pretty huge step, don't you think? I mean, considering you have a daughter, and this affects her life, too?"

Grey tried to control his patience. "Everything I do is with Samantha in mind. I told Cammie that maybe things wouldn't happen right away, but that I wanted to spend my life with her when the time was right."

"I know you've dedicated your life to Samantha, but it's been a touchy thing with her and Cammie so far. I'm not saying it wouldn't ever work its way out, but are you willing to wait; or is she?

His dad sat down at one of the barstools. Grey stood facing him across the bar. He felt sixteen again, defending his love for Cammie. "Dad, I can't lose her again."

Grey heard a small scraping sound and turned, instantly alert, in case Samantha had overheard his declaration of love for Cammie. But as he moved toward the pantry and peeked around the corner, Dane, his boxer came padding from the other room. Grey's relief was physical.

He returned to find his dad still sitting at the bar where he'd left him, wearing a contemplative expression. His father wasted no time. "Grey, you know I want you to be happy; it's all I've ever wanted. But you and Cammie haven't really spent time together in years. Hard to believe you'd even be the same people after all this time and water under the bridge."

Grey had already heard this today. "That's kind of what's she's saying right now, too. I know how I feel about her. I know becoming a father has made me a stronger and more complex person, and her challenges have shaped her, but deep down, we are the same personalities with the same souls."

"Maybe you should bring this up with Sabine at your next appointment."

"Yeah, I plan to. She's been discussing Cammie with Samantha, trying to diffuse some of her resentment from the gossip."

"Sounds like you've got your work cut out for you trying to convince both Cammie and Samantha that this is a good idea."

"Sounds like I do."

Chapter Seventeen

⸙

CAMMIE WAS ON a plane bound for La Guardia. Bruce's assistant had finalized the flight details not two hours after she'd sent her availability. Cammie was amazed at the near-magical ease with which her wishes had been granted.

There would be a car waiting at the airport when she arrived to whisk her directly to the studio for the meeting with the executive producers and other movers and shakers. Cammie hadn't asked too many questions regarding this incredible offer, but Bruce had assured her that she would be blown away at their proposal.

Anything was better than the proverbial doghouse she'd been living under the past several months as the bungling doofus of cooking show land. The television world and media could spin any situation and transform it into something fresh and exciting. From doofus to darling in a day. Wonders never ceased.

The network had requested Cammie keep this meeting under wraps until they came to an agreement. Of course she'd not told anyone besides Grey about the offer. Funny how she knew intrinsically to trust him, though she claimed otherwise out loud.

The flight took only two hours, with Cammie on edge the entire time. The elderly woman in the next seat had recognized Cammie immediately and tried to engage her in conversation about Jessica Green. "I'm sorry. I really can't speak about Ms. Green. My contract prevents me from discussing our relationship." But one day it wouldn't.

"Honey, that woman is a phony-baloney, if you ask me. I'd much rather see you up there cooking on my TV screen than her stupid self." The woman sat back in her seat then, seemingly satisfied she'd said her piece.

"I appreciate your support," Cammie said, not knowing how else to reply. The woman made a satisfied sniffing sound.

But when Cammie turned away, she caught the woman snapping her picture with a cell camera out of the corner of her eye. Maybe this kind of popularity wasn't so great. She'd been removed from the public in Alabama, though everyone there knew her story. At least they'd become used to her daily presence and pretty much left her alone day-to-day.

Not that Cammie was a huge star, but it was surprising how many people tuned in to the daily cooking shows. And Jessica had been so commercialized with Cammie at her elbow for several years; she was well-recognized wherever she went. Maybe not instantly, but rarely did she get through her day without signing a few autographs and taking a photo or two with fans.

As she made her way to the transportation area outside baggage claim, Cammie ducked her head, hoping for anonymity. Fortunately, this was to be a quick trip and she'd not checked a bag.

Her driver held up a sign with only the name, Laroux, which was helpful, until someone standing nearby saw her connect with the driver and his sign.

She dealt graciously with the flurry of smiling photos, comments, and questions, to which she gave her requisite answer of "can't comment." Her driver was obviously a seasoned professional, and aided in taking her bag and keeping her moving toward the car all the while.

"Sorry about that, ma'am." He had a Brooklyn accent.

"No problem. I didn't want to be rude and cause a scene."

"There are some bottles of water and diet drinks in the cooler if you're thirsty. Relax, and we'll be at the studio soon." In other words, *close your eyes and hang on tight.* Cammie had ridden with enough New York cabbies and drivers to know that no matter the size or color of the car, New York drivers were all of the same horn-honking, impatient breed. She wasn't in Alabama anymore. Somehow, that was less than satisfying.

⇥⇥⇥⇤⇤⇤

GREY SAT IN Sabine's outer office. She'd made blueberry muffins again, as was her custom. He supposed it was comforting and homey to the patients who came here feeling anxious about their various situations.

It made him think about Cammie and her constant cooking and baking. She'd left on a plane first thing this morning. He stood and paced the small sitting area. Her flying off to New York made his stomach hurt.

Samantha hadn't been herself the past day or so either. She'd been quiet and withdrawn, like she knew something was up. He'd tried to speak with her about it, but she'd shut him down and been completely uncommunicative.

Forcing himself back down on the flowery sofa, Grey thought he heard crying coming from Sabine's office. He stilled. It was Samantha, and she was sobbing and getting louder. From the beginning of their sessions, Sabine had warned him, "Don't come charging in if you hear Samantha expressing emotion. I will come find you if I think it's necessary."

So he sat outside, listening to his daughter cry her eyes out, catching a fragments here and there, "He said he loves her...I'm afraid if he gets married he won't be happy like when he was married to my mom...I want him to be happy."

Had he heard that correctly? She wanted him to not marry Cammie so he wouldn't be miserable like he'd been with Deb? That was a real kicker.

Samantha *had* overheard his conversation with his dad while they'd believed she was doing her homework, headphones on, in her bedroom. The scraping noise hadn't only been his dog. She'd listened. But she hadn't shared her feelings about what she'd heard. Maybe it was better this way. Sabine had such an effective approach to addressing sensitive issues with Samantha.

It was as if Sabine could say the things that would never

fly coming from him. Things that made sense to a nine-year-old girl, but coming from her dad sounded lecturing and judgmental. From Sabine, it was respectful straight-talk that helped Samantha put the events of her confusing life into perspective. She had a strong sense of fair play. Grey relied heavily on that to help pull her through some of the mucky and confusing emotional stuff.

The door finally opened and Samantha came out. Her eyes were puffy, but she was no longer crying. Sabine maintained her usual serene half-smile and said, "Grey, could you come in?"

He placed a hand on Samantha's shoulder and searched his daughter's bloodshot eyes. "You okay?"

"I'm okay, Daddy." She did seem more relaxed now and less on edge than before she'd gone inside, which surprised him a little. Her body language even appeared somewhat resigned.

"Samantha, you can hang for a bit while your dad and I talk, okay?" Sabine suggested.

"Okay."

Grey followed Sabine into her office and pulled the door shut behind him. "I heard her crying and some of what she said to you."

Sabine sighed, then said, "She's decided to give Cammie a chance."

"What kind of chance?" Grey could hardly believe it.

"Obviously it came as a huge shock to her that you'd told Cammie you wanted to marry her. She's dealing with conflicting emotions right now, but the bottom line is that she's ready for you to stop being sad and worried all the time."

"She said that?"

"Among other things. She's come a long way in realizing that Cammie isn't her enemy and wasn't the true cause of her mother's unhappiness, but this is something that will take some time."

"I'm surprised she's even open to the idea at all."

"After she had a good cry that you hadn't told her how you felt about Cammie—which was the main problem—she opened up that she hated watching you mope around and worry all the time."

"I don't mope around. Well, I do worry, but I try to talk to her about things. I didn't say how I felt about Cammie because I didn't want to upset her."

"She's growing up and wants your honesty, even if she doesn't always like what you have to say. The gossip around town is the worst way for her to get her information. It really should come from you first. And overhearing how you felt about Cammie in her own home felt like you'd been keeping a secret from her."

Grey could understand that.

"How should I approach this with her? I mean, Cammie and I haven't come to a real meeting of minds about where we stand with one another yet."

"Tell Samantha that. Let her know you are uncertain of how things will play out with Cammie, but that you'd like to have the opportunity to give your relationship another chance."

"I guess if she can open up to the possibility of having Cammie in our lives, she'll just know we're all taking things a step at a time together. Maybe she won't worry that I'll spring something on her that she's not ready for."

"Exactly. Right now, Samantha needs to feel like she's in the know and part of what's going on. No sneaking around so that she finds out about it from a kid at school."

"Got it." Grey shifted uncomfortably in his chair.

"She finally asked why you married her mother if you'd planned to marry Cammie all along. I said her mother loved you so much that she made some poor decisions, giving you very little choice but to marry her." Sabine had stayed within the guidelines they'd set up early-on with regards to how much information to supply Samantha when questions arose and explanations were required.

"That was a well-worded understatement. But I don't want her to think her mother was a bad person." Though he believed she'd walked a fine line.

"No, she doesn't. Only misguided to use her own emotions to trap another person into doing what she wanted instead of allowing them to choose. But I made certain she understood that Deb had some serious emotional issues that contributed to her poor decision-making."

"How did she end up viewing Cammie's role in all this?" He couldn't believe they'd discussed it all at such length without his knowing.

"As a somewhat innocent victim, really. Which is pretty accurate, all told."

He exhaled deeply. If Samantha no longer blamed

Cammie for her mother's unhappiness or him for not loving her mother because of his feelings for Cammie, then all of this might potentially work itself out. If only he could persuade Cammie that she really belonged in Alabama.

➤➤➤◄◄◄

"CAMMIE, WE'RE WILLING to run the show five days, twice a day, during the week. You'll have the primo time slot and the most amazing Southern farmhouse kitchen set. We'll incorporate your own brand with cookware, a web presence, and all the fanfare appearances you approve. We're even discussing a future site for a restaurant. Of course that would be your personal endeavor, and the network would support it a hundred percent."

They'd offered her the moon, the stars, and beyond. It was more than Cammie would've imagined. Jessica Green was bound to hate her even more. The public feedback the network had received was overwhelmingly favorable towards her. No contracts had been signed yet, but between the two executive producers and a network vice president, they'd given Cammie the hard sell. She'd been booked overnight into the Ritz-Carlton in Manhattan in a suite, and had tickets for tonight's performance at the NYC Ballet, complete with Bruce as her escort. Several gorgeous evening dresses from top designers were brought up for her to choose from as a gift from the studio.

To say Cammie was overwhelmed by today's events would be an understatement. She truly felt like a princess in a fairy tale. Why did it feel like such a lonely enchantment?

Throughout the entire ballet performance, while Bruce was an entertaining escort now that she'd forgiven him, she expected to lean over and share her enthusiasm or thoughts with Grey. Homesickness had crept into her soul. Home, as in Alabama.

When she returned to the hotel, the desire to call Grey nearly overwhelmed her. Somehow, he'd gotten to her again after all these years. She'd even spent time today wondering how Samantha was faring, hoping she wasn't struggling at school, and worrying that she was happy.

Cammie was terribly afraid this new career move wouldn't be enough, no matter how incredible the opportunity, but she couldn't come up with a way to make everyone happy. Was that even possible?

As she picked up her cell phone, it rang. "Hello?"

"Hi." It was Grey. A deep longing hit her hard the moment his voice came through the speaker.

"Hey there."

"How was your meeting?" he asked.

"Unbelievable, really. They offered me prime time." She winced, thinking she should sound more enthusiastic instead of stunned. Where had her ambition gone? She was not going to give up everything for a man. But the man was Grey, her conscience spoke up. She told it to shut up.

"Wow. That's pretty exciting." Grey said after a pause, but he did sound legitimately happy for her. "Congratulations."

"Thanks. How are things down there?"

"Going pretty well, all things considered."

"Is Samantha alright?" Cammie felt an intense need to know.

"She's fine. Big fractions test in the morning, but I think she's ready for it."

"I—I miss you." Had she really just said that? What an idiot.

"You do? I miss you like crazy, but you know that."

"I'm sitting here in a suite at the Ritz Carlton in Manhattan after an incredible day, and I should be turning cartwheels, but instead I can't stop wishing I was there. It's very confusing." It was a big admission, but she felt like she needed to be honest. With him. With herself.

"I'm so glad to hear it. Not that you're confused, but that you're homesick and miss me. You often give the impression that you can't wait to get the hell outta Ministry."

"Obviously a few things have changed."

"Obviously." His voice was dry.

She remembered opening the curtain in her underwear and seeing him on that ladder outside the window. The horror of that moment, in retrospect, nearly sent her into a fit of giggles.

"What in the world is so funny?" He asked.

"I was remembering the expression on your face when you saw me through the window that first day."

"The look on *my* face? You were standing there in the sexiest bra and panties I've ever seen and glaring at me like you wanted to shoot me."

"I did, kinda. No woman wants to meet her old boyfriend in her underwear without any makeup after ten years."

"Funny, all I could think of was how gorgeous and hot you looked."

"You're such a guy." She laughed.

"Guilty. I'm the guy who loves you, you know?" He became serious.

"Oh, Grey, what are we doing?" She groaned into the phone, more confused than ever.

"I'm trying to persuade you that we belong together. We can make the long-distance thing work, at least until I figure it all out with Samantha."

"I really don't see how." She couldn't commit right now. She wouldn't.

"Just say you'll consider it." He sounded gruff and emotional.

"This is all such a confusing mess."

"Please, Cammie, you don't have to commit. Just don't say no."

"Grey," she breathed, and even she could hear the give in her voice.

"So, you'll be home Thursday?" He asked.

Home, her heart kicked.

"My flight arrives around eight o'clock in the evening."

"I'll pick you up from the airport, and we can grab a bite to eat if you want." He'd backed off considerably, and she felt like she could breathe again, like she wasn't about to burst into tears. She'd never been the weepy type, but Grey did something to her emotions. Always had. Maybe always would.

"Thanks; I'll let you know," she finally said. "I'm likely to be a tired heap by then, but I'll call or text when I land," she assured him.

She should push the end button, but instead she continued to hold the phone to her ear.

"Cammie?"

"Yes?"

"I love you."

He sounded so certain, and with enough emotion that she recognized the sincerity behind his words.

"I know." She nearly said it back. "Grey, I..." She stopped herself before she jumped over that cliff. "I hope you understand that I'm still working all this out in my head." Her words sounded insensitive to her own ears, but she refused to spill gushy emotional stuff only to be hurt again or to commit to anything she wasn't ready to follow through on.

"I can wait." He assured her, but sounded as if she'd stuck a knife into him and twisted it.

Cammie didn't know if that made her feel terrified or reassured.

"Bye." She hung up before she could say more.

⇛⇛⇛⋘⋘⋘

GREY ARRIVED EARLY with a crew of workers at the Laroux house. Today they would begin shoring up an area of the exterior where settling under the foundation had caused some sagging in the floors.

Concrete reinforcement was necessary in a few areas beneath the house, and Grey'd sub-contracted a separate company for that work. Today, they would prep, and tomorrow, pour the concrete. This wasn't his area of expertise, but he oversaw the process to make certain things went smoothly.

Since there wasn't anything else he could do until tomorrow, once the concrete guys left, he locked up and headed out on a personal errand.

Grey returned to the old farmhouse outside of town where he'd found the flooring. He was so drawn to the property still, that he found himself wandering through the barn, making plans for future changes he'd make once this was their home. Grey could picture the three of them here together: Samantha, Cammie, and him. The last time he'd been over, George had given him a key to the house.

He let himself in, took out the camera he'd brought and snapped several photos of the kitchen, hearth, and living areas. It was wonderfully open and airy for such an old place. He envisioned installing stainless appliances and stone countertops, and still managing to maintain the home's charm. The cabinetry was in excellent condition and would only require a deep sanding and refinishing to make it a work of art.

Modern space-making architecture could be implemented without taking anything away from the existing traditional lines. Cammie would require a chef's kitchen in her line of work. Certainly he wanted her input, even if she never lived here. But he didn't want to give up hope. He'd lived for ten years without it.

He took one last glance around at the home's interior, Grey locked up. Today, he'd made a decision. It felt right all the way to his bones. This was to be home.

He dialed George's number to talk specifics. George didn't answer, so he left a voicemail.

Grey then e-mailed the kitchen photos to Cammie, asking her opinion as to what sorts of changes she would suggest to make this the perfect magazine-worthy, modern farmhouse kitchen. He intimated in the message that it was a local home where he was to begin renovation soon. So, when she got the chance, he'd love to hear her professional opinion. He'd included an exterior shot of the front as well.

Of course he didn't expect to hear back from her until sometime tomorrow, but he was eager for her reaction to the farmhouse photos.

He then headed to pick up some items from the local builder's supply.

Grey made it back just in time to meet the bus. "Hey there, how was school?"

"Okay, I guess."

"Got any homework?" Grey took her heavy backpack from her, and they began walking down the drive toward the house.

"A little."

"Feels like a lot." He laughed.

⁂

MAUREEN WASN'T QUITE sure what to do with Howard.

She didn't doubt her feelings, not in the least. In fact, if they could spend every waking moment together, it would suit her fine. She had no doubt it was the same for him.

But he couldn't exactly move into Evangeline House immediately with her. And he lived an hour and a half away. He owned his parents homestead two counties over, and had used a property manager most of his career so the place didn't fall to ruin when he was away for long periods.

Neither was ready to separate—not yet. They were too busy getting to know one another again. He'd told her he wanted to take care of her until she was a hundred percent from her surgery. If he stayed here at Evangeline House, she could only imagine the stink it would cause with her children, not to mention the gossip in town. Maureen was something of a civic leader around here.

Her reputation was important, but she didn't want to be a hypocrite either. Living with a man who was her first child's father, unbeknownst to the world until now, was bound to cause a stir in a place like Ministry. She was the owner of a thriving business, and this news could hurt that business should it get out to the good Christian people around town.

She would be judged. Whether it was right or not, there remained a rather large and rigid contingency of the small-minded who passed judgment. Of course, Maureen likely retained enough uncomfortable information, should it come to light after all these years, about each and every one of those starchy-butted folks to make them rethink their position should it come down to that. A lifetime without missteps was a very rare thing.

For today, she'd asked Howard to bring her home. He was planning to leave just before dark to head back to his own home near Montgomery. He'd gone back out to the car to retrieve the items she'd brought with her to the lake. Anna had returned a few days ago. Maureen had missed her children, and decided to take a little time to settle back into a routine at the center of her family. They would have a nice Thanksgiving together Thursday and hopefully mend some fences. She had the uncomfortable feeling that she would have to come clean with Cammie as well. Having Howard back in her life showed her more than anything that she shouldn't have used her own pain to make a decision for her daughter that was not hers to make.

***

GREY PICKED CAMMIE up from the airport. It was wonderful to see her, but the dark circles under her eyes told a story. He stowed her bag in the backseat of his truck. "You look tired."

"You're a real charmer."

"Honesty is my policy from here on out. I love you and I missed you."

"No pressure there," Cammie said, biting her lip.

"I know. I'm supposed to be patient," he said ruefully and kissed the corner of her mouth. "But I was always impatient for everything with you."

Cammie smiled softly. She seemed far away.

"I could say it a thousand times more, how sorry I am

that I ruined...."

She linked her fingers with his.

"It's not that," she said slowly. "I don't think you ruined my trust so much as you ruined me for anyone else."

"I'm not sure if that's something else I should be apologizing for." He shifted the truck into gear, not breaking the link of their fingers and headed back to Ministry.

"I meant it as a good thing." She smiled, and for the first time in a while it seemed genuine and happy, not tinged with doubt or sorrow. "Do you know if my mother's at home?"

"She was when I left to pick you up. I think she's cooking dinner for you."

"That wasn't necessary. How does she seem? The last time I saw her was at the cabin when we caught her with Maeve's father, Howard."

"From what I could tell, she seemed happy and looked to be getting around pretty well. I met Howard briefly, when he brought her home early this afternoon. He stayed for a while, but I didn't notice his truck when I left to pick you up."

"Hmmm..." she murmured. "I think I want to ask her about the letter."

"Okay." Grey wasn't sure how to respond. "I don't know what that's going to explain after all this time."

"I want to know," Cammie said, and she straightened in her seat. "I want to move on from this completely."

Grey was quiet. Cammie, too.

"How's Samantha?" she asked.

"Doing pretty well; looking forward to Thanksgiving break. It'll be nice having her home without schoolwork and tests on her mind constantly. I can't believe how much they're responsible for in only fourth grade."

"I'd like to see her again if she'll agreed to it." Cammie suggested, hesitantly.

Grey felt his heart soar, but did his best not to show it. He knew Cammie wouldn't try to make inroads with Samantha if she were planning on running off to New York City in the next week or so. But maybe his hope was making him grasp at straws.

"Sure. It's a good idea for the two of you to get to know each other. The more he thought about it, this request signified to him that Cammie might be considering them as part of her future.

"Just let me know when would be a good time."

"Will do." He tried his best to keep a lid on his excitement for now. "Did you get a chance to look at the photos I sent you?"

Cammie started as if she'd been about to fall asleep, and he silently cursed himself for pushing yet again.

"I saw the one on my screen," she said apologetically. "But I've been too wound up to really look at them and offer up any sort of reasoned, professional opinion. Tomorrow?"

"Of course. Take your time."

They'd pulled into Evangeline House's drive, and she looked ready to drop.

Maureen met them at the door, ushered Cammie inside,

and invited him in. "Thanks for bringing my baby girl home. Would you like to have a late dinner with us?"

"No, ma'am, I'd better head home and check in with my family. It's nearly Samantha's bedtime. I'll see you tomorrow."

"Tell her to stop by and see me while she's out of school next week. I've missed her. And say hello to your dad for me." Maureen had spent quite a lot of time with both Lucy and Samantha buzzing around underfoot since they'd moved back.

"Thanks. She'll be happy to know you're home."

He kissed Cammie on the cheek and promised they would speak tomorrow.

⟫⟪

CAMMIE DECIDED THERE wasn't any time like the present. "Mom, I have to ask you about something."

Her mother raised her elegant brow. Cammie figured she was likely ready for any line of questioning at this point following all that had gone down in the past week. "Of course, darling. Let's sit down and talk over dinner. I don't want our food to get cold."

They sat, poured wine, and served up bowls of lovely potato soup and crusty French bread. "Grey shared with me that he'd left a letter with you for me just after he found out Deb was pregnant." Understanding dawned immediately on her mother's face in the form of a pained expression.

Mom stood. "Stay right here. I realize that I have much to explain, but I need the letter to do that."

Nerves like angry bees began buzzing inside Cammie's gut. At least there weren't any denials regarding the reopening of yet another scarred over wound. Cammie tried to calm her uncertain emotions before her mother returned.

The single sheet of slightly yellowed, and obviously much-handled, notebook paper was placed on the table in front of her. Cammie opened it with trembling hands, her heartbeat thumping as if she'd not known its contents until this moment.

My Dearest Cammie,

By now you've heard about Deb and me. I wish I could have told you myself, so you might try to understand. I never meant for any of it to happen, I swear. We'd had that big fight on the phone and you believed the worst of me. I drove like a maniac from Auburn to explain, but your mother said you didn't want to see me.

I was so upset that I went out to the barn and drank myself stupid. I guess Deb followed me. She'd talked to you after our fight and knew I'd come chasing after you. I swear she had it all planned, Cammie. I was shit-faced off Boones Farm and I felt so sad and alone. One minute she was consoling me, and the next, I'd made the biggest mistake of my life. I'm not even sure how it happened.

You and I made up and I'd planned to tell you just as soon as I got the nerve, but then Deb told me she was pregnant. I couldn't deny it. Cammie, she's having a miscarriage and threatening suicide. She swears the baby is fine one minute and wants to die the next. I wanted to talk to you so badly, but your mom says she hasn't heard from you and doesn't know where you've gone.

I love you. I will marry Deb if I have no other choice, but my heart belongs to you—always.

I'm so sorry.

Grey

The tears streamed down her cheeks, unchecked. Cammie only thought she'd realized how his young, passionate words she'd never gotten to see might affect her. How would she have reacted ten years ago?

Her mother hugged her gently. "I'm so sorry, Cammie. At the time, I believe he'd betrayed you in the worst way, and even if somehow you'd forgiven him, you'd never be able to trust him. My own experience with Howard's desertion colored my judgment."

"I know. I do love Grey. I've just realized that, and I forgive him. But this offer—it's everything I've ever wanted in my career. It's never going to happen again in my lifetime. I just wish—I wish there was a way to do what I love without giving up a chance at a life with Grey."

"You've got to do what your heart tells you. Sleep on it. You're tired and coming off an emotional trip." Her mother hugged her hard. "In the last week or so, I've learned a few new lessons about what's important. Just give it all careful consideration before you make a final decision."

Cammie had calmed down now. "I will, and Mom, as much as I wish you would have given me Grey's letter back then, I know you've never tried to hurt me on purpose. And Maeve knows that too, though it's pretty crazy, this secret father you've kept from her all these years. Is Howard angry with you?" she asked.

"He's upset that he's gone all these years without knowing he had a family, but he understands that once I married your father, there was no going back. I loved your daddy, honey. I hope you know that." Tears glistened in her mother's eyes.

"I know you loved him, and I know he loved you. And as long as there weren't any secrets between you when you married, then I don't have a problem with it." Cammie was living proof of their love.

"You are a wonderful child, and deserving of all the good things life can give you."

They finished dinner mostly in silence, but it was a satisfied quiet that required no words.

Chapter Eighteen

CAMMIE AWOKE, STRETCHED, and burrowed down under the covers. It was still early, according to the bedside clock, but she had events to prepare for this evening. A new peace had settled over her sometime after Grey had picked her up, and she'd enjoyed a quiet evening with her mother over their late dinner. Her nerves had eased.

Especially after her mother's turning over Grey's long-hidden letter. Cammie would have expected to feel angry and bitter at Mom, but there had been too much anger and bitterness over the years. Now was the time for true for-giveness and moving forward. She loved Grey, more importantly, she now honestly forgave him. Still uncertain how things would play out, it seeped into her bones and spread. She immersed herself in the healthy and healing sensation.

Cammie rolled over and picked up her smart phone from beside the bed and checked her messages. She took a moment to really look at the photos Grey had sent her when she was in New York. As she scrolled through them, excite-ment took hold. She wanted to call Grey with a million ideas for his kitchen project. Nearly buzzing with thoughts of transforming that wonderful old farmhouse into something worthy of a magazine, Cammie wondered what had come over her. Maybe it was the idea of helping Grey create something fantastic, or maybe she just adored everything about her craft, and kitchens were really in her wheelhouse. She could hardly wait to speak with him and discuss her thoughts on his project.

This morning, however, Cammie had cooking and preparation for this evening. She would see Grey today while he continued his work at the house, and that was comforting. Her mother would help her do some of the light jobs. Maybe she would get a few minutes to discuss her ideas about the farmhouse with Grey. Her big decision could be dealt with later.

She dragged herself out from under the warmth of the quilt and pulled on a robe. The aroma of freshly brewed coffee led her downstairs. She assumed her mother had made the coffee since she was an early riser and Cammie knew Grey wouldn't arrive for at least another hour. Her assumption was wrong. Grey was already here, and he'd brewed the lovely coffee. He stood in the kitchen, freshly showered and shaven wearing a flannel work shirt and jeans, his gorgeous grin nearly buckling her knees. "Good morning, sunshine."

"I wasn't expecting anyone this early—except maybe people who live here," She said, a little grumpy at his catching her at her most unappealing. Again, she thought darkly.

"You look sleepy and beautiful." He approached her and put his arms around her shoulders, pulling her against him. He'd not embraced her since she'd left for New York.

She mumbled into his chest, "I haven't brushed my teeth yet."

His chest shook with laughter. "That's nice."

Cammie pulled away and made a face at him, but not before inhaling a nice big whiff of delicious, clean man-smell.

He handed her a cup of coffee.

"Thanks. I've got to get cracking—double duty this evening."

"What's on tap?"

"The annual Art Guild dinner and a Cindy Lou's book signing."

"Cindy Lou Snodgrass wrote a book?" He appeared truly shocked.

"I'm surprised you've been back in Ministry this long and haven't heard. She wrote a memoir about her brush with death down in New Orleans during Hurricane Katrina." His expression of disbelief intensified—likely because Cindy Lou had mostly been known around Ministry as a teller of tall tales; Cammie hesitated to call her a liar.

"Someone actually published something written by Cindy Lou as anything other than fiction?"

"Well, she self-published the tale, and she's throwing herself a book signing tonight at Evangeline House."

"Is this an invitation-only event?"

"There are flyers up everywhere, so I doubt it. I've seen

them at the grocery and on the stop sign at the corner. I really can't believe you've not heard about it."

"I might have to stop by this evening out of morbid curiosity."

"You do that. I'll be running around here, fending off snide remarks about Jessica Green from the crowd."

"You can handle these folks. They hardly remember any of that now." He started to leave, then turned and asked, "Get a chance yet to look the photos I sent?"

The excitement was back again, as unexpected as before.

"You sound like a kid." She laughed at him. He always had been so full of enthusiasm. She remembered that now. "Yes! Grey, I have so many ideas for your project."

"So, how about you meet me there tomorrow morning and you can tell them to me in person?" He appeared pleased that she was interested, as he was smiling broadly.

"Okay. Send me the address in a text and we'll set a time." On that note, he whistled his way out the swinging door of Evangeline House's kitchen.

She guessed it was a date, of sorts.

A couple minutes after Grey left the kitchen, her mother breezed in, moving with more grace than Cammie expected. "How is your back feeling?"

"Amazingly well, thanks for asking. It seems every day that passes brings less pain."

"I'm so glad. I meant to ask how you were feeling last night, but we got sidetracked."

"That's a nice way to put it." Her mother smiled.

THE ART GUILD dinner required time and attention to the art of food. Cammie'd prepared most of the items before she'd gone to New York, so she only had to allow most of it to thaw and reheat, then add bread and dessert to the menu. Maureen was most helpful, and since many of the ladies were her cronies, she handled the hosting duties.

The book signing was another matter entirely. Since Cindy Lou's "experiences" had occurred in New Orleans, she'd decided they should serve only authentic creole and Cajun foods as appetizers and desserts during her shindig.

So, the pecan tartlets, bourbon glazed bread pudding cups, mini crawfish pies, and individual servings of jambalaya made for high numbers of tiny dirty dishes. But she had to admit; the high entertainment value of Cindy Lou's oral presentation was worth the extra effort. She read aloud a portion of especially dramatic narrative that had her audience leaning forward in their chairs, anticipating her every word.

Needless to say, Cindy Lou sold every copy of her book. The signing was a success, much to everyone's surprise. Cammie was happy for the woman. Cindy'd worked hard toward her goal and persevered. Whether the story was stranger than fiction, or actually fiction, made no difference. Her gift was telling stories. Until now, it hadn't gotten her far.

Cammie and her mother worked side-by-side along with Jo Jo and Maeve, who'd helped with serving and replenishing food and drink as needed.

Grey had texted to say he wasn't going to make it this

evening but that he'd see her at the farmhouse in the morning, and texted her the address. Cammie hadn't had the opportunity this morning to bring up the letter. She'd placed it inside her nightstand drawer right next to his class ring, which had brought on another flood of memories. Cammie could have sworn it was wrapped in a bandana in the chest of drawers last she saw it.

⋙⋘

CAMMIE'S CONVERSATION WITH Bruce Bernard was short and to the point. "I'm sorry Bruce, I simply can't drop everything at this time and move to New York permanently."

"Are you kidding? They've offered you a dream come true."

"I know. I have lost my mind. But I'm now at a point in my life where the choices I make affect more than just me. Please tell everyone at the network thanks for placing such faith in me."

They'd hung up, and Cammie breathed a sigh of what—relief—maybe? She hadn't put a title on quite how she felt yet, but today she'd realized that her whole world was tied up in the people she loved. Her family, Grey, Samantha. This tiny town in Alabama was the canvas for how she'd been shaped as a human being, right or wrong. She'd escaped, learned so many things about the world, and now knew her place in it.

Cammie hadn't told anyone what she'd intended yet. In fact, until today she wasn't certain of her plan. Or, she hadn't admitted it to herself yet.

Her mother's handing over Grey's old letter had cemented her belief in how deep his feelings had been for her back then, and how epic he'd viewed his mistake with Deb. But if either had done anything different, he wouldn't be the father he was today. And that would be a shame.

She couldn't wish that away from him.

"Cammie, is everything okay?" Her mother knocked softly on her bedroom door.

"Come in, Mom." Her mother joined her on the bed.

"I've made up my mind to stay here in Ministry."

She'd never seen her mother appear quite so deeply happy. "I had a feeling you would make this choice."

"I'm not sure how you knew, because I didn't."

"Have you told Grey yet?"

"No. I had a phone call to make first." She had true butterflies in her tummy in anticipation of breaking the news to him. Of course she didn't have any reason to be nervous, did she?

Cammie was at peace with her decision to break away from her previous career. She had her chef's training from the Cordon Bleu in New York City, for heaven's sake. No one held better credentials for opening a restaurant. She'd been earning a salary as severance since they'd let her go, so her income hadn't suffered thus far, and wouldn't for several more months.

After the morning's excitement, she realized she still had a small event this evening to handle. "Well, I guess I'd better get to work."

But her mother laid a gentle hand on her shoulder. "You go find your young man and make his day. I can deal with the Rotary Club meeting."

"Are you sure?" But Cammie knew Mom wouldn't be dissuaded. And she also knew the event was really only a good old boys' club meeting that ran itself, besides a few snacks and drinks. They were here for the location and had been for thirty years.

"Of course. I could do this one sitting down with hands tied and you well know it. Plus, Howard is coming by later. He won't allow me to overdo."

"Thanks, Mom. Coming back here might have been the best thing I've ever been manipulated into doing." She smiled and her mother laughed.

"I do believe that's what your sisters thought all along."

"I have someone to see."

"Bye, sweetie. Have fun."

Cammie didn't change clothes, worry about makeup, or even spare a glance in the mirror. She knew Grey didn't care how she looked. He'd just be glad to see her.

>>>><<<<

CAMMIE ARRIVED AT the address he'd sent to her phone around ten o'clock. He'd said he had some work to do at the house, so she could come when she was ready. As she pulled into the drive, she was struck by the exterior of the farmhouse, by the property, with its old oak tree down the hill, a tire swing gently swaying in the breeze beside a picturesque pond. She felt like she'd come home. Like she'd driven up to her own house and everything felt right. It was strange.

As she climbed out of the car, Grey emerged from the front door looking as good to Cammie as he ever had in his worn jeans and faded t-shirt. She had to restrain herself from sprinting toward him and throwing herself into his arms. *Easy, girl.*

He held out a hand to lead her inside. And just like that, she was home.

"What do you think?"

Her breathing was quick and her excitement over-whelming. "I love it, Grey. Who does it belong to?"

"Me."

Everything came together in that moment for Cammie. Any lingering shred of doubt dissolved with that one word. Then, she did throw herself into his arms.

"Whoa. What's this?"

"I turned down the offer in New York."

"You did? Why?" But he sounded so hopeful.

She took a deep breath and began, "Because I can't leave you and Samantha. Because I love you, and I love her. I can't choose my job over my family. The two of you are my family. Alabama is where I belong although I can't believe I'm saying that."

He stared at her as if she'd sprouted another set of eye-balls. And he continued to stare.

"Aren't you going to say anything? Grey, isn't this what you want?"

That seemed to snap him out of it. "God, yes! I adore

you. But I didn't want you to have to choose me over your dream. I need for you to have it all. If you give up the things that make you happy for us, you could end up angry and bitter." He ran a hand through his hair.

"I don't do angry and bitter," Cammie said. "And I'm not giving up anything. I still intend to have it all."

"You do? How? "

"I want to open a restaurant, here in Ministry." She said.

He'd continued to hold her tightly the entire time, but now he loosened his grip a bit and pulled away so he could look at her.

"That's not a terrible idea. You're a decent cook." She punched him in the arm. "Ow!"

"You're a butthead, but I love you. And I would give it all up for you, and Samantha." She started toward him, but he suddenly lunged and scooped her into his arms.

"I accept."

She giggled and squirmed in his arms. "You accept what?"

"Your proposal. Yes, I'll marry you."

"Slow down, hot shot. I don't have a ring."

"Hold that thought." He slipped outside but was back a moment later, something clutched in his right hand. Before she had a moment to process what was happening, Grey had assumed the age-old position on one knee in front of her. "I couldn't let you change your mind."

This was all happening so fast. "Change my mind?" Her head had begun spinning from the moment he'd accepted her *proposal.* "What—what are you doing?"

"I'm accepting your generous offer to stay in Ministry and make me the happiest man alive. Cammie Laroux, I would like to do you the honor of becoming your husband. Will you accept the ring I've had since we were twenty years old?" Looking down at the open box, she saw his mother's diamond engagement ring.

"When she was sick, she gave it to me, and said I should hang onto it until I knew the time was right." His eyes were misty. "It was as if she knew something I didn't."

All the years and hurt melted away in that moment. Love and forgiveness enveloped her like a warm blanket. For him, but mainly for Deb, who'd been so ill and misguided. It hadn't all been time wasted, but what they'd had to experience to appreciate where they were at this moment.

Tears sprung into her eyes. Cammie held out her left hand and he slid the ring onto her finger. "Thanks for agreeing to marry me."

He gathered her into his arms. "I've loved you since I was a goofy kid. You've been a part of my heart since we passed notes in junior high and circled yes or no to the important questions." He pulled back and placed his hands on either side of her face. "I can't tell you how sorry I am for screwing everything up, but I promise to make it right."

"It is right. Now it's right," she assured him.

"Oh, by the way, there's this house I wanted to talk to you about..."

Chapter Nineteen

CAMMIE'S CELL RANG as she prepared for bed. She'd just hung up with Grey, so she almost ignored it. But the caller I.D. caught her eye. It was a NYC exchange. Curiosity piqued, Cammie answered.

"Hello?"

"Cammie, thank God you answered." She hadn't recognized the number, but the harried voice was unmistakable.

"Bruce? Is everything alright?"

"No, it's not alright, at least not yet." He said.

"What's up?" She asked, her tone neutral. From experience, his calls could either be really good news or not.

"The network is not happy about your refusal of their offer."

"Sorry I made them cranky, but I'm not committed beyond my original contract."

"Cammie, they have a counter offer." His words made her heart rhythm increase very slightly.

"You know my stance on moving." She managed to maintain her cool.

"Hear me out." Her breathing hitched slightly, as she

tried to control her mounting excitement and anxiety. Bruce continued, "They're willing to film on location in Alabama. Everything else about the offer stays the same. If you have any possible sites that come to mind for filming, get some photos."

"Oh. Wow."

"Let it sink in. Talk to whomever you need, and call me back in twenty-four hours."

"This is—wow. Thanks, Bruce." She hung up. Her first impulse was to call Grey immediately and share the good news. But instead, Cammie wanted to let it marinate for a while, figure out how it might affect all their lives. Bringing a daily, nationally televised show to this town, to her family, would have impact—possibly huge and negative impact on everyone she knew. Especially to those she cared about.

She and Grey had decided to hold off on announcing their engagement until he'd had an opportunity to discuss the idea with Samantha. Getting married too quickly might be a disaster for his daughter's emotional well-being. They would give her as much time as she required to accept Cammie as a permanent part of her life in the role of Grey's wife.

Cammie understood that she could never replace Deb as Samantha's mother and wouldn't want to try. But she sought to help Grey raise Samantha and be a part of all her days from here forward—the important ones and just the every days. She wanted to share Grey, not take him away. Hopefully, Samantha would see it that way.

Epilogue

GREY'D BEEN THRILLED over the counter offer from the network. "The farmhouse is perfect. I can start the renovations as soon as I finish at Evangeline House, since filming won't begin for another several months." Grey had been hired to restore the old courthouse in Greenville next year. It was a huge job that would take upwards of two years and a full construction crew.

Alabama had no shortage of aging historic structures. Of course, he hadn't exactly been forthcoming with Cammie about how successful his firm was. They were responsible for major restorations throughout the Southern states. He had several crews, each led by an historical architect, working on projects scattered about. His time so far in Alabama had been somewhat of a sabbatical, a time to refurbish his family.

"You don't have to do it all yourself, you know," Cammie said.

"But I want it be exactly how you envision it."

"I appreciate that." She smiled. Her tummy did a little flip. This was true happiness. So far, so good. Yes, they would have arguments, ups and downs, and hopefully more children. It wouldn't be perfect, but their happiness was borne of imperfection, so unrealistic expectations didn't factor into this real life.

Bringing the world into their home might not be the best way to begin a life together. If filming inside her own kitchen became a problem, she would recreate the kitchen in the barn outside. The farmhouse had to be renovated anyway; might as well try it inside first. It would be her dream kitchen, thanks to Grey and her new job.

The job and the media attention it would bring was part of accepting such an offer. She'd sat down with both Grey and Samantha to discuss what the likely downsides might mean. After weighing everything, they'd come to the conclusion that Cammie should go for it.

In an obvious attempt to overshadow the media attention Cammie's upcoming cooking show had garnered, Jessica Greene held her own press conference.

"Turn it up," Cammie said to Grey, who held the remote.

The woman did do drama. To keep peace and her job at the same network, she was required to play in the same sandbox. "I've done this poor young woman a wrong turn. It's come to my attention that Cammie Laroux wasn't at fault for setting my hair ablaze, people. She was a victim, and she deserves this second chance." She paused, hand over her heart for effect, "She took the blame for someone else's mistake—she took the fall, y'all"

Each word was deliberate and uttered with perfect evangelical intonation. She'd intimated that she, Jessica Greene, was giving up her own spot in the line-up in martyrdom for Cammie. What a load of horseshit.

A member of the press asked about the accusation of the recipe theft, to which Jessica Greene replied, "A pure misunderstanding." And waved her chubby hand as if a fly were buzzing around.

"Misunderstanding, my as—"

"Easy. You know she's not going down without spinning her own special sauce on this. The network is a hundred percent behind you."

The ads were airing next week, touting Cammie's show, *Down Home with Cammie.* It would be an all-out media blitz. Cammie had filmed ad spots all over town, introducing Ministry to America. The ads would continue airing until the season began in a few months. It really was all good. Amazingly, she'd made a meteoric jump back to town celebrity, as opposed to town embarrassment. Jessica was simply someone she'd have to smile and endure.

Howard and Mom were getting married on New Year's Day in a couple weeks, so their wedding was top priority right now. The siblings were on board, even Emma. Howard, they'd discovered, was pure gold. He'd won them over with his obvious love for their mother and newfound excitement at a ready-made family. You'd have thought he'd just discovered they were all his biological offspring the way he wallowed in his new family. His obvious enthusiasm for getting to know them all was truly irresistible. He refused to miss a single football or soccer game, not to mention Suzy's dance recital.

Grey hadn't given Cammie an opportunity to change her mind. They'd tied the knot in a small, family-only ceremony at Evangeline House within days of Grey's Thanksgiving announcement. They were living temporarily with Grey's father because he'd insisted they stay until the closing on the farmhouse. It was working out well enough that they would wait to move until the renovations were complete.

Cammie had come back to Alabama, wanting nothing more than to escape the past misery this town and Grey Harrison represented. But as her sneaky, but wise siblings had predicted, she'd rediscovered her roots by making peace with the one person who'd been able to truly heal her heart. Alabama was now her happy place—again.

Discussion Questions

Again, Alabama

1. Would you run if you found out your boyfriend cheated and got someone pregnant or would you wait for an explanation?

2. Would you be willing to take someone back after he cheated?

3. How would you feel about raising someone else's child?

4. How would you feel if you found out the man you thought was your father really wasn't your father?

5. How would you feel if you found out your mother wanted to get back together with a man she almost married before marrying your father?

6. If you were Cammie, could you forgive Grey and forget, or just forgive?

7. Do you think Cammie's reasons for coming back to Alabama were good ones? Why or why not?

8. Who is your favorite character in this story? And why? Your least favorite?

9. What do think about Cammie's relationship with her siblings? How did these relationships help flesh out Cammie' character?

10. Does the woman on the front cover fit the vision of Cammie you have in your mind? Why or why not?

About the Author

Susan Sands grew up in a real life Southern Footloose town, complete with her senior class hosting the first ever prom in the history of their tiny public school. Is it any wonder she writes Southern small town stories full of porch swings, fun and romance?

Susan lives in suburban Atlanta surrounded by her husband, three young adult kiddos and lots of material for her next book.

Visit her website at SusanSands.com.

For the latest news from Tule Publishing, sign up for our newsletter or check out our website at TulePublishing.com

TULE
PUBLISHING

48960856R00216

Made in the USA
San Bernardino, CA
09 May 2017